Pat,
To such a friend
Joan

The Locket Watch

St. Croix Mystery Series

Joan Mallgrave

IBN: 13: 978-1497403246
ISBN-10: 1497403243

DEDICATION

This book is dedicated to my sons and grandchildren.
They haven't figured me out yet, but they're getting close.

ACKNOWLEDGMENTS

I owe a large debt of gratitude to friends Jeanne Buckingham and Diana Graham. They spent hours proofing, correcting my grammar, and making gentle suggestions.
Their assistance was needed and appreciated.
I also thank my son Ron – he bugged me until I finished the book.

Chapter 1

Anyone would think the tall gangly man was a tourist in his tropical print shirt, sloppy tan cargo shorts, a Phillies baseball cap, and sneakers with white socks. He had long dirty-blond hair and a scrawny face with nondescript brown eyes. A skimpy mustache perched between his pencil thin lips and his wraparound sunglasses.

Roland Coombs walked as far as the security gates leading to the cruise ship. The white and red liner at the dock had arrived in port an hour earlier. Hyped tourists poured off their floating hotel prepared for a day of sightseeing, snorkeling and shopping.

Three thousand potential wallets. Lucky me.

As the first horde of island visitors passed through security, he merged into a cluster and studied the women's purses.

Ah, lots of nice tote bags. No zippers!

As he strolled down the beige brick sidewalk leading to the picturesque town of Frederiksted, he took note of which men had the fattest wallets.

What an interesting variety of marks. Few challenges in this collection of dimwits.

Excitement among the tourists grew as tropical music floated through the tall black wrought iron fence surrounding the entire pier area. Huge concrete fence posts covered with yellow stucco served as sentries for the enclosure.

Tourists grabbed their cameras as they passed through the main gate. Greeting them was a macko jumbie wearing a mask both eerie and cryptic. Representing an African spirit, the man dressed in a purple and yellow satin costume with pant legs covering his six-foot high stilts. The entertainer cajoled the tourists into the town.

As the visitors waited for a break in traffic, they noted the quaint street with palm trees lining both sides. In one direction they saw a colorful array of buildings in shades of blues, greens, corals and golden yellows. Most had red or white roofs. Many of the structures had graceful arched overhangs that provided shade from the tropical sun for those on the sidewalk. From the other direction, they noted the Frederiksted Fort, a structure built during the colonization era. Next to it, a small circle of white circus-style tents set near the yellow clock tower. Various vendors peddled a variety of island wares in addition to souvenirs and tee shirts.

On any other day, the vacationers would peruse the offerings under the tents. But today, the sounds of nearby Calypso music and a glimpse of a passing parade lured them into town. They joined the crowds lining the parade route.

A SNEER formed on Roland's stubby face.

The pickings will be good today.

He ambled by the old Customs House toward King Street. He used the glass of a souvenir shop to study a heavy-set man walking toward him. He had noted the man and his wallet on his walk down the pier. The man was rotund and wore dark red Bermuda shorts. He had fat, hirsute calves.

A hairy ape – my kind of chimp.

The tourist waddled his way toward the parade along with his equally rotund wife. The passenger's stateroom key card swayed back and forth, as it dangled from a white plastic necklace around the man's thick, sunburned neck. As the tourist passed, Roland artfully relieved the man of the wallet in his back pocket. He smirked.

You know what they say about a fool and his money ...

Roland surreptitiously emptied the purloined wallet of cash and driver's license and then buried the leather inside a nearby trashcan. As he headed for King Street, he tucked the license in a makeshift pocket sewn inside his shirt, and deposited the cash in one of the pockets of his pants. He stopped to enjoy six macko jumbies. They stood high above the crowd as they performed acrobatic stunts and dances on their towering stilts. Several of the stilts were long enough to enable the men to shake hands with the spectators on a second-floor balcony. Costumed in flashy red satin outfits with magenta silk waistbands, green plumed headdresses, and dark foreboding masks, the men waved in acknowledgment of the crowd's applause.

IT DIDN'T take long for the new visitors to absorb the parade's atmosphere by sheer osmosis. They watched the cavorting troops enjoy their day in the spotlight as they shared their African souls and ancient dances with the spectators.

The parade participants swaggered, strutted and sashayed their way through town. At times, the marchers prismatic costumes were a bit skimpy and suggestive, but the more they pranced, the louder the ruckus from the crowd.

ROLAND crossed King Street when there was a pause between a performing group of majorettes and their high school band.

He found an outdoor bar under a temporary pagoda near the corner of Market and King. As the customer in front of Roland turned to leave with a tropical rum concoction in each hand, the two men accidentally bumped shoulders. Both men said a quick "I'm sorry." The tourist returned to his girlfriend with two partially splattered drinks and an empty back pocket.

Roland strolled to a corner house. It had a convenience-type store on the first level and living quarters on the second. He leaned against the wall under the arched overhang. As a group of feathered dancers passed by, he noticed a short black man in his late teens or early twenties. He stood across the narrow street in cut-offs, white tee and loafers. Roland knew exactly what the man was about to do as he recognized one of his own maneuvers – a classic trick of his less than honest trade. The young man had a cloth bag draped over his right hand to hide his busy fingers. Within seconds, the lady next to him no longer had a wallet in her fanny pack. The movement of his concealed hand went unnoticed by the crowd around him, so the young thief strolled down the street. Roland watched his every move.

With eyes hidden behind dark sunglasses, the young man unobtrusively glanced to his right and watched a middle-aged tourist stuff money in his shirt pocket as he left an ATM. The thief nodded toward his young pretty accomplice. It didn't take Roland but a second to pick her out – a lithe woman about fifteen feet away from the young thief. She was dressed in tan shorts and a sleeveless blue cotton top. On cue, the young woman accidentally tripped in front of the traveler with the cash-filled pocket. As expected, the unsuspecting tourist played the role of hero and prevented the young woman's fall. During those few seconds of distraction, she fished the cash from his shirt.

Roland was pissed with the success of his competition so he decided to have some fun at their expense. Still on the opposite side of the street, he followed the confident and cocky young man and his girlfriend. Roland watched them try to cross the street to his side. The couple paused for a second while a troop of turquoise-feathered dancers frolicked past the crowd amidst hoots and applause.

Roland emptied the recently snatched wallet belonging to the man with the drinks. He pocketed the cash and license. He continued to hold the wallet in one hand. He correctly anticipated where the young thief would be after he crossed the street. As soon as the man stepped on the curb, Roland stepped behind him. There was a second well-orchestrated shoulder bump. The young thief was unaware that the wallet and the ATM cash were gone from his cloth bag.

Roland again pocketed the cash and license. Now with a cashless wallet in each hand, he followed the young thief and his partner to the corner. As the couple waited for a break in the parade, Roland stuffed one empty wallet in the cloth bag. He tapped the young thief on the shoulder, "Excuse me, did you drop this?" He handed the younger thief the second empty wallet.

Roland bowed his head with a smile, turned, and scurried away through the door of a nearby shop. He went directly to the rear exit. He saw an officer standing by the road and told him about the thief. He even pointed him out in the crowd. As anticipated, the officer approached the man and woman as they stood on the corner trying to figure out what had just happened.

Chapter 2

Charlie Mikkelsen joined her island cousins, Elin Mikkelsen Kingston and Alyse Mikkelsen, on the second floor balcony of Alyse's King Street home.

"Party time!" Charlie sang as she handed Alyse a bottle of their favorite rum drink, Cruzan Cream. She stared at Elin's bulging tummy, "On second thought, it is party time for Alyse and me. Pregnant ladies don't get to drink alcohol."

"But pregnant ladies are always hungry," Elin laughed. "What did you bring me to eat?"

"A whole box of chocolate covered TastyKake mini-donuts and one delectable pineapple and mango iced oozy served with a swirly pink straw in a hollowed-out coconut shell – sans the rum, of course."

Without hesitation, Elin grabbed the box of goodies and tore into the calorie-laden treats.

"How was the traffic from your place?" Alyse asked Charlie as she motioned her to sit.

Charlie, who had returned to her maiden name after her divorce, ran her fingers through her tightly cropped silver hair before she spoke. Shrinking in the wrong places fast, she was now down to five-six. Her aqua top was hip length to hide a tummy bulge in her white slacks. "Since everyone on the island is at the parade, the roads were almost empty. Finding a parking space was the challenge. I'm blocks away and my knees hurt from all the walking."

"How can metal replacement knees hurt?" Alyse asked.

"That's one of those mysteries of life that defies all logic."

Elin offered Alyse some doughnuts. She declined. Charlie confiscated the snack Alyse turned down. She began to nibble as an occasional brown crumb fell onto her shirt.

Ms. Charlie, your knees hurt a lot more since you put on those last six pounds.

Did you forget chocolate is good for our heart?

A dozen chocolate mini-doughnuts a day? I don't think so.

I don't count and neither should you.

Well, I do count. And I also know about the cache of chocolate treats hidden on the top shelf of your bedroom closet!

CHARLIE and Elin inhaled their treats as they watched a group of men whoop their way down the parade route dressed as native Indians, complete with war paint and breechcloths. After the women applauded, Charlie said to Alyse, "Give me an update on this lawyer friend of yours."

Alyse, the only dentist in Frederiksted under the age of seventy, kept her office on the first floor of her home. She was short and petite with medium dark skin. She and her sister shared their most striking features – high cheekbones and luxuriant thick eyelashes.

"Neither my mom nor my sister like him," Alyse said. "They claim he's conceited."

"And what do you think?"

"He seems okay to me."

"Sis," Elin said, "you and Charlie are two of a kind. Her retired police chief and your lawyer buddy both seem like okay guys, but neither of you ever mention the M word."

"I'll consider the M word when I'm good and ready and not one second before," Alyse said as she winked at Charlie.

Charlie responded, "And the Chief and I do have a commitment of sorts."

"Come again?" Elin said as she glanced sideways at Charlie.

"What exactly is a commitment of sorts?"

"It's quite simple. Victor cares for me and I care for him. Fortunately or unfortunately, we live in two different worlds. Each of us has our own children and grandchildren to distract us. Victor likes coffee and a full breakfast at six in the morning. I'd like a Diet Pepsi and doughnuts at nine. He reads the paper; I read the Internet. He keeps his house impeccably clean and tidy. I, on the other hand, keep my house somewhere between almost tidy and not quite dirty. Victor prepares three nutritious meals a day; I dig for a Lean Cuisine in my freezer. He likes the barbecue pit; I like my microwave. At the moment, neither of us wants to upset the status quo."

Alyse chortled and asked, "But you do love him, right?"

"You may call it love. I'm amazed I even repeated the L word. Frankly, our biggest problem is we both liked living alone. When I'm living in St. Croix and sharing a home with my son, I do things because I feel I have to, not because I want to. When I'm at my own condo in Pennsylvania, I spiffy things up when I get the urge, not before. I don't live in squalor or filth, but I do prefer the luxury of deciding the time and the place to do my housework. I sometimes think if Victor and I melded our lifestyles, we'll both go postal within a week."

"Pete and I have issues to work on also," Alyse said. "He wants to move his law practice to St. Thomas, but my dental practice is well established here. I don't want to move."

Elin shook her head and said, "The next time he stops admiring himself in the mirror, you need to talk to him about the move. You need to come to an agreement or you need to move on."

"I'll ignore your wisecrack for now. If I do decide to move on, I will adopt a baby or two. My sibling is very pregnant and she gets all of our mother's attention. I'm jealous."

Charlie and Elin smiled as Alyse proudly patted her sister's tummy.

Charlie stood for a few minutes so her knees wouldn't become stiff. As she peered over the balcony railing, she looked down upon the crowd and noticed some kind of action on the sidewalk. She wasn't sure what it was she saw.

Ms. Charlie, did you see what I saw down there on the sidewalk?

I think so. The tall blond tourist stole something out of the other man's bag. He then gave something back to him. Is that what you saw?

Yeah. Isn't that a bit weird?

Sure seems so.

Missy, write down a description of the tall man in case we both saw what we think we saw.

Elin interrupted Charlie's thought process, "Did you hear me, Charlie? What do you think I should name my baby?"

"Isn't that a selection you and James should make?"

"James claims he's in shock. I think he's in total denial."

"Oh he knows the baby is the real thing," Alyse guffawed. "James was waiting for Steve and Mark to produce grandchildren and never expected to start a second family at his age. It's the last part that put him in shock."

"Second wives deserve to have a baby, too, you know. I was so busy with my shop I never thought about children. When I found out I was expecting, I was delighted and so was James."

"What do Steve and Mark think about a sibling?" Charlie asked.

"They were excited when they came home for Christmas break. Their own mother has been gone for years, so they call me Mama Two – two like in the number and not the Roman numeral."

The glow of motherhood was evident on Elin's face. Her once slim and seductive figure transformed into a full-figured mother-to-be. She exuded happiness and delight over her first baby. As the successful owner of Island Elegant Apparel Shoppe, Elin not only ran the company and its branches, but also designed the high-end, sophisticated frocks that drove tourist into a shopping frenzy. At the moment, however, her mind was more on clothing ranging in sizes from zero to six months.

Ms. Charlie, look! Officer Bob Thompson just collared the young man who had something stolen. He should've caught the blond tourist, don't you think?

Maybe we didn't see what we thought we saw.

Give Bob a call. We might get to play detective again, Missy.

We won't have time. Jake and the girls will be here tomorrow for a week's visit.

That's never stopped us before. We're good at all kinds of detective stuff.

If we're so good, then why am I the only one who ends up in the emergency room?

Charlie refocused on the parade. The three women roared as they watched a tourist with a rum-spiked oozy in his hand join a cadre of dancing women in elegant magenta costumes. One of the dancers grabbed the man, hugged and kissed him. The onlookers hooted and clapped as they filmed the antics on their camcorders or cells.

After the parade resumed, Charlie asked, "Alyse, what do you think will happen between you and Pete?"

"Good question. Hopefully, I'll find out soon."

"Spare me, you two," Elin said. "You and Charlie are more alike than you and me. And I'm your sister!"

Charlie retorted, "Were not exactly alike – I'm white and you two are black; I'm old and gray and you two are young and sassy; your buns are still convex; mine are now concave. We may be distant cousins, but I believe people can still tell us apart."

Chapter 3

In St. Croix's town of Christensted, Jeremy Bauer stood on one of the piers at his marina and watched as the Chief pulled his boat into one of the slips. The athletic young bachelor was in his mid-thirties and had collar-length brown curly hair, dark brown eyes, and a thick chest and arms. His hobbies were his weights, his jet skis and his favored blond in Savannah.

Jeremy wore a white polo shirt with the Pirate's Cove Marina written in dark blue script above the pocket. He had owned the marina for almost two years. During that time, he expanded the number of slips and elongated several of them to accommodate some of the larger yachts trolling the Caribbean. He also built the Shanty, a covered pavilion surrounded by palm trees and sand.

The Shanty served two purposes: in the morning, it was an à la carte breakfast bar. It enticed its marina guests with the addictive aroma of specialty lattes and the inviting fragrance of freshly baked sweet breads. In the afternoon the bar underwent a metamorphosis and offered its guests, as well as locals, a psychedelic array of tropical island rum drinks in addition to all the traditional concoctions found stateside.

Jeremy closed the Shanty when his nightclub, located just outside the marina's fence, opened to the drinking and dancing public.

"Good afternoon, Jeremy. It's a fine day for boating," the Chief said after he reduced the power of his twin Cat engines to a gentle purr.

THE CHIEF was about the same height as Jeremy and stood straight and tall. Only a touch of gray in his hair and a few deep-set wrinkles on his tan face gave away his age. Now retired, he had been a former deputy police chief with the Virgin Islands Police Department.

"Your craft is in good shape, Chief. Why do you want to sell her?"

"It's very simple. Now that I'm retired I don't seem to have time to do anything. *Gertie* requires more TLC than I can give her."

"So you had more time for *Gertie* when you were the deputy police chief?"

"I find it amazing, but I did. Days seem to go by so fast anymore. By evening, I can't even remember what I did during the day."

"Did you name your motor boat?"

"*Gertie* was a toddler when I got her, so I had to keep the name. It's unlucky to change your boat's name, you know – check with Gil Cliver. He'll tell you."

"Once that old sailor starts on his tales he goes on forever," Jeremy said as he grinned. "I'll check with him the next time I have three or four hours to spare."

"Hop in and let's go for a spin. You won't have any doubts about buying *Gertie* after you've spent an hour at her helm."

JEREMY learned to power a large boat when he was a teenager and worked at a marina in Ocean City, Maryland. Later, he kept a large catamaran on the Susquehanna River when he lived in York, Pennsylvania. He sold the craft and his investment properties in order to purchase the Pirate's Cove Marina. He was now a permanent year-round resident on the island.

It took a while for Jeremy to warm up to his mother's suitor,

Victor, better known throughout the three U.S. Virgin Islands as the Chief. Both Jeremy and his mother would be the first to admit that as the island's deputy police chief, Victor had serious attitude problems. To say he was a bit bossy and bombastic would put it kindly. Those traits, mixed with an overabundance of opinionated remarks and unsolicited advice, was an almost lethal combination between a man and a woman who were each independent, confident, and used to being the decision-maker in the family.

As time moved forward, Jeremy was actually pleased his mother had the Chief in her life. After her own retirement she was restless and out of sorts. It wasn't until she got into some serious genealogy and discovered she had family on St. Croix that life changed. She decided to visit the island and meet her newly discovered family. Everything may have turned out differently if she hadn't tried to play wannabe detective, pissed off the Chief, and actually went after some bad guys herself.

ROLAND considered the possibility that the young man recently arrested could identify him, so he walked from the center of town to the next block on the parade route. He stopped to admire a troupe of dancers in scanty costumes. They moved seductively to the sounds of quelbe – folk songs containing innuendos and double entendres.

Nice!

Roland buried himself in a group of onlookers. As a mother bent over to tend to her baby in the stroller, Roland extracted the exposed wallet from her open diaper bag. He moved on and crossed King Street just as a Caddie convertible passed in the parade with the governor waving to the crowd.

The thief sought cover from the sun under an overhang housing several soda machines. He emptied the young mother's wallet of her cash and license and disposed of it in a covered trashcan filled with half eaten food.

He watched a squadron of National Guard troops march by, and then leisurely strolled to the next block. Two elderly locals sat on aluminum chairs with orange canvas seats. They shaded themselves with colorful umbrellas as they smiled and waved to a float filled with smiling young teens in long white gowns.

One of the seated onlookers had her purse on her lap; the other had hers nudged neatly between the legs of her chair. As Roland approached, he took a few coins from his pocket and deliberately dropped them on the sidewalk. As he bent over to retrieve them, he opened the purse under the chair and extracted the wallet. Five seconds later, he was on his way.

As he walked, he watched a group of young women in amber sequined costumes. The young ladies had multicolored butterfly-shaped wings strapped across their backs. The hoops spanned three feet in each direction. The young women smiled despite the effort it took to keep their wings from flying away.

ON THE other end of King Street, Charlie, Elin and Alyse didn't solve any world problems as they chatted and watched the parade, but they did discuss the perfect nursery Elin and James had built onto their home.

It was now almost three in the afternoon and the parade was not even close to over. Charlie was on stimulus overload. She checked her Princess Summerfall Winterspring watch and decided it was time to leave the music and festivities so she could head to her son's marina. After she said her goodbyes, she called Victor, a.k.a. the Chief, to see if she could meet him and have dinner at one of the harbor's restaurants. There were no answers on his home phone or his cell.

Charlie had parked on the outskirts of town on the street in front of the Frederiksted Cemetery. She headed for her car. When she reached the cemetery wall, she could see the huge white marble slabs that outlined her ancestors' resting place. She walked inside to pay her respects to her great, great grandparents – two of the original Danish settlers who came to the Danish West Indies to seek fortune and fame on a sugar plantation. One of their sons remained on the plantation, married a freed slave, and sired Elin and Alyse's family. The youngest son chose to immigrate to Savannah where he met and married an Irish beauty and started his own family.

Charlie stood quietly at the gravesite remembering the first time she realized that she had relatives on St. Croix. She had put a bulletin board post on a genealogy website. She requested information on her family. Elin saw the post and answered it. As Charlie smiled with her memories, she sensed movement. She looked up and saw a man walk by the cemetery fence about ten yards away. She saw him throw something in the gutter as he continued down the street. She recognized the tropical print shirt he wore.

He's not a tourist, Ms. Charlie.

I think you're right. At least he's not from the cruise ship anyway. Let's be thankful he didn't notice us standing here.

As soon as the man disappeared out of sight, Charlie left the cemetery and started down the old cracked sidewalk until she could see what the man threw away. A wallet was partially wedged in the sewer grate.

We did see what we thought we saw, didn't we?

We sure did.

Now we have a bad guy to catch, Missy.

I'm not supposed to play detective anymore, remember?

That never stopped you before.

I know. I'll just help the police a little bit this time.

Charlie dug for a tissue in her tank-sized purse. She used the tissue to extricate the wallet without getting her fingerprints on it. She held it gingerly and headed for her car. Instead of going to the marina as initially planned, she headed for police headquarters in town. While she sat in a traffic jam at an intersection, she grabbed her phone and speed dialed Elin's husband, Deputy Police Chief James Kingston.

"James, we have a crime to solve!"

"Charlie, please tell me you haven't encountered any murderers today."

"Not so far. How about a thief picking pockets all day? I even have his fingerprints."

"Where are you?"

"I just left the Frederiksted Cemetery. I'll be at the station in ten.

If Bob Thompson is around, tell him this concerns him, too. He arrested a man earlier today that may not be guilty."

Chapter 4

It took twenty minutes before Roland arrived at his dilapidated trailer located in an antiquated mobile home park on the outskirts of Frederiksted. There were only a few patches of white paint left on the surface of his decrepit abode. The tires on his trailer were so flat they resembled pools of hardened cracked tar. The interior of his box was confining and bug-ridden. There were a half-dozen other trailers within close proximity. Ear-piercing music blared from several of them.

Once inside the twenty-feet long trailer, Roland brushed several empty Chinese take-out boxes off a chipped tabletop. The ancient burnt-orange Formica had brown cigarette burns all over it. A half-inch coat of dried food adhered to parts of the top, and a foot-high pile of used paper plates and cups were scattered under it. He sat on an equally gross built-in vinyl seat and removed the cash from his pockets.

There is always the boardwalk this evening if my fingers get itchy.

He counted his cache – eight hundred and forty-two bucks plus drivers' licenses. Four of the licenses had stateside addresses, one was Japanese, and four were local.

Not bad for a day's work. If we only had a nice big parade every week.

ROLAND retrieved his Elmer's glue from an overhead cabinet stuffed with wrinkled dirty clothes. He bulldozed his way through the trash on the floor to the bathroom. It was composed of a small round sink and a miniaturized toilet sitting close to the floor. The throne had a thick crust of brown around the waterline. An annoying drip echoed from the tank. The cold water spigot was the only thing working on the sink. Around the cracked oval mirror over the sink, Roland glued the licenses to the moldy, moisture-stained, wood-paneled wall. He stood back and admired his collection.

Whoa. I got me sixty-three licenses from forty-two different states. Wonder how many states I have left to go?

THE parade-related traffic was far more intense than Charlie anticipated. Frustrated, she found an empty spot, parked, locked her car, walked two blocks, wiggled through an opening in the parade, and trudged another block to police headquarters. James had his office door open and Charlie could see Bob Thompson inside.

James, a man in his mid-forties, was six feet tall and had a lean torso. He wore a crisp blue uniform shirt and dark blue slacks. A picture of his wife Elin sat on top of his desk.

"May I join you?" Charlie said as she tapped on the steel doorframe with her manicured candy apple-red nails.

"So you've been out chasing bad guys, huh?" James said as he smiled. A gold cap twinkled on one of his incisors.

"Not exactly, but I did observe a pocket being picked and later saw the real thief throw this wallet away." She placed the tissue-covered wallet on James' desk.

"It can't be the thief I arrested," Bob said as he showed her a mug shot.

Charlie took the picture from the six feet-six man whose frame filled a doorway.

"The man in your picture was the man the thief robbed. I saw a tall white man with long frazzled blond hair rob your younger, dark-skinned man."

"The kid I arrested said something like that, but I didn't believe a word he said. I checked our system, Charlie, and this man has a record a mile long – all for petty theft and picking pockets."

"When you arrested him, I bet he had a cash-void wallet on him, didn't he?"

"How did you know? He also had an empty wallet in a bag. Credit cards were inside, but no license or money. My man was neither Lenora Stewart nor Hans Jansen."

Charlie explained in detail what she saw at the parade and outside the cemetery fence.

James probed as he leaned forward on his desk, "Can you describe this man?"

"Sir, I'm Charlie Mikkelsen, crime stopper extraordinaire. Do you doubt my powers of observation?"

Extraordinaire? Ms. Charlie, get real.

I always wanted to say that.

You're such a dweeb sometimes!

James tapped the fingers of his right hand on his desk as Charlie dug for the notebook stuffed in her cross-body pumpkin-size orange cloth purse with a wide, lime green zipper. She pushed aside a bottle of vitamins, a crossword puzzle book, and a checkbook she never balanced. As soon as her fingers touched the spirals of her notepad, a look of triumph transformed her face.

Her little book contained a multitude of critical facts about her private world, plus information she deemed important, like phone numbers, list of meds, contact names and numbers, and a description of the thief written in her own private version of Gregg's shorthand. She transcribed her notes orally.

"When I saw what I thought I saw, I checked my trusty Princess Summerfall Winterspring watch and wrote down the time." She held up her arm so the two officers could see a native Indian princess with big fat hands pointing to the time.

"Charlie," the younger officer said, "who or what is a Princess Summerfall Winterspring?"

"Howdy Doody and his gang was well before your time, Bob. Television was quieter and gentler then. No one dared to curse or make a sexual comment. Even Desi and Lucy slept in twin beds." Charlie began to sing the opening song of the puppet show.

It's how Howdy Doody time ...

James laughed as Bob's mouth dropped.

Charlie said, "Don't look so shocked, Bob. Princess Summerfall Winterspring was a character on the show, as well as Buffalo Bob and Clarabell the Clown."

"Okay, if you say so," Bob said as he almost hid a smile behind his hand. His Joe Biden white teeth were in sharp contrast to his almost black skin.

Bob turned to James, "Charlie's description fits the tourist the young man told me about. I guess I'd better release the kid, Boss."

James said, "If Charlie's thief was up by the cemetery, I think we have a local thief on our hands and not a tourist."

James shifted his gaze from Bob to Charlie, "If we get our sketch artist over here from St. Thomas tomorrow, could you work with him to produce a pretty picture?"

"Benny and I have a good track record, in case you've forgotten my valorous feats of the past few years. I'll be here between nine and ten in the morning. Afterward, I'm due to pick up my son Jake and my granddaughters at the airport."

"I'll ask Benny to get here as early as possible so your visit won't be spoiled. The Virgin Islands Police Department respects your time, ma'am."

CHARLIE was excited to be involved in a crime again – even from the sidelines. She knew she best not show her enthusiasm in front of James. Both Victor, James and her three sons had told her many times to stay out of police affairs. In the past she had been kidnapped on a cruise ship, had a midnight brawl with a low life in a cemetery, and fought off a serial killer in a gas station. Even she admitted that none of those events had been the highlight of her detective career.

James interrupted her thoughts, "Let me call Benny now.

Meanwhile, Bob needs to interview you before you go home."

After a fifteen minute Q & A session with Officer Thompson, Charlie headed for the door.

James called her and she stopped. "Charlie, thanks for all your help. But remember, this is official police business, so please, no extracurricular activities on your part. Understand?"

Charlie's answer was a smile.

"Charlie, I don't like that look on your face. Don't you get involved and don't get my pregnant wife involved. Understand?"

Charlie didn't answer. She waved as she left.

JEREMY tried to decide if he wanted to buy the Chief's boat.

"There's a lot of grunt work involved in restoring a fifteen year-old boat, Chief."

"But there is a lot of boat here for the money. You'll never find another this size in this condition at this price. I've taken good care of *Gertie* and she's never let me down."

"One of those Cat engines sounds like it may have a problem."

"They were both reconditioned two years ago and she's been in dry dock at Ole Luther's since then. Both engines need to run for a while, and I need to replace her oil. Try *Gertie* for a week and see for yourself. I'll even fill the tank for you."

Jeremy liked the looks of the powerboat. He knew its size would give it stability in the ocean. He also knew if those Caterpillar engines were good, *Gertie* would be around for at least another fifteen years.

The Chief changed the subject and asked, "How do you like sharing a house with your mother? She said you've been on your own for a number of years, but now the two of you live together."

"I miss my own place, but I don't miss those icy Pennsylvania snowstorms. In reality, mom and I do pretty well together. I might have to do the housekeeping on occasion, but at least mom keeps her stuff almost picked up. She may not cook on a regular basis, but she does come up with a mean Thanksgiving, Christmas and Easter dinner. Did she tell you she was returning to her condo for Easter?"

"She broke the news. I'll miss her."

"I'm headed for Savannah to see Laurie over the holiday, but my stay will be short. Now about the boat ..."

"Like I said, try *Gertie* for a week. If the engine doesn't sound better, I'll have Luther take a look."

"Deal. I must admit I do feel a little stupid. I own this marina, but the only boat I have at the moment is a nine year-old speedboat."

The Chief's cell rang. He answered and listened for a few minutes. "Why were you at the police station? Charlie, what are you doing?"

Jeremy rolled his eyes. "Tell mom she better not be chasing criminals."

"Charlie, did you hear what your son said? He mirrored my sentiments exactly. I'll wait here until you arrive." When the call ended, he put his cell back in his pocket.

"Chief, my mother was a perfectly sane and responsible woman until the day she retired. Never missed a day at work, cooked healthy food, raised my brothers and me, kept our house clean, washed our clothes, and raised fresh veggies for our dinner table. She smiled as each one of us left the nest. Then she retired.

"Now she travels, reads nothing but mystery novels, does crossword puzzles for hours, buys herself wild and colorful clothes, wears jeans to church, and chases criminals as a hobby. What happened?"

"Your mother wears jeans to church?"

Jeremy nodded.

The Chief tried to envision Charlie in jeans but gave up. "Let's go for a short spin before your mother gets here. I'm starting to get heartburn."

Chapter 5

Roland decided he needed a beer so he headed to the nearby Palm Shack. Before he left, he exchanged his touristy shirt for an equally smelly black tee he found on the floor of his closet. He drove his wasted '88 Camero. Billows of fumes puffed out of the exhaust as he started down the narrow lane out of the trailer park.

The bar was a bit on the dingy side and catered to the island's locals. It was located on the main road and Roland recognized most of the clunkers in the gravel parking lot. They belonged to dedicated regulars of the establishment.

"How's it going, Bert?" Roland asked.

"Little slow earlier. I guess everyone was drinking at the parade. The action started here about an hour ago."

Bert the Bartender, the owner of the Palm Shack, finished drying a glass with the edge of the dirty apron wrapped around his pudgy waist. The short, squat bald man always wore blue trousers, a grayish-white tee shirt and brown loafers.

Roland spoke, "Everyone at the parade was looped – even the tourists."

"You're not juiced. How come?"

"Well, I was busy, Bert. I'm a working man, you know."

"Don't tell me what you work on. I need to plead innocence every time a cop comes in here. Usual?"

Roland nodded.

Bert filled a pilsner glass with island-brewed beer and slid it down the bar. It stopped directly in front of Roland. He took a long swig. "Cold and wet, just like I like it."

Bert saw a young couple enter the bar and sit at a table in the rear. He headed for them as he wiped his hands on the dampish apron tied around his waist.

Roland watched Bert through the smoke-glazed mirror over the bar. Tiny white Christmas lights edged the glass. Two six-feet high neon Palm trees flanked each end of the mirror. One tree had a brownish monkey clinging to the trunk.

Roland recognized the two newcomers as he stared in the mirror. They were the young thieves at the parade. He tilted his head toward his beer so they wouldn't see his reflection in the mirror, but he kept his eyes upward and glued on the couple.

"What can I get you?" Bert asked.

"Beer for both of us," the man answered.

"You're not from here, are you?" Bert asked. "Don't look familiar."

"We took the ferry from St. Thomas so we could watch the parade."

"You two young ones missed the last ferry home, you know."

"We know. Got held up by some stupid cop. Where is a cheap place to stay overnight?"

Bert proceeded to tell the couple about several places they could stay. The young man nodded and thanked the bartender. Bert turned and headed for another table where a man needed a refill. He didn't notice Roland watching the young couple.

JEREMY and the Chief putted along the coastline for a half hour before turning around and returning to the marina.

"Are you sure you want to sell *Gertie*?" Jeremy asked.

The Chief grinned as he spoke, "Yep. I figure if I get the urge to do some deep-sea fishing, I can always talk you into taking me out."

Jeremy smiled. He knew he would do just that. The Chief moored his boat. "If your mother gets here while I'm gone, tell her I won't be long. I need to pick up some cleaning supplies to make *Gertie* shine."

Jeremy nodded and then went into his office to tackle a desktop of paperwork. Both he and the Chief wondered how and why Charlie morphed from a responsible, hard-working citizen into an insouciant senior citizen who wore purple clothes with red hats and a brown and orange Princess Summerfall Winterspring watch – all at the same time.

CHARLIE arrived at the marina as the Chief and Jeremy stood in front of the marina's office. Charlie gave Victor a quick peck on the cheek.

"What have you been up to today?" she asked.

"Jeremy and I took my lady out for a spin." The Chief turned, and swept one arm outward toward his boat. "Ta-dah! Won't Jeremy look good behind the helm?"

"You sound like a salesman, Victor."

"At the moment I am," he chuckled.

"So let's see, your trading in *Gertie*, your old boat, because you now have *Rubee*, you're almost new red Mustang convertible. Do you plan on trading in Charlie, the old broad, for a young Chickie Poo?"

The Chief put his arm around Charlie, "What I do that to you?"

"Hope not."

Jeremy shook his head and grinned when he heard the mush talk. He finally said, "It's a nice boat, Chief. Reduce the price another $2,500 and it's a deal."

"Done."

The Chief and Jeremy shook hands. "I'll come to town the first thing tomorrow and clean *Gertie*. Then I'll sign the title over to you."

The Chief turned toward Charlie, "Ready for dinner?"

"Always am. Let's head down to the boardwalk and go casual

tonight."

Ms. Charlie, what's a Chickie Poo?

A sexy woman who flirts with men.

Would the Chief look at a Chickie Poo?

Does the Chief wear pants?

Stop with the clichés! That dribble is older than you are.

The Chief and Charlie casually strolled to the crooked boardwalk that followed the natural coastline of the harbor. They passed a few hotels and a couple of restaurants before they settled on a casual eatery near the armless windmill. After climbing the steps to the second floor, they sat next to the balcony so they could gaze at the harbor.

"It's always so pretty at this time of the evening," Charlie said. "The waters are so calm."

"That's because hurricane season is over. I think Jeremy got a bit jittery during our last storm."

"It was his first big one on the island."

"But not his last."

"I need to hit the ladies room for a minute. Order me a Diet Pepsi, a fish sandwich and some of those salty, curly fries. Don't forget to ask for a big bottle of ketchup. I haven't had my lycopene today!"

While Charlie was gone, Victor took out the small crossword puzzle book he had in his back pocket.

If Charlie can do these things, so can I. I need to keep my mind sharp.

Victor had started on the puzzle over breakfast, but most of the little white boxes were still blank.

I can't believe this is all I know. What on earth is half a zwei? I don't even know what a whole zwei is, let alone a half.

Charlie returned a few minutes later. "What's a zwei?" Victor asked. "It's not in my pocket dictionary."

"Don't know. I know what a half of a zwei is."

"How can they use words when they aren't in the dictionary? It doesn't make sense."

"Crossword puzzles aren't designed to make sense. Some insidious creature snickers for hours as he or she designs a crossword puzzle that will stymie your mind and addle your soul for all eternity. These things are meant to challenge your plaque-filled brain and test the depths of your memory. And since when did you start doing crossword puzzles anyway?"

"Charlie, you're not much of a conversationalist when you have your head in front of the monitor or eyes glued to your Kindle. I decided to fight fire with fire, figuratively, of course. And besides, you do a dozen crossword puzzles a week."

"We have to keep the gray matter upstairs extra sharp, don't we? The seventh decade is scary," she said.

"Yes, it is. I even started to use those stickies you gave me on my birthday in that goodie box. My refrigerator now looks as bad as yours."

"You use those stickies to write the meanings of words like zwei and otiose and verisimilitude. You'll need to refer to them, I promise."

The waiter served the meal and then left. Before Victor picked up his fork, he sighed and asked, "I give up. What is half of zwei?"

AFTER Jeremy double checked *Gertie*, he buttoned down the marina for the night. He checked to ensure all the piers were clean. Where there was some debris or a dead fish in the water, he used a net with a long handle to scoop it out. After everything was in its place, he headed for the small on-site gym and ran three miles on the treadmill. He showered and changed.

He headed for the Pirate's Lair dressed in black slacks and a white polo shirt with a pirate's head logo. It was the standard attire for all the wait staff and bartenders. The Lair was a popular spot for his marina guests, plus the hotel and resort crowd throughout the island. A number of locals patronized it and religiously coveted the same barstools four or five nights a week.

Jeremy had built the bar on the second floor of an abandoned, hurricane-damaged restaurant near the marina. While not huge, he decorated it in a pirate's theme and had a large plaster pirate's head featured above the mirror on the bar. The pirate looked suspiciously like a movie pirate without his legendary eye makeup. Live music had begun at nine and a fair size crowd had already gathered.

Gil Cliver, the former marina owner, greeted him at the door, "Evening, young fella."

"Hey, Gil. I see the action began without me this evening."

"Not many dudes here yet, but there will be now that the parade is over."

Gil had just turned eighty. He had spent much of his life at sea before his father died and left him the marina. Jeremy was convinced Gil was St. Croix's version of Popeye with his thick chest, arm muscles, and a few chin hairs. Instead of Olive Oyl, Gil had his crystal blue Danish eyes on an energetic and spunky senior citizen named Jeanette.

"How's your lady?" Jeremy asked.

"Young fella, an ole salt like me doesn't kiss and tell, you know."

"I didn't ask for any details of your love life, only about Aunt Jeanette."

"She's fine and so is my love life." Gil giggled with delight as he slapped the front of his thighs with the palms of his hands.

"Is Jeanette still making her famous mango mousse pie?"

"Oh yeah. You'll never guess what she told me," Gil whispered.

Jeremy whispered, "Did she say she loved you?"

"Better than that. She told me she wouldn't make her mango mousse pie for anyone but me!"

"You're in trouble then, Gil," Jeremy teased.

Gil's forehead tightened into a mass of creases. "I ain't done nothing bad. I'm in no trouble."

"Deputy Police Chief James Kingston, also known as Jeanette's favorite and only nephew, loves her mango mousse pie. You don't want to piss him off, do you?"

"Holy Moly, you don't think he would put me behind bars, do ya?"

"Gil, I'm needling you. But it really isn't fair that the rest of us can't enjoy Jeanette's pies."

"I do feel bad for ya, but I'm a man in love. When my heart starts thumpin, it drives the kid in me wild."

Jeremy started to tease Gil again. Suddenly, he felt two arms go around his waist from behind. He pivoted and saw blond, blue eyed Laurie Glass smiling up at him.

"Guess who just quit her job at COX TV in Savannah? And guess where I moved?"

Chapter 6

Roland sipped his drink as he watched the young thieves leave the Palm Shack. Once they were out the double glass doors, he watched them go to the side of the road and begin to hitchhike as they walked.

Roland hesitated for only a second before he made a decision. He left the bar, got in his gas-guzzler, and drove out of the parking lot by the rear exit. He turned onto the main road. The two young thieves had their backs to him. They were far enough down the road they could not be seen by anyone in the bar.

Should I or shouldn't I? Of course I should. Those two can identify me. Go ahead, Ro. Eliminate your competition.

Roland looked up and down the road. Seeing no oncoming cars, he revved his engine and accelerated. The young thieves realized two seconds too late there was a car aimed at them. Roland plowed into the couple. They both fell under the car. Roland stopped and glanced around to ensure no one watched. Then he backed over the two bodies. Just to be sure the young couple were dead, he drove forward over them again. He left the scene of his crime and sped to his little trailer. He pulled his car behind two trees so no one could see it from the road.

Punks. I'm king of my domain again.

JEREMY studied Laurie. Her baby blues, pale blue boat-neck shirt, and white tailored slacks fit the bill. The blond curls didn't hurt the picture either.

"Quit your job! Was that producer with the roving hands after you again?"

"He finagled a trip with me to Atlanta next week. I was supposed to be there to cover a big clown convention. To make a long story short, I quit."

"Honey, I can't say I'm sorry. In fact, I'm kind of glad."

"I didn't think I had anything to lose, Jeremy. After I sold the fifteen-minute clip of Gil and his rowboat race, I didn't think I'd have trouble getting another job. And I didn't!"

"So where is this new job?"

Laurie stood tall and proudly announced, "The U.S. Virgin Islands Department of Tourism. I'll be doing all the videos for their website, including storyboarding, scripting, producing and starring. I'll even have a say in the filming and editing."

An ear-to-ear smile appeared on Jeremy's face. He gave Laurie a big congratulatory smooch on her glossy pink lips. He then motioned the music men to slow the tempo. He snuggled up to the cute and pert lady in his arms for the next set of up-close-and-personal dances. Having Laurie Glass permanently in his arms had been a recurring thought lately.

Maybe I'm not the confirmed bachelor I've always claimed to be!

After the dance ended, Jeremy asked TJ, the bartender, to close the bar at the end of the evening. The two lovers left hand in hand and walked toward Christensted to find an open restaurant.

"I need to find a small apartment," Laurie said.

"Now that the new wing on my house is done, mom and I have an empty bedroom. You can stay with us tonight and we will go apartment hunting tomorrow."

"Would it upset your mother if I stayed overnight?"

"She'll welcome you. But don't expect her to cook breakfast in the morning."

Jeremy and Laurie found a small restaurant about to shut down for the evening. They both ordered takeout sandwiches, curly fries and slaw. They picked up several bottles of beer and headed back to the marina.

"You and I will share our first meal on my new boat."

"New boat? When did this happen?"

"Today. The Chief hasn't used *Gertie* for several years, so she's been in dry dock. He brought her by this morning, and we took her out for a spin. She runs well for being fifteen-years old, and she is about as stable as you can get for her size."

Jeremy swiped his key card to get them inside the marina fence and led Laurie to the pier next to his office.

"Laurie Glass, meet *Gertie* – the other woman in my life."

Jeremy pulled one of the mooring ropes and the boat inched closer to the dock. He helped Laurie step onto the stern and then he followed. Laurie sat on one of the built-in seats located on the deck of the open stern. Jeremy arranged a small table in front of her. He sat and snuggled up close to his young love. Neither Laurie nor Jeremy tasted a thing going into their stomachs.

Chapter 7

James had left a message on Charlie's answering machine at the home she shared with Jeremy. She was to meet Benny, the sketch artist, at the police station at nine in the morning.
She rose early, dressed in white slacks and a magenta top. She stood before her bathroom mirror and put on her makeup.

Ms. Charlie, you missed a sunspot on the side of your cheek. Put on some more cover-up before you apply your foundation.

I hate all of these spots.

I hope you noticed I said sunspots instead of age spots.

I noticed. Are you trying to be nice to me for once?

I want us to work this pickpocket case together. We haven't hunted criminals in months.

I've been thinking the same thing.

PETE Hummel, Alyse's boyfriend, was in his mid-thirties. The young lawyer thought he looked exceptionally good in his new tan linen suit, dark brown shirt and tan silk tie.

Around five feet-ten, he considered himself a lady's man. He thought he somewhat resembled Will Smith. In reality, he looked more like a well-dressed black version of a young Fred Mertz.

The four years he had been with Murray Sedge and Associates had proven profitable. Pete had already treated himself to a snazzy silver BMW and a sleek new speedboat. He operated the Sedge office on St. Croix, but hoped to transfer to the main office on St. Thomas. He knew Sedge was around retirement age, and he wanted to buy the practice.

Pete had dated Alyse for the last six months. He liked her looks, her figure, and her taste in men, namely – him. He knew Alyse wouldn't leave her dental practice, so he figured his latest fling would die a quiet death when he switched islands.

After he finished admiring the man in the mirror, he turned on his computer. He double-tapped the icon for the VIPD's site, and then clicked on Recent Arrests. He reviewed the arrests made in St. Croix that week. Since he was a defense attorney, he made a potential client list. After researching the addresses and phone numbers of the names on his list, he left the office to drum up some business.

FIVE feet-three inches, dark-skinned and slightly overweight, the only female detective in the entire Virgin Islands Police Department knocked on the frame of the open door of James Kingston's office.

"Boss, I need to update you about a young couple who were run down last evening. The two were killed a short distance from the Palm Shack."

"Come in, Detective Benton. Did you identify the victims?"

"Do you remember the man whom Bob Thompson arrested yesterday on pickpocket charges? He later released him."

"The one Charlie told us about?"

Chamaign nodded. "He and his girlfriend were run over while next to the road. I talked to Burt the Bartender and he said they were in his bar. He also said they missed the last ferry back to St. Thomas yesterday. The man asked Bert about a place to stay overnight. I suspect they were hitchhiking."

"Was this an accident, Chamaign?"

"Don't think so. The bloody tire tracks on the bodies, berm and road indicate the driver drove over them from behind, and then backed over them. He or she then went forward a second time."

"Since it was near the bar, did anyone see them?"

Chamaign shook her head.

"Can we ID the tread?"

"The tires were almost bald, but we might get something. The tires were large and the distance between the wheels indicates the car is a full-size sedan. We also found specks of gray primer paint on the victims so the car is probably old."

"I'll assign Bob to help you," James said. "A double homicide will have the police commissioner on our backs before the end of the day. Do what you can to wrap this up quickly, Chamaign."

"I'll get Bob and we'll inspect the scene again in daylight. I also want to talk to Burt again. I read Bob's report from the pickpocket incident yesterday, and now I want to know if this tall, blondish man was in the bar."

"Charlie is the one who saw him. She will be in this morning to work with Benny," James said. "We'll have a good likeness in an hour or two."

"Bob and I will put Charlie on our list to interview. Why does she always seem to be around when a crime occurs?"

"Good question. If you figure out the answer, let me know. Let's keep her out of this case. We don't need Charlie poking around and putting herself in danger again."

"That's for sure. Thanks for assigning Bob to help. He and I make a good team. In fact, we've kicked some serious butt with that serial killer last year."

"Yes, you did, with Charlie's help, of course. Now get out of here and kick some more butt – this time without Charlie."

Chamaign left the room and paged Bob. They agreed to meet at the crime scene. She visited the ladies' room and pinned her hair into a tight bun. She called her husband and asked him to pick up their second grader after school. She knew her day would be busy.

THE CHIEF headed to the marina in his old black Toyota truck. The sky was a grainy blue. The morning's cool air and calm ocean waters seemed so perfect, the Chief decided to take one last run on *Gertie*.

The retired officer arrived at the marina with a box of motor oil, some tools, and a small portable carpet vacuum. As soon as he stepped onboard, he noticed there were empty food containers in the trashcan and several empty bottles of beer in the sink. He called Jeremy's name to make sure he wasn't in the tiny stateroom under the bow of the boat.

Looks like Jeremy celebrated last night – first of many good times, I hope.

The Chief immediately dragged the mattress from the stateroom to the stern. Then he pulled the seat cushions from the built-in booth to the stern also. He shampooed everything and then leaned the pieces against the side of the stern. He wanted the hot tropical sun to perform its magic.

The Chief hummed as he worked on his self-appointed task. He had never enjoyed squeezing into the snug confines of the engine compartment, but this would be his last time. After the oil was changed, he wiggled out and wiped the oily residue off his hands. He carefully put the empty oil cans and paper towels into a trash bag and set them on the pier. The Chief grimaced when he noticed two small gas cans stored near the twin engines. He moved them to the open deck on the stern.

That was careless of Jeremy. I'll have to warn him he cannot store gas so close to the engines. No point in allowing hot engines to ignite and blow Gertie out of the water.

When he started the twin Cats, they ran smoothly. He sighed.

Maybe I should've kept this old girl!

While allowing the engines to gently putter and distribute fresh oil throughout, he pulled up a cushion from the built-in seat on the stern to retrieve additional cleaning supplies. Cotton hand towels, a bottle of an eco-friendly window cleaner, and a container of polishing wax sat on top of a black plastic bag.

Haven't seen the bag before – Jeremy must have moved some of his things on board last night.

As the Chief bent over to retrieve his supplies, a speedboat zipped out of the marina. The Chief anticipated a nasty wake and braced himself by placing his hand on the black bag. *Gertie* rocked hard when the wave hit.

Some people never learn. Five miles an hour means five miles an hour until they are out of the wake zone.

The Chief scrubbed the canvas over the fly bridge, hosed it, cleaned the windshield, and used boat polish on the hard surfaces. The area sparkled.

He tackled the kitchen next. He unplugged the refrigerator and removed several bottles of beer, several small packets of ketchup and a wrapped bag. He wiped down the interior of the fridge and defrosted the tiny freezer compartment. When done, he placed everything back inside and plugged in the small fridge.

Before I finish today, I'll have to borrow one of those beers.

He removed the contents of the overhead cabinets and wiped down the shelves. He returned the contents like Jeremy had them. Then he tackled the small stainless steel sink and built-in two burner stove, followed by the windows. After all the small portals glistened in the sun, he retrieved the seat cushions and mattress and replaced them.

He scoured the small head, and lastly, he wiped down the walls and swabbed the interior flooring.

I'll clean your stern, old girl, after we go out for a spin.

The Chief undid the lines, put the engines in reverse, and deftly maneuvered his way out of the slip.

This is it, Gertie, our last adventure together.

With the expertise of a seasoned boat pilot, he turned *Gertie* around until she faced seaward. He moved the throttle forward a bit and slowly crept out of the no-wake zone at the posted five miles per hour. Once out to sea, he headed west and hugged the coastline. *Gertie* behaved beautifully. The Chief reminisced about the good times he and his family had had on the boat.

The Chief continued his pleasure trek for almost an hour before he spotted a police patrol boat about to pass him on his starboard side. He noticed that the boat slowed, so he did, too. He had always enjoyed boat patrol in his younger days while on the force.

The patrol boat puttered closer. Two uniformed men and a dog were onboard and the Chief knew both men and Snuff the dog.

"Carlos, catch any drug traffickers this morning?"

Carlos Martinez grinned as he spoke, "Been a quiet week, Chief. How is retirement treating you?"

"I decided to go back to work so I can get a few things done."

The Chief looked at the second officer, "Bill, heard you have a new baby."

"My very own little Billy Boy Browning. Snuff already loves him and doesn't allow any strangers near him."

The Chief looked at Snuff. "Remember me, boy? I gave you treats when you went through training. You did great when you passed your drug sniffing trials."

The German Shepherd's tail wagged rapidly as his long tongue hung out the side of his mouth. He jumped from the patrol boat into *Gertie*. The Chief knelt on one knee, patted the dog, and rubbed his neck fondly.

"Good boy, you did remember me, didn't you?"

The Chief and the two officers chatted for a few more minutes as Snuff chose to investigate *Gertie*. He moved around the deck sniffing, as Bill had trained him to do. He stopped next to the built-in seat. After sniffing for another few seconds, he sat down next to the seat, barked once, and looked at his master in anticipation of a reward.

"Snuff, what are you doing, boy?" Bill asked.

"Maybe he thinks I have drugs hidden under the seat cushion," the Chief said with a wide grin.

"Come over here, Snuff. Come now."

Snuff didn't budge and he didn't bark.

"Chief, do you mind if I board your boat?" Bill asked.

"Not at all. Come over. You're more than welcome."

Bill pulled the patrol boat closer to *Gertie*. He stepped on board and went over to Snuff. He lifted up the seat cushion. Beneath the cleaning supplies, he found a black plastic bag. When the officer checked inside, he found a partial brick of black tar heroin.

For the first time in his life, the Chief panicked.

Chapter 8

Benny, the sketch artist from headquarters, walked down the ramp of the ferry after it docked in Christensted. He knew he would be working with Charlie Mikkelsen. It would be the third time she would provide the information he needed to do his job. He carried his laptop loaded with software that would build a computerized portrait of the killer as it was fed information.

Benny looked forward to spending time with her. He enjoyed Charlie's unique and gregarious personality. He knew his finished sketch would be close to perfect because she was fastidious about her observations and details.

From the dock, Benny took a cab to Frederiksted and met Charlie in the lobby of the station. They went into a conference room and worked for almost an hour before Charlie had to leave. Before Benny returned to headquarters, he left a disc with the sketch of the murderer in Chamaign's office, greeted every officer in the building by name, and left for the ferry to return to police headquarters in St. Thomas.

OUTSIDE the marina, two men stood on the far side of the security gates. Both were dressed in khaki cargo pants and torn, but washed, tees. They weren't as interested in their beers as they were in the empty docking slip next to the owner's office.

"It took us all day to locate the dumb boat yesterday, Zeke. Then those people were on it last night. Where did the boat go? What do we do now?"

"Keep your voice down, Wizard. I don't see anyone around so maybe the owner has taken the boat out. We need to get our stuff off it somehow."

"How? We can't even get into the marina. We need some kind of key or something to get through the gate."

"We'll get in," he said. "We have a big investment stashed on the boat. If we don't sell our drugs, we can't replace all the money I swiped from Nana's savings account. The old lady's almost blind, but she'll figure out what I did sooner or later."

Wizard was Zeke's younger brother. A dark-skinned high school dropout, Wizard was a roly-poly nineteen-year-old. A classmate had bullied him out of his lunch money all through grade school. On the days he bought his lunch and had no cash, he went home bloody. By age fifteen, he attempted to rob a bank when two friends dared him to do it. He was caught, tried as an adult, and sent to prison. Wizard was now out on parole.

Zeke was taller and thinner, but not a whole lot brighter than his baby brother. Both men lived at their grandmother's house and were out of work more often than they held jobs.

"What are we going to do and when?" Wizard asked.

"Let's hop over the gate. We need to check the rest of the marina to see if the boat is docked elsewhere. Pretend we're looking at the boats, so act casual."

Both brothers climbed over the gate and sauntered toward the piers. Jeremy was in the middle of processing payroll when he noticed the two strangers on one of his security monitors. He went outside to see who they were and what they wanted. As he approached the men, Jeremy asked how he could help them.

"We were looking for the boat docked next to your office yesterday. We're interested in buying it."

"Sir, that boat is not for sale. As far as I know, none of the crafts at this marina are on the market. You should try Ole Luther's Marine

Repair Shop. He has used boats for sale."

"Can we walk down the piers and see a couple of boats," Wizard asked. "We're not criminals or anything."

Zeke glared at his brother as he kicked his ankle. "It's time to go, bro. We'll let this man get back to his job."

Jeremy headed back to his office. He stood outside until the men were on the other side of the gate.

"I had to ask, Zeke. He might have let us stay."

"Do you realize what you did?"

Wizard shook his head. The way his brother spoke to him made him look down at the ground. He realized he had done something wrong.

"When you started prattling, the man in the office took a good hard look at both of us. He could identify us to the police if asked."

"What are we gonna do? We need to get our heroin."

"Lower your voice. After it is dark, we'll return and see if the boat is at the marina. If it is, we'll climb the fence again, board, and retrieve our stuff. No one will ever see us."

CHARLIE headed for the airport carrying her brand-new Barbie-pink leather purse. It was a smidgen smaller than a hot air balloon. The pocketbook had a white leather flap on the front and a wide white over-the-shoulder strap. There were gold metal snaps, zippers, and sundry other decorative hardware weighing a half-ton.

Before leaving the house earlier, she stuffed it with her large digital SLR Canon camera, three bottles of water, and a zippy stuffed with chocolate mini-doughnuts. She arrived in time to see the 757 swoop in for a perfect landing.

She parked and walked directly to the outdoor baggage claim area and stood near the carousel. It was a wondrous morning with a light cerulean blue sky. The soft ocean breeze would keep everyone comfortable until the tropical sun reached its peak in the sky. Charlie knew her family would enjoy a taste of paradise after a horrific winter filled with back-to-back snowstorms from the mid-West to Philly.

Ms. Charlie, I hear buzzing and I'm afraid of bees.

I don't see any bees, but I do hear buzzing.

What's the noise?

Aha! My new smart phone.

Why is it vibrating?

Don't know.

Charlie retrieved the phone from her purse after a significant amount of digging.

I have a text message.

What's a text message, Missy?

It's when you write something in code and send it like email over the phone. When they publish a Texting for Dummies book, I'll let you know more.

Charlie kept pushing buttons until a message appeared: BRT CWYLA.

What's that supposed to mean, Missy?

I don't know, but I bet it's from one of my granddaughters.

A second message appeared: RUT M.

Ms. Charlie, you're not in any rut! What are they telling you?

Got me. This isn't the shorthand I learned in high school.

Charlie didn't know how to reply to the text or how to decipher the texting lingo. While she pondered her dilemma, she heard two happy voices yell in unison, "Grandmom!"

She saw Jake and two grinning granddaughters emerge from the airport and head for baggage claim.

JAKE, Charlie's oldest son, was six feet-two with broad shoulders and a well-honed gut. He was divorced and in his mid-forties. His hair was salt and pepper with more emphasis on salt than pepper. He wore his favorite black shirt with the orange Harley-Davidson logo on the front. Like many tourists, he wore jeans.

Molly, now fourteen, inherited her dad's perfect smile. She had a thick mane of long, dark brown hair with a hint of curl. Like many teens, she spent an hour each day straightening her hair before leaving for school. Her most distinctive feature, however, was her wide, stately shoulders – the envy of every model world-wide.

Annie was the sixteen year-old daughter of Charlie's middle son JJ. He had driven Annie from their Indiana home to Pennsylvania so she could travel with her uncle and cousin to see grandmom. The three planned a one-week stay.

Annie was petite and naturally thin. Her light brown hair was full of curls, and the teen let them drape down the side of her face almost to her shoulders. Her smile was sweet and gentle. Whenever she flashed it, she captured a heart or two.

While Molly was outgoing, Annie was reserved; while Molly walked into a room and made a new world of friends, Annie cultivated friendships one by one. Both girls loved their BFFs and would kill for a sleepover seven nights a week.

CHARLIE couldn't give and get hugs fast enough. It had been five months since she had been stateside, and she hadn't realized how much she missed the other two-thirds of her family. After all the appropriate greetings, the four of them divvied up Molly's three jumbo pieces of luggage. Jake attached Annie's carry-on on top of his trunk-size suitcase.

Grandmom listened to the girls' incessant chatter all the way to the parking lot. After stashing the luggage in the trunk, the family slid into the used silver Camry Charlie had bought for her snowbird months on the island. The girls continued to prattle.

"You didn't answer my text, Grandmom," Molly said.

"I wasn't sure what you said. What does RUT mean?"

Molly looks sideways at her grandmother. She didn't want to call her grandmother a dolt, but she did think grandmom was a bit obtuse. "R means ARE. Y means YOU."

"And T means THERE. Right?" Charlie asked with a pleased grin spread across her face.

Molly nodded as she curled a tress around her finger.

"What do you think of my text?" Annie asked.

"BRT CWY A. You got me, Annie. I don't know."

"It means I'll be right there and chat with you."

"And how was I supposed to know that?" Charlie asked.

Annie tittered as she beamed her best smile.

"Grandmom, you've got a get with the program," Molly said as her fingers arranged her hair on the side of her face behind her ears.

On what planet do these two live, Ms. Charlie?

Good question. It definitely isn't earth.

Does the "i" in iPhone stand for intelligent, Missy?

I only have a smart phone, so what do I know?

Charlie didn't want to appear too dated, so she changed the subject. "Molly, you brought enough luggage to spend the month!"

"Can I stay a month?" Molly asked, knowing full well spring break lasted only one week. "I brought my laptop so I can get my homework assignments, and I can keep up-to-date by texting my friends."

Jake responded, "Don't think so, kiddo. When I go home, you go home."

"Annie, how did you manage all your clothes in a single carry-on?" Charlie asked.

"I only needed shorts and tops and a couple of bathing suits."

"You're amazing, Annie," said Jake. "You need to teach Molly how to pack small."

"Da-ad," Molly said. "I brought what I needed."

Jake slipped into the driver's seat. As he turned the key in the ignition he said, "When I was here before, Mom, you showed me the home of my great, great, great grandparents."

Charlie nodded as she wondered why he alluded to the house in Frederiksted.

"Can we go there now? I want to check something."

"Is there any particular reason we need to do it now, Jake?"

"I'll tell you when we get there."

Jake's unexpected request made Charlie curious, "Good idea. We can show Molly and Annie the house."

As Jake headed out of the parking lot, Molly screeched, "Dad, you're driving is crazy!"

Simultaneously, Annie yelled, "Uncle Jake, you're on the wrong side of the road! Move over before we're all killed."

Jake chuckled. On purpose, he had not told the teens how people drive on the left side of the road instead of the right. He explained the local custom.

"Why on earth would they drive on the wrong side?" Annie asked as the whites of her eyes grew bigger.

"Good question," Grandmom said. "I haven't figured it out yet myself. On occasion I still find myself in the wrong lane."

After the first left turn, Annie and Molly decided to keep their eyes closed so their stomachs wouldn't turn inside out. Jake teased them, but he found himself in the wrong lane twice as they weaved their way toward the town of Frederiksted.

As they drove down King Street, Charlie pointed to her ancestor's home from 1846 until her great, great grandmother's death in the late 1890s. Jake pulled the car into a space and parked.

"It's so big, Grandmom. Can we go inside?"

"Unfortunately, no. Someone else owns the house now."

Jake said, "Mom, remember this?"

From his pocket, Jake retrieved a large, solid gold woman's locket watch. Attached was a thick gold rope chain. As Charlie took the watch she said, "It's as beautiful as I remember. It's too bad the front and back are so worn. I can barely make out the etched design." She pressed the tiny tab on top of the watch. It opened the casing. "The watch is working! You fixed it."

"Those watch tools I bought came in handy. It keeps perfect time now."

Molly and Annie glanced at each other with dropped jaws. "Where did the watch come from, Dad?" Molly asked.

"Grandmom gave it to me to save. It belonged to grandmom's great-great-grandmother – the very one who lived in this house. You've never seen the watch before because I've kept it in a safe deposit box."

"It's been decades since I've seen it," Charlie said. "Now that I see the house and watch at the same time, the etching on the front looks like this house."

"It's what I was thinking, and it's why I brought the watch with me."

Molly asked, "How old is the watch, Dad?"

Jake showed the teens the inside of the rear gold casing. "See, here – it says from CJM to CJM 1867."

Charlie explained to her granddaughters that the initials were those of their ancestors – Christoffer Jacob Mikkelsen and Claudine Joan Mikkelsen. "And see ladies, the gold assay number is also included as well as the production number. The assay number tells us how pure the gold is. Years ago, I took it to a jeweler whose hobby was locket watches. He looked up the production number and told me when it was manufactured."

"Remember the back casing, Mom?" Jake asked.

Charlie turned the watch over and read aloud, "X Marks My Heart." She showed her granddaughters the inscription engraved below an etching. She told them she never knew what it meant.

"Awesome," Molly said.

"Romantic," Annie said.

Charlie examined the etching closer.

Jake said, "I know it's worn, but I think the etching is a fireplace."

"That doesn't make sense. We're in the tropics and the houses down here don't need fireplaces. I was inside this house once and it doesn't have a kitchen or running water."

Jake said, "Before I left home I cleaned the watch and polished the gold. I kept looking at the rear casing and thought I spotted something. I used my jeweler's loop and found an X on the upper left side of the fireplace." Jake handed his mother the loop. "Tell me what you think."

Charlie put the loop in front of her right eye and scrutinized the rear of the watch. "It is most definitely an X, and the X is engraved in the middle of a stone. That's a bit bizarre."

"Maybe the X means a treasure is buried inside the fireplace," Molly said.

"Maybe that's wishful thinking," Grandmom replied as she watched her granddaughters in the rear view mirror.

"But it must be important to have it engraved on the watch," Annie said. "I bet the X has something to do with love."

"We need to find the treasure, Dad," Molly said.

Annie said, "There may be a treasure, Molly, but I bet the saying means our ancestors loved each other. How romantic is that?"

The exuberant teens were so preoccupied with their fanciful visions of love and treasure, they ignored their vibrating cells and text messages arriving by the dozens from their friends stateside.

JEREMY stopped his truck in front of a small hotel on the boardwalk.

"This looks pretty nice," he said.

"Once I check in, we can go apartment hunting," Laurie said. "When I find something, you can help me shop for some used furniture."

"You register and I'll go to the marina. If Gil can take over, I'll join you. Be right back."

Laurie smothered Jeremy's lips with a wet sloppy kiss and then both of them slipped out of the truck. Jeremy wiped the lipstick off his face with the back of his hand. He then carried Laurie's suitcases inside. Once back in the truck, he headed for the marina. He parked and went through the security gate. Once he opened his office, he checked his phone messages before he went to find Gil.

Meanwhile, Gil, the former owner of the marina, was sitting on a stool at the Shanty gassing with his childhood buddy, Sammy Berger.

"Sammy, you're one of my oldest pals who is married. I need some expert advice from a pro. This ole heart of mine thumps away every time I think about my little bowl of puddin."

"Did I just hear what I thought I heard? Puddin? Gil, it sounds like the love bug has gone and bit you."

"Holy Moly, Sammy, do you realize I'm now eighty? I think it's time to settle down and take me a wife."

"Sure you want that? You always liked being single."

"I did like my bachelor days, Sammy, but now it's nice to jist sit on Jeanette's front porch swing and hold her hand. It's almost like I'm sixteen again." Gil pushed out his chest and pounded it like Tarzan. Both men hooted in amusement.

"You damned ole fool," Sammy snorted. "Got me a good woman

over sixty years ago. Now we get to watch our grandchildren have children. Yeah, Gil, a good woman does make a difference."

Engaged in his conversation, Gil didn't hear Jeremy come up behind him.

"Gil, can you keep an eye on the marina for me today?"

Gil recognized Jeremy's voice and turned, "Howdy, young fella. Where are you off to?"

Jeremy told him about Laurie and her apartment search.

"You're in love, too. I can tell," Sammy laughed. "Love must be contagious around here."

"Why do you think I'm in love?" Jeremy asked as he tried to hide the stupid grin on his face with his hand.

Sammy snapped his suspenders on his chest and guffawed. "Three things. The first clue is you have lipstick on one ear. The second clue is you have a tell-tale glint in your eyes."

"I admit to the lipstick," Jeremy said as he rubbed his ear and studied his shoes.

"And we haven't even told you the third clue yet," Gil said as he slapped his thighs in merriment. Jeremy looked at Gil and his buddy.

Sammy said, "The third clue is …"

"Let me tell him, Sammy," Gil said amidst a belly laugh. "Jeremy, the third clue is you're floating on air. We didn't even hear you come up behind us!"

Sammy and Gil roared with laughter at Jeremy's expense. Finally Gil stopped his shenanigans. "I'll take care of the marina, young fella. I can tell your heart is thumpin, too!"

"Let me out of here," Jeremy said as he fled the scene. He knew his crimson face burned from embarrassment, and not from the searing sun. There were rounds of laughter behind him as he walked away.

As he left the marina, his thoughts turned to Laurie. He didn't even notice his new boat wasn't at the pier.

OFFICER Bill Browning was flustered. "Chief Hanneman, I'm sorry. I have to impound your boat. I'm sure there is a good explanation."

The Chief nodded his head and looked away. As a young cop, he had impounded any number of boats transporting drugs.

Bill stepped aside as the Chief climbed into the patrol boat. Bill and Snuff followed. Officer Martin tied a towline to *Gertie* and headed to the police dock. The Chief stood on the stern and shook his head at the incredulity of the situation.

OFFICER Chamaign Benton called St. Thomas Detective Marlboro Man Carmen at his office. The headquarters for the Virgin Islands Police Department was located in the Criminal Justice Center in Charlotte Amalie. The St. Thomas police force was part of the same complex.

"Marlboro Man, I have the names and addresses of the two hit and run victims I called you about. The man is Thomas Otts. He has a long rap sheet. Let's hope his family is on the island. The woman is Carolyn Rodriguez. Her license expired four years ago. She uses a Post Office Box, so you'll need to do a trace on her."

Man asked, "Where does the perp live?"

"We think he lives in St. Croix because he has access to a car. Bennie and Charlie got together this morning and did a sketch. I'll fax it to you in a minute."

"Charlie? Charlie Mikkelsen?"

"Yep. One and the same. Charlie witnessed one of his hand tricks and wrote down his physical description."

"Chamaign, the VIPD would save a lot of time if they simply hired her. She comes face-to-face with more bad guys than we do."

"I'm sure the Chief will lock her up if she gets involved in this double homicide."

The two detectives shared VIPD gossip for a few minutes before they disconnected.

Chapter 9

Deputy Police Chief James Kingston blurted into the phone, "What!" when Officer Bill Browning told him that he was bringing the Chief in for questioning.

Bill explained as James paced and listened intently.

James had been a detective under Hanneman for several years. He had started his career with the St. Thomas PD. He transferred to St. Croix to go undercover for a big drug bust. During this time, he met and fell in love with Elin. He applied for Hanneman's position when the Chief retired.

"Sir," Bill Browning said, "we weren't looking for drugs on the Chief's boat. Carlos and I first saw *Gertie* as we exited the Salt River, so we slowed down to say hello. Snuff recognized the Chief and jumped from our boat to his expecting a treat. As we talked, Snuff picked up a whiff of the drugs and did exactly what he was trained to do."

"What did Chief Hanneman say?"

"He stood there with his mouth agape," Bill said. "He didn't speak all the way to the dock. Sir, I asked permission to board, and Chief Hanneman motioned me onboard. Carlos Martin witnessed everything.

"Snuff found one partial brick and the rest of the skag was in individual packets hidden everywhere. I told Chief Hanneman I had to impound the boat and we towed it in. I called you directly because I wanted to warn you before we got to the station."

"Did you cuff the Chief?"

"I know I should have followed police procedure, but I didn't think it would be right."

"This is one time I'm glad you didn't follow protocol. Who knows about this, Bill?"

"Our men at the dock."

"That means everyone in the entire VIPD will know about this in the next five minutes. Gossip travels between these islands faster than the winds of a hurricane. When you get here, casually escort Chief Hanneman to my office and don't discuss this anymore with anyone on your way in or afterward. Got that?"

LAWYER Pete Hummel was speaking with the desk clerk at the police station when an officer tacked a wanted poster on the lobby bulletin board.

"What's the poster all about?" he asked the clerk. The clerk told him the man was wanted for picking pockets.

"Got an extra copy of it?"

The clerk handed him one.

"And the cops don't know who this is, right?"

The clerk nodded. Pete rushed out of the station, jumped into his BMW, and gleefully left town.

The cops don't know this man, but I do. I got me a new client.

AFTER Chamaign faxed Marlboro Man the sketch of the suspect, she and Bob Thompson left the station to interview Bert the Bartender. She took a copy of the sketch with her. She hoped Bert might be able to identify him since so many locals patronized his bar.

When she and Bob got there, the Palm Shack hadn't opened yet. Bert was inside wiping tables. When he heard the knock on the back door, he peeked outside and saw a dark blue VIPD SUV. Bert opened the door, "What do you need, officers?"

"Some cooperation from our favorite bartender," Chamaign said.

Bert stood back and motioned the officers inside.

Six feet, six inches in height and two-forty in weight, Officer Thompson squatted on a bar stool. Sitting, he was taller than Chamaign.

Bob spoke, "We have two things we want to discuss, Bert. A theft and the double murder. Let's start with the theft. We have this sketch." Bob slid the image out of a large tan envelope. Chamaign saw Bert wince when he saw the likeness.

"Don't know who he is," Bert said.

"Sure you don't know, Bert?" Chamaign replied. "Usually everyone stops in your bar sooner or later."

"Nope. Don't recognize him."

"Officer Thompson," Chamaign said without looking at Bob, "do you have any contacts at the health department?"

"Sure do – a couple people, in fact."

"What do you think they would think of that filthy rag Bert is using to wipe tables?"

"I suspect they would test it for botulism or something even worse."

"Are those droppings under the table next to you?"

"Could be. If they are, the Department of Health would want to identify the rodent and make Bert fumigate the place."

"What would happen to the bar while all this testing and fumigating went on, Officer Thompson?"

"Okay, okay, okay. I get it," Bert said. "This is how I earn an honest living, officers. I can't afford to close down. I've seen the guy before and he was in here yesterday."

"How good is the sketch?" Chamaign asked.

"Really good. His hair is a little lighter, and he has a small light-colored mustache."

"Thank you, Bert. Now what's his name?"

"What did he do? Are you going to protect me if he finds out I told you?"

"His name, Bert. Consider this your civic duty and good deed for the day," Chamaign said.

"Roland something. He never told me his last name. I've heard some people call him Ro."

"Come in here often?" Bob asked.

"About once a week, maybe. Sometimes twice."

"Where does he live?"

"Never said."

"What kind of a car does he drive?"

"Old Chevy, really old. The tires are almost bald. We're talking a late eighties model. He must have started to paint it, but only got as far as the gray primer paint."

Mathematical formulas like two plus two started to float through Chamaign's head.

Large car with bald tires. Could this be connected to the murders? That would be too easy.

"Bert, was this Roland in here when the young couple came in? I'm talking about the two who were run over," Chamaign asked.

"Yeah. Didn't notice when he left because things picked up after the parade."

"Was he here at the time of the accident?"

Bob Thompson noted Chamaign's line of questioning and realized where she was going with her questions.

"Didn't notice," Bert said.

"Where were you when those two young people were killed?"

"In here working. Didn't know about it at first."

"How did you hear about it?"

"An old geezer stopped in and asked me to call nine-one-one. He didn't have a cell phone. Can you believe there are people who still don't have a cell phone?"

"Bert, let's stick with the topic. Did you go to the scene of the accident?"

"Sure did. Locked the cash draw and went out. All of my customers did the same thing. Sure wish I hadn't gone – got sick afterward."

"Was this Roland at the scene of the accident?"

"Don't think so."

"Did you see anyone other than the people in your bar?"

"Only the old geezer."

"Anything else we should know?"

"I'll call if I think of anything," Bert said. "By the way, what did Roland do?"

"He picked quite a few pockets at the parade," Chamaign said as her mind churned.

Chamaign and Bob left. As they went out the door, Chamaign said, "We'll be back, Bert."

A few feet outside the bar, Chamaign explained her math formula.

"So the pickpocket had a beef with the young couple, and therefore decided to kill them when he saw them. Yeah, Chamaign, the answer is four," Bob said.

GIL Cliver slipped into Jeremy's office to use his phone.

"Miss Jeanette, this is Gil," he said.

"Oh Gil, I knew who you were a soon as I heard your voice. How is my handsome Popeye today?"

"I'm doing good. And you?"

"Fine, just fine. I started thinking about you so decided to make one of my mango mousse pies. Can you come over tonight?"

"Not tonight, Sweetie. I'm helping the young fella at the marina. Can I come tomorrow? I sure do miss my sweetheart."

The short and plump bundle of energy with light brown skin and kinky gray hair said, "Oh Gil, you always make me blush. I'm a little disappointed I won't see you tonight, but tomorrow is fine."

After Gil hung up, he rubbed the palms of his hands together and then slapped his thighs in excitement.

Holy Moly! I'll see my Olive Oyl tomorrow. Can't wait.

TERRY Mitchell, a reporter for the Virgin Island Press, approached the duty officer behind the front desk and identified himself.

"Sir, I'd like to speak to the detective who is handling the double murder."

"That would be Detective Benton. She is out at the moment. You can have a seat and wait."

Terry sat on a nearby bench. From where he was perched, he could see the office of James Kingston through a glass wall. Terry watched the Chief pace, sit, tap the fingers of his right hand on top of his desk, and then get up and repeat the cycle. Terry smelled a story. He looked around and saw several other officers in the corner huddled together. He had seen the same thing outside when he entered the station, but hadn't thought anything about it.

He saw retired Chief Hanneman and another officer come down the hall and enter James' office. He noticed the body language of the officers in the area. They all diverted their eyes as the Chief passed. He saw Chief Kingston close the blinds in his office windows and shut the door.

Something is going on! I've got some digging to do.

THE CHIEF'S foot tapped the floor as he folded and unfolded his hands. He started to speak before James, his protégé, asked a question. "James, I know absolutely nothing about those drugs."

"I believe you, Chief. We need to figure out what is going on."

James looked at Bill Browning. "Bill, would you get a tape recorder and bring it in here?"

"The boat's been in dry dock for the last two years, James. Yesterday and today are the only times I been on *Gertie* in those two years."

"Chief, let's wait a second until the tape recorder arrives."

"James, my fingerprints are all over my boat! I spent two hours cleaning her today and wiping the other prints way."

Bill Browning returned and set up the tape recorder. James had the Chief identify himself and then he identified Bill and himself as present. He gave the date and time of the session. The questions began and Victor's right foot tapped the floor the whole time.

"Chief, we need you to fill in the blanks. Give us some basics first, like how long you have owned *Gertie*, and where she has been docked for the last two years." The Chief sighed and his eyes lowered. His body language was that of a worried little boy as he slid down in the seat trying to disappear. He answered the questions.

Midway through the Chief's story, James asked, "Has anyone else been on the boat recently?"

The Chief answered, "Luther and his crew help me set her back in the water yesterday. Later that day, Jeremy and I did a spin down the coast."

"Let's clarify this, Chief. Are we speaking of Jeremy Bauer, the marina's owner?"

"Yes. He and I went for a ride before he decided to buy *Gertie*. I returned to the marina this morning to change the oil, take one last spin, and clean out my personal things."

"Has anyone else been on board recently?"

"Jeremy was on board last night. At least I think it was Jeremy. There were food containers in the trash bin and two empty bottles of beer in the sink. It looks like he was with someone. James, Jeremy would never be involved in drugs – you know that."

"Bill, make a note to ask Jeremy about last night," James said.

"Chief, you said the boat was not docked in the water for two years. Where was it?"

"I stored it on the side lot of Ole Luther's Marine Repair Shop. It was kept inside his fenced yard."

James asked questions for the next half hour. "Chief, we will get this resolved. Forensics is going over things now. Let's see what prints we get."

"Am I free to go?"

"Yes, but there will be more questions later. You might want to talk to a lawyer before this thing goes any further."

Frustrated, Victor said, "I haven't done anything wrong, James."

"I know. Get a lawyer just in case. We might have to prove a negative."

REPORTER Terry Mitchell watched as Chief Hanneman left Kingston's office. He noted Officer Bill Browning stayed inside. The officer at the front desk and four other officers had clustered in a small circle in the hallway. All lowered their eyes as the Chief passed, but watched him as he exited the front door. What Terry observed next was even more bizarre. The Chief hailed a cab.

That's odd. Where's his car? What was he doing here? Why is everyone acting so funny?

As Officer Benton entered the building, Terry stopped her before she went down the hall to her mini-office.

"Detective, can you give me an update on the double murders?"

Chamaign invited the young journalist into her small area. She identified the two victims. She told Terry both of the deceased lived on St. Thomas.

"Has the action moved to St. Thomas now?" Terry asked.

Chamaign told Terry that Detective Marlboro Man Carmen would interview the families and neighbors over there; she and Officer Thompson would work the case on St. Croix.

"Do you have any suspects on either island?"

"We have a source who gave us some information, but I can't mention any names. We also have a lead on the perp's car. I need to get information into our computers to see if we get a hit."

"Is the autopsy report on the couple back yet?"

"I haven't seen it. Give me a couple of hours and I'll tell you what I can."

"Thanks, ma'am. One other thing, is there something else going on at the station?"

Chamaign wrinkled her brow, scrunched her shoulders, and said, "Not that I know about."

After Terry left, she opened the folder on her desk.

I don't need any more on my To Do List. I need to hide. Where is that invisibility cloak I borrowed from Harry Potter?

THE CHIEF took a taxi to the marina so he could pick up his equipment and get his own truck. As he entered the parking lot, Jeremy was leaving on one of his little blue rental scooters. The Chief stopped him.

"Hey, Chief, I noticed *Gertie* wasn't around. I thought you might be out on her. What's going on?"

"We need to talk, son. Got a minute?"

"What's up? Did *Gertie* sink or something?"

"No, but maybe I should have deep-sixed her." The Chief explained about the oil change, his housecleaning, his last outing, and about Bill Browning and Snuff.

"Someone stored drugs on *Gertie*?"

"Black tar heroin. There was part of a brick in the storage area under the seats on the stern. Also, the police found filled zip bags in the cabinet over the sink, the refrigerator, and in two gas cans. They actually found some paraphernalia stored behind the toilet tank."

"Chief, your fingerprints have to be all over the boat, correct?"

The Chief nodded, "And worse yet, it was in all the places where the drugs were hid. I thought the bag in the refrigerator was yours so I removed it when I cleaned the inside. If that isn't bad enough, I put the bag neatly back in place. I even touched the brick under the seat when I removed my paper towels and window cleaner. It was wrapped in black plastic. Would you believe I moved the two gas cans to the deck when I wanted to start the engines? I'll be in jail by tomorrow – if they wait that long."

"Laurie and I ate on *Gertie* last night, Chief. Our fingerprints will be there too,"

"Did you touch the paper bag in the fridge or the outside of the gas cans?"

"No, I thought the bag and cans were yours."

"Well, you can expect an officer to wrap on your office door any minute now."

As the Chief spoke his last syllable, Officer Browning interrupted the conversation.

"Mr. Bauer, may I speak with you privately?"

ROLAND hosed the front and rear bumper of his old car, as well as the entire chassis. Afterward, he used a dent repair kit and a rubber hammer to repair most of the dents caused by the two bodies.

It's a good thing none of my lights broke.

He hand-wiped the car dry, but noticed there was a tinge of pink on the towel.

I better pick up a couple gallons of bleach and rewash tomorrow.

He put the hose and rags away and went inside to change his clothes. He showered in cold water before he changed into tan pants and a wrinkled blue cotton shirt covered with tiny white sailboats. It, too, had a special pocket sewn inside. He pulled half of a sub out of the mini-refrigerator. He ate it standing up because he didn't feel like cleaning his mess off the bench seat.

CHAMAIGN rapped on James' door. "Boss, is something going on? People are acting a bit funny around here. I went to the copy machine and the place is as quiet as a mouse. Why is everyone whispering?"

"Your radar is working well. Chamaign, have a seat."

"What did I miss?"

"You missed the Chief being brought in for questioning. Drugs were found on his boat."

"You couldn't possibly think the Chief is a seller or distributor, do you?"

"No, but the lab reports show the Chief's prints were on several containers where the drugs were stored. The whole thing makes me very uncomfortable."

"Who knows about this?"

"You're probably the last person to know." James explained about the patrol boat, the Chief, and how Jeremy had been onboard the night before. "That gives us two strong suspects, but I don't think either is guilty."

"Did anyone else have access to *Gertie*?"

James explained about the boat in dry dock.

"Who's going to run with this case?"

"At the moment, Bill Browning. I spoke to my boss, Bill Farrow, and he requested the Commissioner appoint someone outside of St. Croix to take the case. Because of the relationship between this department and the Chief, we need an independent third party to handle it. I don't think even your fellow detective, Marlboro Man Carmen, will be allowed on the case even though he's from St. Thomas. He's been too close to our people in those last three big cases."

"I'm dumbfounded, stupefied and flabbergasted. What can I do?"

James smiled before he answered, "Those words all mean the same thing, Chamaign."

"I know, I know. You got my drift, right?"

"I got your drift. You and Bob work the double homicides for now. Anything new on that front?"

"We're running a trace on the car. It's so old, there shouldn't be many on the island. Bob and I will interview the owners and inspect the cars." Chamaign then explained her two plus two theory.

"Good work, detective. Continue. I'd like this case wrapped up so we can concentrate on the Chief and the drugs."

As Chamaign headed for her office, she passed Officer Browning and Jeremy. She gave Jeremy a thumbs-up.

LAWYER Pete Hummel drove to the small trailer owned by his old high school buddy, Roland.

I often wondered how Ro earned his living. Picking pockets, huh buddy? You sly ole rat. Hope you're home. Believe me, you want me to find you before the police find you. You need a lawyer and I need a good case if I want to buy out that fossilized old goat Murray Sedge.

Pete parked in front of the trailer. "Ro," Pete yelled from the front seat of his convertible.

Roland was inside when he heard Pete call his name. He peeked out the door and then smiled as he trotted to the BMW.

"Ro, the police have a BOLO out on you. They even have a sketch – a darn good one too."

"How did they get it?"

"I don't know, but I do know you need a good defense attorney."

"I wonder how they know what I look like."

"Someone saw you."

"It was an accident. I didn't hit the couple on purpose."

"Are you talking about that hit and run last evening, Roland?"

"It was an accident."

"Stop right there. I thought they were after you for picking pockets."

"That was earlier at the parade."

"I don't think the police connected you to the accident yet. Get hold of your mother, father, brothers and sisters, and aunts and uncles. You're going to need all the money you can get your hands on. You need my skilled and specialized services even more than I thought."

Pete handed Roland a business card: Murray Sedge and Associates, Peter M. Hummel, LL.D, Defense Attorney.

Pete drove away with a grin on his face.

Forget the pick-pocketing. I've got me a double homicide, and better yet, I know things the cops don't. I'm a rather nice-looking winner if I say so myself.

JEREMY wiped the fingerprint ink off his fingers as he sat down in the interrogation room. Officer Browning thanked him for his cooperation.

"Mr. Bauer, how often have you been in the Chief's powerboat?"

Jeremy told him how he and the Chief took the trip up the coast and about the evening he spent with Laurie.

"While you were on the boat, can you tell me what you may have touched?"

"Pretty much everything. I was at the helm, the Captain's chair, the deck chairs, the table, and the refrigerator."

"Were you in the head?"

"No, the Chief had told me the pipes were drained."

"Let's go over each activity in order, Mr. Bauer."

Step-by-step, Jeremy retraced every step he took while onboard.

"What about your girlfriend? I need to know her personal information and how I can reach her."

Chapter 10

While pacing on his enclosed sun porch, the Chief called Charlie. "I'm in big trouble and my name is anathema at the police department right now."

Ms. Charlie, what does anathema mean?

I'm trying to remember ...

Why is he using such a big word?

Because he's now into crossword puzzles to keep his mind sharp. He is trying to remember everything he's forgotten. Now shush, I need to listen.

"What happened, Victor?"

Charlie spent the next fifteen minutes listening to Victor's tale. Her anxiety level grew exponentially, especially after he mentioned Jeremy's name.

"What did James say? He couldn't possibly believe that either you or Jeremy is involved in drugs!"

The Chief told her what James said and explained that the police commissioner would probably assign someone from another island to work the case.

Ms. Charlie, I missed what the Chief said. I'm still on anathema.

The word means no one at the station wants anything to do with him right now. He's been ostracized.

Ostrich what?

Not ostrich, stupid. Ostracized. Like no one will speak to him.

I think you're the one who has been doing too many crossword puzzles, Missy!

"Victor, how long do you think Jeremy will be at the police station?"

"Until Bill Browning finishes his questions."

"You were a cop for almost forty years, Victor. I don't see how anyone can question your honesty."

"I was a cop long enough to know they already have enough evidence to arrest me."

"Do either you or Jeremy need a lawyer?"

"Jeremy doesn't, but I do. I called Murray Sedge. He is the best defense attorney on our islands. Sedge has an office on St. Croix, but the attorney here is an ambulance chaser. I'm headed for St. Thomas to meet with Sedge."

"Are you staying overnight?"

"I'm sure I'll miss the last ferry, so I'll stay. I'll call you from my hotel."

"I'll be at dinner this evening with Jake, Jeremy, Laurie and the girls. Call me around ten."

THE police computer burped. Five names appeared as owners of the possible cars involved in the hit and run. Chamaign and Bob took the list and started their investigation.

They stopped at the home of Josh Hopkins. With his permission, they inspected his old Chevy. There was no evidence of recent damage to the already dented old clunker. Bob used his Polylight to look for signs of blood. There were none.

They drove to the residence of both Roland Coombs and Abe Bissler. Neither person was home nor were their cars. The officers visited Edie Walters. Her car had been in a wreck and it was in her backyard on blocks. It, too, proved negative for damage and blood. On their last stop, Shaquille Montour refused to allow them to inspect his car. From the street, there seemed to be no apparent damage, plus the paint was a dull red instead of the gray primer.

"Any thoughts, Bob?"

"I think we can scratch the Montour car off the list, but I'll get a warrant to check for blood anyway. I think we need to visit Mr. Coombs and Mr. Bissler early tomorrow morning with warrants in our hands."

CHARLIE, Jake and the teens picked out a casual restaurant for dinner. It was located on the small boardwalk in Christensted. Laurie joined them. They slid into a corner booth. Jake and his mother were inside flanked by Molly, Annie and Laurie.

"Where's Jeremy?" Laurie asked. "He didn't answer his cell."

Charlie explained the events as relayed by the Chief.

"They will find my prints, too," Laurie said. "I guess an officer will be rapping on my door soon."

"Jeremy should be here in a minute," Jake said. "If not, we'll get takeout and go down to the jail and join him in his cell for dinner."

"Let's not even use words like cell and jail, Jake."

"You don't really think either Jeremy or the Chief is involved, do you, Ms. Mikkelsen?" Laurie asked.

"I don't. And Laurie, please call me Charlie, okay?"

Why do I have to call you Ms. Charlie if she can call you Charlie?

Because I have to separate you from me.

What do you mean?

If you're Charlie and I'm Charlie, which one of us is the real Charlie?

Both of us, Missy.

Then one of us is delusional.

Not me!

Yes, you. You exist for the sole purpose of my mental health!

"I'm baaack," Jeremy said as he hugged Laurie and kissed her on the cheek. He sat down next to her.

"Jeremy," his mother said, "tell us all you know and don't you dare skip one detail."

Jeremy chronicled everything that happened and then answered two dozen questions. “It was an interesting experience. They do need an interior decorator to redo their ugly gray interrogation room.”

“I’m not sure you should be so blasé about this,” Laurie said. “Did you speak to the Chief at all?”

Jeremy told his audience everything the Chief told him before officer Browning showed up at the marina.

“This is a real mess,” Laurie said.

“The police aren’t wasting any time on this and neither is Victor,” Charlie said. “He went to see a defense attorney on St. Thomas today.”

Charlie told her family that an officer from St. Thomas would be assigned to the case. “They believe someone from another island would be impartial.”

You don’t think the Chief is guilty, do you, Ms. Charlie?

No retired man who irons his tee shirts, jeans, sheets and towels could possibly be guilty of such a crime.

If he ends up in jail, you’ll have to buy him a dozen crossword puzzle books, Missy.

Shush or I’ll vivisect you – that’s an eight letter word that means I’ll slice you in half!

OFFICER Bill Browning entered James’ office.

“Anything new, Bill?” James asked.

“They finished examining *Gertie*. Someone removed her inboard fuel tank and installed a new one. It had split compartments – one half for gas and one half for drugs. There were no drugs inside.”

“Prints?”

“The Chief's prints were all over the boat, including the bow area and the head. Only two prints were on the fly bridge. The Chief did have his prints on the gas cap.”

“What about Jeremy Bauer?”

“He had a few prints, but most of those were on the stern. If the Chief cleaned the boat like he said he did, it helps to explain why there were so few prints for Bauer or anyone else. The prints we have are being run now. I need to visit Luther Scott tomorrow and see if he'll volunteer his prints. Also, I need to get prints from Jeremy's girlfriend."

"Bill, Luther was in the service. He will be on file. Call me tonight if anything pops up and hits you in the face. By tomorrow you'll be off the case and a third party will have taken over."

Chapter 11

The main office of Murray Sedge and Associates was in the harbor town of Charlotte Amalie and close to the Criminal Justice Center. The Chief checked into a hotel in town before his appointment. He walked to the lawyer's office. As soon as Sedge's administrative assistant told her boss the Chief had arrived, he opened his office door.

"Good afternoon, Chief Hanneman. I believe our paths have crossed a number of times in court," Sedge said.

"Yes, they have, but I was always on the prosecution's side of the room. You were on the defendant's."

"True enough. I certainly never expected to see you in my office. Fill me in on the details of this case."

The older heavyset lawyer had thick white hair and alert blue eyes tucked under bushy white eyebrows. His reddish complexion and large bulbous nose made the Chief think Mr. Sedge indulged in more than one drink every evening.

Sedge listened intently as the Chief spoke. At each pause in the conversation, he took notes on a yellow legal-size notepad. "When was the last time you were on the boat before yesterday?"

The Chief disclosed as many details as he could remember.

"So if I understand this right, anyone could have accessed your boat over a period of two years while it was at Luther's shipyard. Correct?"

"I suppose. During the day, the boat yard is open. Anyone can enter. Luther locks it at night. He does live above the shop, so if his dogs barked, I'm sure he would have checked on things."

"I can understand fingerprints on the gas cans and fridge, but not on the plastic under the seat. Go over that part of your story again."

The Chief explained about the wake that made him lose his balance.

"Does Luther have any employees?"

"At least eight or nine, maybe. I know the two older guys. They helped Luther and I get *Gertie* back in the water."

"Chief, call me Murray, please. Would you prefer me to call you Chief or Victor?"

"I answer to either."

"Good. I'd like to do some homework on this. It's your dime so you decide. Do you want me to wait to see if the police decide to file charges, or should I go ahead and start my work?"

"To be brutally frank, those prints have me worried."

"Is that a yes?"

"It is."

"I have a private investigator who works for me and he is very good. I'll have him check on some things. I do have an associate on St. Croix, but I believe I am more suitable for this type of thing. Meanwhile, you try not to worry and keep me informed of everything you hear."

The gentlemen shook hands and the Chief left. Victor felt a little encouraged, but not enough to slow down the gastric juices surging through his system.

AFTER dinner and before dessert at a restaurant on the boardwalk, Jake extracted the gold watch and chain from his pants pocket. "Remember this, Jeremy?"

"It belongs to mom, doesn't it?"

"It belonged to her great, great grandmother."

"May I see it?" Laurie asked.

"It's a clue to a buried treasure," Molly declared definitively.

"And it is about true love," Annie added as her face lit up in a smile.

Jake handed the heirloom to Laurie. She opened the casing and examined the timepiece inside.

"This is quite an antique, isn't it? What a treasure!"

Charlie said, "It was made in 1866. That's why the etchings on the casings are so worn."

"What does the *X marks my heart* mean? Is that the part about love, Annie?"

Annie nodded as her cheeks became little red apples and a wide grin appeared. "It's got to be about something romantic."

"I think the *X* means there is a treasure," Molly said. Her big dark brown eyes gleamed with excitement and mischief.

"Jeremy, examine the front," Jake said. "Kinda squint a little and tell me what you see." Jeremy's squinched his eyes and said, "Isn't that the house on King Street?"

"Both mom and I think so. Now look at the back and tell me what you see."

Jeremy squinted again and said, "I'm not sure what it is. What do you think, Laurie?"

Laurie examined the timepiece, "It looks like a fireplace to me."

"That's what I thought," Jake said. "Now look for an X."

Surprised, Laurie blurted, "I see it. I see the X!"

"I think it's a treasure map! Don't you?" Molly asked. Her grin widened and her thick black eyelashes flashed as her excitement grew.

"What kind of treasure do you think it is?" Laurie asked.

"We don't know," Jake said. "It could be anything – our grandpop always talked about Spanish gold. The Spanish did inhabit the island at one time. Maybe there really is buried gold."

"But what about the fireplace?" Annie asked.

Charlie shrugged her shoulders.

"How did they cook?" Jeremy asked.

"Many homes had cookhouses in separate buildings. A

cookhouse! Ohmagosh! Of course, a cookhouse. There is a small building in the back of the house. It is used as the shed, I believe. Maybe it was originally a cookhouse."

Ms. Charlie, why don't you and I go and claim the treasure!

Why don't we win the Power Ball, too? The odds are about the same.

"Let's go check the cookhouse," Molly said. "I bet we'll find the treasure!"

Charlie said, "I believe we would all end up at police headquarters with the Chief. It is a little matter of breaking and entering. The house and the cookhouse are privately owned."

There was silence at the table for a few seconds. Charlie saw Annie texting, "What are you texting?"

"My friends might know what the X means."

Molly added, "I'm texting my friends to see what they think the treasure is."

Ms. Charlie, help me here. How do their thumbs work so fast?

Evolution.

Huh?

It means we descended from the apes.

Apes? I'm glad you didn't say ostriches.

Apes were the first primates with opposable thumbs. If it weren't for apes, thumbs couldn't be used to text today.

Why can't I text?

You don't have fingers, remember? You exist only inside my mind.

"Grandmom, we gotta go check out this treasure," Molly said. "Can't we, please?"

Laurie said, "You have to be practical, Molly. If there is a treasure hidden inside the fireplace, the owner isn't going to hand it over to us."

"Killjoy!" Jeremy said.

"Spoils sports!" Jake said.

"Party pooper!" Annie giggled.

"Wuss!" Molly laughed.

"Realist!" Charlie said.

TERRY Mitchell waited in the police parking lot until the deputy police chief emerged. Chief Kingston winced when he saw Terry with a microphone in his hand.

"Chief Kingston, may I have a moment?"

"A very short moment, Terry."

"According to scuttlebutt, the Chief's boat was impounded."

"True."

"Were there really drugs onboard?"

"Yes, Terry."

"My source said it was black tar heroin. Is that correct?"

"Yes. At the moment, I don't know the exact amount."

"Is the Chief a suspect?"

"The boat was in dry dock for the last two years until a day ago. A lot of people had access to it."

"Did you interviewed the Chief?"

James nodded as he said, "I can't tell you anything else, Terry. Commissioner Dylan will appoint an officer from St. Thomas or St. John to investigate the case. We don't want any appearances of special treatment by the Chief's former staff."

"What is your opinion, Chief Kingston?"

"My opinion doesn't count. Once all the facts are known, the right person will be arrested. Please do me a favor and don't print what you don't know."

Chapter 12

After legal-eagle Pete left the trailer park, Roland returned to his cubby hole. He had a stash of emergency supplies in case he found himself in trouble. He dug through a small closet until he found a box of hair dye. He cut his hair short before he darkened it. After he shaved off his mustache, he attached a fake soul patch he had used from time to time when he was picking pockets. He exchanged his touristy print shirt for a tan cotton one, and cut-offs for khaki pants. He wanted to appear as a typical island native.

Roland packed a duffel bag with dirty clothes along with his weed and what money he had. He headed for his brother's house, but decided to see what action he could find along the boardwalk first. He chose an open-air restaurant where only a railing separated the tables from the popular boardwalk. As he sipped his beer at the bar, he slowly eyed the entire room to determine where the ladies kept their purses and where the men carried their fat wallets. One large straw pocketbook leaned against a leg of the table.

A bit chancy, but a possibility.

There was a man seated at the bar engrossed in a football game. The outline of his wallet was clearly visible.

Not even a small problem.

Roland noticed the group in the corner.

Grandmas are perfect targets because they so often pick up the tab for the whole clan.

Roland spied the gold locket watch on the table.

The price of gold is astronomical. It's worth the risk if I could get out of here fast enough.

Roland took his beer and sat at a table near the group in the corner. He took care not to touch anything. He overheard spasmodic bits of conversation. He tuned in harder when he heard the word *treasure*. A second later he heard *Spanish gold* and *fireplace*. He stood and walked to the railing that separated the restaurant from the boardwalk. There was very little foot traffic as most people were in the restaurants or bars.

He visualized an escape route: out the front entrance, right on the boardwalk, past the ice cream stand, and another right up the dark alley to his car.

Roland returned his beer glass to the bar and asked for a refill. He told the bartender he needed to use the restroom and would be right back. Instead of the restroom, he went out the rear exit and headed for his car. He turned the engine on and let it run. He got out, closed the door and returned to the restaurant. He paid for his new beer and sat down. He deliberately spilled a little beer on the bar so he could ask the bartender for a dish cloth. He cleaned up the beer while he unobtrusively wiped the bar clean of his fingerprints.

Can't be stupid about this.

Roland strolled to the edge of the boardwalk with his beer. It was void of visitors. He furtively poured his beer into a planter box, but kept the glass.

Got to watch my prints.

Charlie & Family were in the midst of a second conversation about the watch when Jeremy excused himself for a few minutes. Molly, Laurie and Annie had all dug into their desserts. Jake and Molly spoke about potential treasures hidden behind the fireplace. Laurie and Annie talked about affairs of the heart. Charlie listened to both conversations. No one noticed the tall man who inched his way toward the table until an arm reached and grabbed the opened heirloom locket watch.

With the treasure in his hand, Roland hightailed it out the front exit. As he ran, he tossed the beer glass onto the rocks in front of the harbor.

Jake was boxed in the booth by Molly and his mother, so it took him a few seconds before he could bolt after the thief. He, too, scampered out the front, past the ice cream stand, and looked up the inky alley. He saw movement and sprinted forward.

Roland had opened the car door, slid in and was about to slam the door shut as Jake caught up to him.

Jake grabbed the locket watch through the partially opened door. Roland held onto the rear casing as the car backed out of the parking space. The hinge on the casing broke. Jake had the front and the actual watch and Roland had the rear casing.

JEREMY returned in time to see Jake run out of the restaurant. Charlie yelled for him to follow. He caught up to Jake as the old junker sped away belching a cloud of oil fumes. The brothers returned to the restaurant as Charlie finished her nine-one-one call.

"Dad, what happened?" Molly asked as tears moistened her cheeks.

Jake opened his hand and showed his family his half of the watch. "He got away in an ancient gray Chevy."

"I'm scared," Annie said. "He might come back for the other half." She hiccupped as her petite body trembled.

Charlie said, "He won't be back, Annie. The police will see to it. He was the man I saw picking pockets at the parade yesterday. This morning, I sat with a sketch artist so the police already have his picture. He's cut his hair and darkened it, but he'll be caught."

"You didn't tell me about this," Jeremy said. "You got yourself involved in another crime, didn't you?"

"I'm not involved in police work. I saw what I saw and I reported it to the police," Charlie countered.

Officer Paul Simpson entered from the rear of the bar. Jake immediately filled in the details and Charlie told him about the man at the parade. Simpson used his handheld to notify the station. They discussed the BOLO already issued.

Molly overheard the officer and asked her father, “What’s a BOLO?”

“Don’t know. Grandmom is the sleuth in the family.”

“Grandmom, what’s a BOLO?”

“It means to be on the lookout. The dispatcher will notify all the police officers to look for the man in the car.”

“They say the word BOLO all the time on NCIS,” Annie said.

“I watch the show, too,” Molly said. “Tony DeNozzo is too cute.”

“I prefer Timmy,” Annie said. “He’s so sensitive and caring toward people.”

“Tony is too, really. He doesn’t want people to know how sensitive he is, so he acts like a jerk sometimes.”

“That’s true, but don’t you think Timmy is deep?”

Charlie hid her smile. She was glad the conversation had shifted from the thief to NCIS.

Officer Simpson asked Charlie a few questions. She described the changes to the man’s appearance.

“I have his picture in my car. Be right back,” the officer said.

Charlie saw Molly texting again. “What are you telling your friends now?”

“This is a big news event and I’ve witnessed a crime. I need to notify the press in York, Pennsylvania.”

“Make sure you include WGAL-TV!” Jeremy laughed.

Annie said, “Grandmom, I told my dad you’re involved with bad guys again.” She giggled as she texted a second message to her dad. Officer Simpson returned with the sketch and showed it to Jake. Jake immediately identified the man, despite the haircut, dye job and fake soul patch. The bartender hurried over and looked at the sketch. He agreed with Jake, as did four other customers.

When Officer Simpson left an hour and a half later, Charlie said, “Let’s head home, gang.”

Jake looked at Molly, “Are you okay now?”

“Yeah, but we lost part of the watch, Dad.”

Annie said, “But we’re the ones who know it’s a treasure watch.

The thief doesn't know that. All we need to do is find the fireplace." She giggled as she texted her dad.

ROLAND used back roads to get to his brother's house. He backed the Chevy into the pole barn. He quickly changed his shirt, put on a baseball cap and borrowed his brother's car. He returned to the crime scene and sat on the boardwalk facing the ocean. He was already seated when Charlie and her family left. He followed them home. Once he learned the address, he decided to follow them the next day.

Hidden treasures, huh? Not without me.

THE Virgin Island Press lay on James Kingston's desk when he arrived at work the next morning. It had a large front-page picture of the Chief at his retirement ceremony.

RETIRED POLICE CHIEF A DRUG DEALER?

ST. CROIX. Water Patrol Officer Bill Browning yesterday impounded a powerboat belonging to retired Deputy Police Chief Victor Hanneman. Hidden onboard was black tar heroin.

According to Deputy Police Chief James Kingston, the police interviewed Hanneman at the station. Hanneman had told the interviewing officers the boat had been in dry dock for the past two years. Multiple people had access to it.

Kingston said he expected Commissioner Dylan to appoint an officer from St. Thomas or St. John to investigate the case.

"We don't want any appearance of special treatment by the Chief's former staff," Kingston said. "Once all the facts are known, the right person will be arrested."

CHAMAIGN entered her boss's office.

"I see the Chief made the front page," Chamaign said as she placed her copy of the paper in her lap. She sat across from her boss and discussed the theft-homicide case. Lynette Speers, James' administrative assistant, entered. She handed him a report from the team that inspected *Gertie*.

James read Chamaign the details.

"This doesn't look good for the Chief, Boss. Someone is going to nail him on those prints."

"Tell me about it," James said. "We've identified three sets of prints so far, the Chief's, Jeremy's, and Luther's. There are a number of other prints and at least one of those belongs to Jeremy's girlfriend, Laurie. I don't know about the other prints yet."

"Any word as to who will investigate the case?" Chamaign asked.

The phone rang on James' desk. Chamaign stood to leave the office. James motioned her to stay.

James answered the phone, listened for a second, and said, "Chief Farrow, I expected to hear from you this morning. Did you read Bill Browning's report?"

"Yes, and so did Commissioner Dylan," Bill Farrow said.

"Who is going to run with the case?"

"Manny Powell."

"But he's with Internal Affairs. That doesn't make sense, Bill."

"It does if you remember he was a detective before he transferred to Internal Affairs."

"What you said doesn't make me happy. Manny and I never got along. I wanted to put criminals in jail and he wanted to be the Police Commissioner."

"It's out of your hands now, James. You and your staff have to keep out of this."

As James hung up, Lynette entered and interrupted, "Sorry to bother you. I think you need to see this." Lynette handed James the report compiled by Paul Simpson. "It's about Jake Bauer."

"Jake Bauer? Isn't he Charlie's son?" Chamaign asked.

James nodded. He read the report to her.

"That's too bad," Chamaign said. "The locket watch must have been very important to Charlie and her family."

"Don't miss the next page, you two," said Lynette. "See who

identified the thief."

James quickly reviewed the report as Chamaign read over his shoulder.

Lynette said, "Charlie told Officer Simpson the thief was the man picking pockets at the parade. Officer Simpson had the sketch with him and showed it to everyone at the restaurant. Four other people identified him despite shorter, darker hair."

James picked up the phone to call his boss.

ROLAND arose around nine in the morning. He stayed in bed until his brother left for work. He didn't want to explain too much to his family. He shaved his head in the bathroom, but didn't bother to clean the sink. He used Instant Caribbean Tan to darken his white bald skull to match his already-tanned face. His piece de resistance was the wire-rimmed glasses perched on his nose. He attached a pair of flip-up sunglasses over the lenses for an added touch.

He went through the kitchen and smiled at his sister-in-law, Tess, as he took her car keys off the wall rack. "See you later," he said as he dashed out the door and headed for the car. Once inside, he waved as Tess stood at the kitchen door with her hands on her hips and a glare in her eyes.

Catch Me If You Can! Gosh, I loved that movie.

CHAMAIGN found Bob Thompson in his cubicle. "We need to get this car identified. Our suspect, the pick-pocketing murderer, robbed Charlie's son last night."

Bob stood and folded his arms, "You got to be kidding!"

"No, I'm not. Did you get the paperwork to search the cars?"

Bob grabbed the materials from his desk, stashed it in his shirt pocket, and left the building with Chamaign. He followed her in his own squad car.

Upon arriving at the Montour house, the officers presented the warrant. The man reluctantly allowed them to check his car. The officers did not find the evidence they wanted, so they left.

"Did that car ever stink," Bob said. "What was that's smell?"

"It smelled because he sprayed the interior with Lysol. He probably smokes his pot in there!"

The Coombs trailer was empty again so Chamaign and Bob went to the Bissler residence. The mother said her teenage son drove the old car. She nervously watched as the officers inspected it.

"Nada," Bob said. He and Chamaign thanked the relieved mother, got in their squad cars, and left.

"Let's go back to the Coombs place and show our sketch to some of his neighbors," Chamaign said.

Six trailers surrounded Roland's trailer. The officers were able to speak with the occupants of three. Two denied recognizing the man in the sketch and claimed they knew nothing about the car. The last person agreed to answer the questions as long as she didn't have to testify to anything. She identified Roland Coombs and the car.

Chamaign called for backup and officers Paul Simpson and Axel Stevens responded. They parked off the road to wait for Coombs while Chamaign and Bob returned to get an arrest warrant.

MANNY Powell, the officer assigned by the police commissioner to work the drug case, arrived at police headquarters in Frederiksted.

"How are you doing, James?"

"Just fine, Manny. Welcome to St. Croix." James greeted Powell with a handshake.

Manny Powell was about six feet-two, thin, and had dark skin. He was well groomed and bordered on being handsome. While he was not happy to be in St. Croix, he felt he would enjoy making James feel uncomfortable.

"I'm going to need the case file, James."

"It's on my desk waiting for you. There were a lot of the Chief's prints. We also have some unidentified ones. One probably belongs to Laurie Glass. Her address is in the file. Jeremy Bauer agreed to buy the Chief's boat, and he and Glass were on *Gertie* the night before it was impounded."

"What kind of a nerd would name his boat *Gertie*?"

James ignored Powell's sarcasm and pretended he didn't hear.

Powell moved on, "Has this Bauer been eliminated?"

"His prints were where he said they would be. They were not on or near the drugs. Another set of prints belonged to Luther Scott. He is the owner of Ole Luther's Marine Repair Shop. *Gertie* was in dry dock there. Luther can identify his employees and the remaining prints may belong to them."

"Do you have an office I can borrow?"

"I have a small room with table and chair. I scrounged around for a file cabinet and found a key to the door. It's not wired for either a phone or computer. Our tech guy is going to string some wires for you shortly."

"AC, I hope."

"Yes, Manny, we have air conditioning in St. Croix. My administrative assistant is Lynette Spears She can get you any materials you want; however, she is not available to help you in any other way."

Manny followed James to a small room. He dismissed him with a wave of his hand, sat down, and started to read the file. An hour later, he completed the paperwork to have the Chief's house searched.

Now to find a judge with some sense!

AROUND seven that evening, Gil arrived at Jeanette's home. He waltzed his way up the front walk and met his gal on the porch.

"Sure missed ya, Sweetie. You sure do look adorable today in your cute little violet print dress and your fancy white apron with all them ruffles."

"Oh, Gil, you always say the sweetest things to me. My heart has been fluttering all day just thinking about you. I'm so glad you're here. While making your favorite pie, I actually found myself singing that Zip-A-Dee-Doo-Dah song. That's how happy you make me."

Gil said, "Wow" as he scratched his head and tried to figure out what she was talking about.

"Do come in the kitchen and have a piece of my pie."

THE CHIEF made his regular late-night phone call to Charlie.

"I feel somewhat better now that I've spoken with the defense attorney."

"Then the attorney is not concerned?"

"He's very concerned about the prints. I've been a cop long enough to know he should be concerned."

"What did he say about a possible defense?"

"He didn't. I don't see much of a defense besides a few character witnesses. The prosecuting attorney would probably want to argue I was a distributor or the intermediary who sold the drugs to the street sellers. The fact that *Gertie* was in dry dock would cause some measure of reasonable doubt, I would hope."

"Victor, a jury of your peers would not convict you."

"You're only saying that because you like me," he said. "I'm not so sure."

Chapter 13

Wizard Cort looked at his brother, "What are we going to do about our drugs?"

"Nothing we can do," Zeke replied. "We're out all the money."

"Think the cops have a bead on us? I sure don't want to go back to prison."

"They don't know about us unless you screwed up and left prints somewhere on the boat."

"I was careful," Wizard said.

"The cops will interview Luther's employees and that includes me. If they have your print, it won't take a rocket scientist to figure out you are my brother."

"We don't have to worry, Zeke. According to the paper, it looks like the old cop will be arrested."

"Yeah, but he ain't the guilty one."

JAKE woke around ten and eventually made his way to the kitchen.

"Hungry?" Charlie asked.

"Cooking, Mom?"

"There is a frying pan somewhere in a box in the closet and there are eggs in the refrigerator."

"You always were the perfect hostess," Jake joked as he gathered ingredients from the refrigerator. He then slit the tape on a closed packing box in the pantry. He poked around until he found a brand new frying pan with its label still attached. After washing the pan, he made omelets for the girls.

I'm ashamed of you, Ms. Charlie

Why?

Because your son is cooking breakfast.

And if I'm lucky, he'll also make lunch and dinner.

"I'm still upset about the watch, Mom," Jake said. "It's an heirloom. What do you think our chances are of finding the man?"

"I honestly don't know. Remember, you still have the most important half."

"But not the treasure half," Molly said as she stood in the doorway in tan cutoffs and a red tee. Annie followed Molly into the kitchen and was dressed in a similar outfit except she had on a pink halter top.

Charlie looked at her almost-awake granddaughters. Molly plopped on a wooden bar stool next to her grandmother as Annie perched on a stool on the other side. Charlie put her arms around the girls and gave them good morning hugs.

"Why aren't you texting, ladies?"

"Oh – my cell!" Molly screamed as she turned and ran into the bedroom to look for her phone. After a minute she yelled, "Annie, I can't find my cell. Call me on yours so I can find mine!"

Ms. Charlie, can you believe what the girls are doing?

It doesn't exactly fit the definition of sane, does it?

It's definitely weird.

No, it's a six-letter crossword puzzle word beginning with lun and ending in acy.

After the teens were fully engaged in their morning texts, Jake said, "How can we find out who owns the house and the cookhouse?"

"I'll ask Elin. She got me inside once before and she'll do it again, I'm sure. What do you have planned for today?"

"I booked a trip to Buck Island so the girls and I can snorkel."

Can we go, Ms. Charlie? I want to snorkel, too!

Stop acting like a teenager.

But it works for Molly and Annie! Can we go, too? Pleeeze.

"Can I go, Jake?" Charlie asked.

"I didn't know you still snorkeled."

Your son is insulting us, Ms. Charlie. We're not in the older-than-dirt category yet. You tell him.

"Jake, I'm not so old I can't snorkel," Charlie said as she stood with her hands on her hips, feet eighteen inches apart in a make-my-day stance. A lowered head, a Clint Eastwood clenched jaw, and a do-or-die stare completed the picture.

Molly interrupted when she yelled from her bedroom, "The Internet says there is coral taller than me on Buck Island. Is that true, Grandmom?"

Charlie picked up her cell and texted Molly her version of texting, "WILL SHOW YOU."

"Can you keep up with us as we snorkel?" Jake asked.

He insulted us again, Ms. Charlie. We might have replacement knees, but we're not helpless.

"Jake, I might have replacement knees, but I'm not exactly helpless," she said as her hands returned to her hips.

"I know. I don't want you getting tired. We've had a lot of excitement around here."

Ms. Charlie! You were up later than he was last night talking goo-goo to the Chief!

"I was up later than you last night, Jake."

"Don't think so, Mom."

"And you know this how?"

"I could hear you snoring while I was answering my emails from work. I went to shut your bedroom door and you were passed out in your La-Z-Boy."

Charlie's lips clenched tight as she searched for a clever retort. She could only come up with a weak, "So?"

Why do we always sleep in the La-Z-Boy, Ms. Charlie?

So our acid reflux won't back up.

So why did we buy a bed?

So our room would look like a bedroom, silly!

That doesn't make sense, Missy. We don't use the bed.

Read the real estate section sometime – have you ever heard of a home with two baths and three La-Z-Boy rooms?

"Jake, what time are we leaving?"

"Now."

"Perfect. I'm meeting Victor at the ferry dock at three. He's returning from St. Thomas. He called late last evening and is still upset about the drugs."

ROLAND parked amidst a row of trees off the main road leading to the home owned by Charlie and Jeremy. He sat and studied the inside of the watch casing while he waited for her car to leave the driveway.

X marks my heart. How stupid.

He turned the casing over and studied the worn etching on the back.

The one kid said something about a fireplace. Yeah, this could be a fireplace. And there's the X. Well, I'll be damned. So there's a treasure buried behind a stone in the fireplace. I'll let those dummies lead me right to it.

CHARLIE and Jake took separate cars to the snorkeling pier. Charlie wanted her car because she needed to pick up the Chief. She pulled out of her driveway first, followed by Jake and the teens. Everyone was dressed for snorkeling. Charlie had insisted the girls wear heavy tees over there bathing suits to protect their backs from the searing tropical sun. She also saw to it everyone wore wide-brimmed hats to protect faces and necks. Each of her family members received a tube of sunblock.

Roland followed the mini-caravan into Christensted. When the two cars reached the gravel parking lot of the snorkeling company, he watched the family turn in. He drove past the entrance, stopped down the road, turned around, and drove back. He entered the lot.

I need to stay close and keep my ears open. They may have plans

I don't know about.

Roland parked and opened the trunk of his borrowed car. He found fishing equipment and a pair of his brother's old pants. He used a knife to cut the legs off the pants mid-thigh. He entered the office and asked if there was room on the next snorkeling trip. There was. Roland changed pants in the men's room and then went on the pier to wait for the catamaran. He sat on a bench across from Jake and the girls. He kept his wire-framed glasses with drop-down sunglasses squarely on his nose.

Nothing like hiding in plain sight!

Roland listened to the teens talk about treasures while he pretended to study the horizon.

"Maybe we'll find some sunken treasure while we snorkel, Dad."

"If we do, we'll split the treasure – seventy percent for me and thirty percent for you and Annie."

"Dad, if you keep the seventy, you'll get to pay my entire college tuition." Molly laughed.

Annie piped up, "And you get to pay for a private trainer as I prepare for the next Olympics."

"Olympics?" Molly said, "I forgot you were into track. Good going."

Charlie interrupted the girls as they jabbered, "Wait a minute, all of you. I get a piece of the pie, too. How about fifty percent of your take, Jake?"

Jake didn't hear what his mother said. He had noticed the bald man, but couldn't figure out why red flags appeared in the back of his mind.

"Grandmom, when can we go to the cookhouse?" Annie asked.

"Grandmom's working on it now," Jake said. "She'll find a way to get us inside."

Roland casually glanced over his shoulder at the teens. He didn't miss the cookhouse comment, but he also didn't realize he was being watched.

The snorkeling guide appeared and introduced himself. Everyone followed the leader as they headed to the docked catamaran. They climbed on board one by one. The large vessel sat sixteen people. Once everyone had a seat, the operator used his engines to get the bulky vessel out of the harbor and into open waters. He obeyed the five-miles an hour speed limit. He then used his sails and the engine for the next twenty minutes as the craft glided toward the coral deposits surrounding Buck Island.

The teens had lathered gobs of sunblock over their bodies before they left the house. They wanted tans instead of angry sunburns. At their grandmother's insistence, they wore their protective shirts. As the vessel neared the island, the girls put on their snorkeling gear. They belted themselves into flat vests. Then they blew air into the air chambers of the vest to keep their bodies afloat without hampering their maneuverability in the water.

As the excited snorkelers neared Buck Island, they watched the waters turn from a deep teal blue to an azure as the depth of the waters dropped.

As the catamaran sailed past the island and headed for the east end, Charlie explained to her family how the island was actually in an arid zone and experienced very little rain.

When their turn came to slide into the water, they each slipped the goggles over their eyes and tested the breathing apparatus. They slipped into the warm Caribbean.

That day there was barely a hint of a current. The guide instructed everyone to form a line. He gave Molly and Annie a red life preserver to hold onto with one hand. Jake held the end of the tethered rope attached to the flotation device. They proceeded on their journey.

Ms. Charlie, this is so surreal.

Check out those blue tangs feeding among the coral. Aren't they beautiful fish?

We should be as long and thin as they are, Missy.

What? And do without our doughnuts?

Ms. Charlie, do you really want me to answer you?

At first, the ocean's floor resembled the moon's terrain – pristine sand with an occasional deep depression. More and more metaphoric rocks appeared as they continued. Soon they saw jagged coral with long arms reaching out in all directions. Looking more closely, dyads and triads of azure yellow silverfish fed between the arms of the coral. Jake gave Molly and Annie the thumbs-up sign. Charlie snorkeled with Jake behind the girls. She snapped picture after picture of her granddaughters. Jake noted that the man with the bald head snorkeled behind them.

Molly pointed to several small brain corals. They resembled little round tan puffs dotting the ocean floor. As the larger pieces of brain coral came into sight, the exterior surface of the coral was more visible. It resembled the folds of the brain as seen in anatomy books. The convolutions in the coral twisted and turned in all directions. Some corals were so bulbous they grew into other coral and resembled long, bloated worms.

At one point, the guide led the snorkelers through a narrow passageway between two large Elkhorn corals with sharp serrated arms. The living coral was capable of permanently scarring anyone who scraped against it. The area between the two corals commanded the full attention of the snorkelers as they dodged its many outreached arms. After the snorkelers maneuvered their bodies through the area, there was a deep depression in the ocean's floor. There sat the huge brain coral Molly had wanted to see. She dived as deep as she could.

The coral was an almost perfect ball and its height was the least as tall as Molly. Jake and Annie dived, too. Charlie snapped more pictures from her little yellow waterproof underwater camera.

As the exhausted snorkelers began to return to their catamaran one by one, Jake pointed to a cluster of blue and yellow iridescent fish. The school was attracted to the strange floating monstrosity above. The floats of the catamaran had reddish-orange carpet glued to them to protect the vessel from contact with the piers. Much to everyone's delight, the carpet had the added bonus of beckoning the curious fish. More pictures.

Too soon, it seemed, it was time to go. Once the adventurers hoisted their tired bodies back on board, Charlie & Family devoured the bottled water they had brought. Molly and Annie wrapped their towels around their lower bodies. They each had about fourteen ounces of sunblock across their face and arms.

Jake still tried to figure out why the man who sat opposite them looked somewhat familiar.

Chapter 14

After Charlie left her family in the parking lot of the snorkeling company, she headed to Gallows Bay to meet Victor's ferry. On her way, she stopped at Luther's shop. She and Luther discussed what happened with *Gertie*. Charlie asked if there were any security cameras in the area where Victor's boat had been stored. There was. Luther warned her that his system was old, and there was only one camera recording the dry dock area. All tapes had been recycled with the exception of the last three. She found the one she needed most. It was dated the night before the Chief launched *Gertie*.

Luther didn't know how to make a copy of the tape, so Charlie made one. She tucked it into the crevices of her cloth chartreuse and yellow shopping cart-sized purse trimmed in yellow felt flowers with lime-green leaves. She left the shop.

Oh goody, goody, goody, Ms. Charlie.

What's so good?

We're doing police stuff. Why else would you want a copy of the tape?

This is a just-in-case action on my part.

Just in case what?

Just in case Plan A doesn't work. The tape is Plan B.

Huh?

Plan A is Murray Sedge. If he can't keep Victor out of prison, I'll step up to the plate for the home run.

CHARLIE hugged Victor after he walked off the ferry. "How was the ride?"

"A little rough. Or maybe it was a little rough because I didn't sleep last night."

"Sounds like your anxiety level is high today."

"Very high. My lawyer called me this morning and told me Manny Powell is in charge of the case. I never thought too highly of the man. Unfortunately, what I think doesn't matter."

"Why don't you like him?"

"He somehow discovered I gave him low grades during his training. His weapon trials were not great and his detail work was beyond sloppy. Anyway, he always seemed to have an attitude around me and he probably still does."

"I'll say it again – how could anyone possibly believe a former police …"

"My prints are on the containers. This is trouble, Charlie."

"I can always find the bad guys if the police can't do it."

Victor's glare gave Charlie a non-verbal warning.

"I know, I know. You're about to tell me to stay out of this."

"Exactly, and I mean it."

He hasn't figured out yet that it doesn't do any good to tell you what you can or can't do, Ms. Charlie.

But he gets an A for trying.

LUTHER and Gil hovered around the cash register and jabbered away about the Chief's impounded boat and the big drug bust.

Gil said, "Ya know, don't ya, the Chief didn't have anything to do with those drugs?"

"Course he didn't," said Luther. "I've known the Chief for forty years at least. He was a young cop on the beat when I started my business. We were about the same age."

"I remember back then. Ya put your Ole Luther sign up and I came in here 'specting to see an old man with gray hair. Here you was a young kid."

"Needed people to think I had experience. Fooled you at least 'cause I got your business, didn't I?"

The two men laughed as they sipped their coffees. A clean-cut young man dressed in tailored tan slacks, brown dress shoes and a white short-sleeve shirt entered. Luther went to greet him and held out his hand. The man didn't reciprocate.

"Luther Scott?"

"Yep. How can I help you?"

The man didn't answer. He glared at Gil until Gil got the message and moseyed to the rear of the shop.

"I'm Lieutenant Manny Powell with the Virgin Islands Police Department. I have a few questions for you."

"I can tell you right now the Chief is innocent. He's a good and honorable man and an outstanding citizen. My buddy Gil and me were discussing what happened. We know he didn't commit any crime."

"Well, Mr. Scott, I'm not convinced. I understand his boat was in dry dock here."

"Yep, you're right. I expected someone from the police would be by to ask questions, so I pulled the Chief's account. *Gertie* was here two years, three months and twelve days."

"Who had access to the boat?"

"Pretty much everyone. I made a list of employees who have been here while *Gertie* was here."

Luther handed Powell a list of nine men. "Now look at the list," Luther said, "John passed last year, so he don't count. Ya know, officer, John was standing right where you are when he had a heart attack and …"

"I'm not interested in where John stood. I want to know about the next name on the list."

Luther didn't appreciate the abrupt response, but was he was determined his thoughts would be heard. "Anyway, John was a good man."

Luther then proceeded to give a brief background for everyone on the list. There were five viable leads by the time Luther was done.

"I need prints from these men."

"George and Tom have both been in jail for drunk driving, so you have their prints on file. The men left are Joey Mills, Jeremiah Peale, George Thrush and Zeke Cort. Their address and phone numbers are under their names."

"Did any of these men have access to the boat?"

"They all did."

"Anyone else?"

"Sure. People come here looking for boats all the time. Especially nice ones like *Gertie*. People were always asking me if she was for sale after they took a peek inside."

"You get those men down to the station for prints today."

"Lieutenant, I can't tell those men what to do."

"Do it anyway," Powell bellowed as he started for the door.

"You're not as nice or as polite as the other guy."

Powell stopped dead in his tracks and pivoted. "What other guy?"

"That nice, polite young man. I think he said his name was Michaels."

"Who is he?"

Luther hustled over to his desk and found the man's business card. "His name is Kevin Michaels and he works for Murray T. Sedge, Attorney at Law."

"Sedge," Powell sneered." And you think Hanneman is innocent! What a joke."

Powell slammed the door as he left the shop.

Gil made a beeline for Luther. "Sounds like that there cop thinks the Chief is guilty."

"That self-appointed mini-God thinks he's someone important. I think he's a jerk."

"Nincompoop," Gil snorted. Luther nodded in agreement and both men roared.

JAKE didn't leave the snorkeling company's parking lot until after the bald man left. He didn't know why he didn't trust the man, but he knew he wanted to keep him away from the girls.

Roland wasn't worried about the family and took off for his brother's house.

AFTER Charlie dropped the Chief off at his house, she headed to the town of Christensted. She went to the store owned by her island cousin, Island Elegant Apparel Shoppe.

Even with her belly ready to burst, Elin was determined to sell her high-end clothing to every tourist who peeked in the door. She had received a new shipment of her latest fashion statements the day before, and she was in the process of steaming items before she racked them.

"A new selection?" Charlie asked.

"Right out of the box," Elin said as she put the steamer down and stretched her back.

"The colors are perfect. This orange and navy blue goes so well together," Charlie said.

The two women talked shop for another fifteen minutes before Charlie recalled why she came. "Remember when we toured the house on Market Street last fall?"

Elin nodded.

"How did you get the key?"

Elin told Charlie about the lady who owned the house.

"Can you borrow the key again?"

"Sure, I'll get it for you this afternoon."

Afterward, the ladies began to discuss babies. Elin showed Charlie her new digital camera and camcorder. Then she itemized every new piece of clothing she bought for her anticipated new bundle.

Were you as happy as Elin when you were pregnant, Ms. Charlie?

I was until all three of my sons went three weeks past their due dates.

Was that really bad?

Let's put it this way – the stock prices on hemorrhoid cream went through the roof.

THE CHIEF no sooner entered the front door of his home when a VIPD SUV pulled up his driveway. Two officers showed the Chief a search warrant. The Chief allowed the officers inside to search his property for drugs. After he made himself a mango rum and Coke, he sat on his sun porch and stared at nothing.

Chapter 15

For his special assignment, Manny Powell reported directly to St. Thomas Police Chief Dwayne Philippe. Dwayne's boss was the Police Commissioner.

"What do you have, Manny?" Philippe asked over the phone.

"The boat was pretty clean on the interior. There were a few good prints and one partial, but the only ones around or on the drugs belonged to Hanneman. There are several dozen on the exterior of the boat. The remainder of the interior and all the exterior prints are being run now. The last will be the partial."

"What about Bauer and his girlfriend?"

"He had some prints, but not anywhere near the drugs. I don't have the girlfriend's prints yet. Went to the place where the boat was in dry dock and got a list of several men. I need to track them down. You'll never guess what I learned. Sit, you'll like this, Chief."

"Stop with the dramatics, Manny. Get to the point."

"I found out Hanneman hired that two-bit defense attorney – Murray Sedge. That blowhard Sedge has his own little serf doing his dirty work for him. The grunt is Kevin Michaels."

"Didn't take him long to hook up with a lawyer," Philippe said.

"He would only do that if he was guilty, Chief."

Philippe wasn't so sure he agreed. "Manny, don't pat yourself on the back yet. You need to play this by the book and be as objective as possible."

A silent sneer spread across Manny's face.

The Chief will rue the day he ever met me. I'll have his butt in jail in no time.

OFFICER Bob Thompson had taken over the watch at Roland Coombs's trailer. He called Chamaign and told her Coombs had not returned.

Chamaign said, "There is a Richard Coombs who had a record as a teen. He's been clean as an adult. Anyway, he happens to have the same birth date as our Roland Coombs. We need to check him out pronto."

As soon as the relief officer arrived, Bob left to meet the detective. He and Chamaign each took their own squad car to Richard Coombs's house. Before they left the safety of their cars, both checked their weapons.

After Bob knocked on the front door, a man answered and a small boy peeked out behind his father's leg.

"Sir," Thompson said, "This is Detective Benton and I'm Officer Thompson. We're looking for Roland Coombs. May we speak to him?"

Chamaign watched the child. The small tot strained his neck to look up adoringly at his daddy.

"I don't know any Roland Coombs."

"But Dad …"

"We don't know any Roland Coombs, now be quiet, son, and go finish your lunch."

"I assume it is a coincidence you and Roland have the same birthday."

Richard looked down and to the left for second, but stuck to his story.

"Mr. Coombs, this involves a double homicide. If your brother is here, or if you even know where he is, you are aiding and abetting a fugitive. You could be guilty of a serious crime if you are rendering aid to your brother."

"I don't know the man, officers."

Richard started to shut the door when Chamaign said, "Mr. Coombs, may Officer Thompson and I look around your property?"

"Got a warrant?"

"Not yet. We didn't think you'd mind, and it would be for your family's safety."

"I don't know the man, so he wouldn't be here. It's time for you two to go."

Richard Coombs shut the door. As the officers left, Chamaign noticed the mother and the little boy looking out the side window. The woman tilted her head in the direction of the pole barn. Chamaign acknowledged her signal with an almost imperceptible nod as she returned to her squad car.

Chamaign stayed in her vehicle at the bottom of the driveway while Bob left to get the warrant so they could search the property.

ELIN called the friend who owned the big house on King Street. She asked about borrowing the key so Charlie & Family could get inside. The friend agreed and Charlie went to pick up the key.

JEREMY and Laurie sat in her tiny new office located in a narrow alley in town. It was rented by the U.S. Virgin Islands Department of Tourism.

Jeremy said, "This Powell will be giving you a call, I'm sure. He's as annoying as a vuvuzela."

"I already ran into him. I stopped by the station earlier today to have my prints taken. Are we suspects, Jeremy?"

"Who knows? I can't believe the Chief's prints are actually on the drugs. Here he was cleaning *Gertie* as a favor to me and look where it got him."

"I'm worried."

"Let's try to forget about it for now and go meet mom, Jake and the girls. She should have the key to the cookhouse and I want to be in on this treasure hunt."

"Me, too. I want to film it for a possible story for my new job."

ATTORNEY Pete Hummel drove to Roland's trailer. He wanted to be sure Ro left. The trailer was empty so he asked the neighbor if he knew Ro's whereabouts. The man said he didn't know, but told Pete about the series of police vehicles in and out.

I wonder if the cops figured out where Ro is. Nah, they're too stupid.

MANNY Powell was looking at the backgrounds of the men who worked for Luther. An officer tapped on the door and poked his head in. He told Manny the report on Chief Hanneman's boat was now on the VIPD's network.

Manny located the file. It said all of the interior prints were identified. As expected, most of them belong to Chief Hanneman and a few belong to Jeremy Bauer and Laurie Glass. Several others belonged to Luther's employees. The partial print belonged to a young man in his late teens. He had a prison record – Willard Cort. He went by the nickname of Wizard.

Cort? There is someone else with the same name.

Manny checked the notepad in his shirt pocket.

Just as I thought – Ezekiel Cort, Zeke for short. And he works for that old goat Luther. This Willard and Zeke must be related. Have to track Zeke down and get his prints. I bet they are brothers and I bet they both work for Hanneman.

Those two will be happy to implicate Hanneman if I threaten them. I've got me a slam-dunk case here. Guilty as charged!

Powell called the phone number for the Cort home and left a message with the grandmother. He told her he wanted her grandsons at the station immediately.

ROLAND Coombs sat in his sister-in-law's car. He followed the

Mikkelsen family to King Street and watched them enter the house with the concrete staircase in the rear of the home.

The old hag has a key to the iron gate leading to the steps. I wonder how she got it.

He watched the family enter the house and open many of the tall double wooden doors leading to a balcony surrounding the front, side and rear of the home.

As Ro watched, Richard called. “Bro, you can’t come back here. The cops are at the end of the driveway and probably are waiting for a warrant to search the property. The cops know you are staying here.”

“Keep them away from my car in the barn. I need scrub it with bleach.”

“Where are you?”

“Parked on King Street. Don’t ask why – you don’t want to know.”

“I have no way to get your car out of my pole barn without it being seen by the cops. Besides, I don’t want my prints anywhere on it. You leave my car where it is on King Street. I’ll pick it up. You’re on your own, Roland. Sorry about that, but I don’t want to end up in jail over this.”

“Where am I supposed to stay, Richard?”

“You have cash?”

“Some.”

“What about that buddy of yours who went to Miami to see his parents? You said he left you his apartment key. Can you hide there?”

“If I have to.”

“Ro, do it. If the police trace my calls, they’ll figure out I called you. Keep your cell turned off so they can’t locate you.”

Chapter 16

Charlie & Family toured the home of her great, great grandparents. Laurie filmed the event to use for a television series on the older homes on the island.

"What do you think of the house, Laurie?" Charlie asked.

"It's so lovely. I can't believe a house built in the 1840s could still be in such good condition. The floors are beautiful and the detail work is incredible. If they lived on the second level, what did they do with the first floor?"

"Christoffer Mikkelsen was in the import-export business, so I assume they used the first floor for buying and selling merchandise. I would assume they lived upstairs because the house is so close to the water. During a bad hurricane, I would think the water could easily rise to the first floor level."

"I wonder if the stained glass in the door is original."

"I assume so. I would like to know how many coats of paint are on the doors. Glad I don't have to strip and paint them."

After everyone duly admired the charm of the house, they closed the house and went down the old worn concrete steps to the ground level and headed for the shed that used to be the cookhouse.

"Now is the good part," Molly said with an enthusiastic smile that spread across her face from ear to ear. "Let's go find our treasure."

"Stand in front of the cookhouse, Molly and Annie," Charlie said. "I'll take your picture."

Ms. Charlie, why do phones have cameras in them now?

To confuse my generation. We still think cameras take pictures and phones plug into walls. That's why I still lug my camera around.

But you use your cell and read books on an electronic gadget, Missy.

That's so I can pretend I live in the twenty-first century. I also pretend I don't really need those refrigerator stickies to remind me what I've forgotten.

Boxes and old building materials filled the old cookhouse. Jake and Jeremy pushed the boxes aside so they could get to the stone fireplace once used for cooking. Both men scrutinized the stones.

"There has to be at least one stone that is different," Jake said.

"There are a lot of small cracks in the old mortar," Jeremy said, "but all of the mortar looks the same. It doesn't look like any stone has ever been removed."

"To be absolutely sure, we would have to chisel out the mortar and check each stone," Jake said. "Then we'd have to repoint each and every joint. I don't think the owner would appreciate that very much."

Charlie said, "Jake, this fireplace isn't shaped like the image on the watch. The etching on the back appeared to have an arched fireplace. This one is a big rectangle."

Jake agreed with his mother. "Sorry, guys. Maybe our treasure really doesn't exist."

"Oh Dad, there is a treasure – somewhere!" Molly said. "We have to find it."

Annie chirped, "And this treasure is about romance. I just know."

"I'm hungry." Jake said. "Let's go to a restaurant. I need to think about this some more. Molly and Annie are right, the X means something. We need to figure out the mystery."

"It has something to do with love, Uncle Jake," Annie said with certainty in her voice.

"Let's take a break from love for a second," Charlie said, "us girls need to cool down."

Charlie, Laurie and the teens rushed across the street to a corner stand. Charlie treated the girls to a strawberry oozy. When Jeremy and Jake saw the thick, icy drinks, they each bought one, too.

As everyone started to cross the street to return to the car, Officer Axel Stevens pulled up.

"Hi, Axel," Charlie said, "I didn't get a chance to read the news today. Anything new with our thief?"

"When I got back to the station, I found out your thief is now officially a murder suspect. He ran down the young couple he robbed yesterday. Killed both of them. It wasn't an accident, either. He ran his car over them three times. I also read a report on the wallet you found. The prints belong to the same man – Roland Combs."

Charlie's shoulders twitched with horror. Goosebumps appeared on her arms. "When did all this happen?"

"The man you saw picking pockets was Roland Coombs. After he left the parade, he went to the Palm Shack and saw the young couple. He must've thought the two could identify him, so he plowed his car right over them. Afterward, he went to the harbor where he robbed your family."

Let's go get him, Missy.

Yeah.

"An informant told Chamaign and Bob what kind of car he drove. We tracked him to his trailer, but he had already deserted the place," Axel said. "Chamaign and Bob are on his trail now."

"I'll keep an eye out for our murdering thief."

"Now Ms. Charlie," Axel said, "it wouldn't be wise for you to get involved with this murder case."

"Thanks for the words of advice, Axel. That being said, if I can help the police without putting myself in danger, I'll do so."

Don't listen to him. Let's find this guy. Pleeeze.

Grow up.

Axel laughed, "If you're not going to follow my advice, please don't tell anyone I told you about this."

Jake said, "Mom, I know what you're thinking. Your criminal chasing days are over."

"I agree with Jake," Jeremy said.

Are you going to put up with your sons telling you what you can or cannot do, Missy?

No. I simply won't tell them what I'm up to.

Charlie gave Axel a big wave as he drove away. She turned to her family, "Since our dinner was spoiled last night by one Roland Coombs, why don't we have a nice dinner tonight at the Harbor View Seafood Restaurant?"

Everyone agreed.

Me too, Missy. I love the Caribbean lobster.

And I love their wicked desserts. We'll need lots of calories to solve this case.

ROLAND sat in his brother's car and watched Officer Simpson talk to Charlie. He studied the interaction between the officer and the old gray-haired hag.

She's tight with the cops. Who is she? What is going on here?

TWO officers waded through the trash in Roland's trailer taking prints, hair samples, and any items that could be important. They didn't miss the collection of driver's licenses surrounding the bathroom mirror. They found a wad of cash hidden in several shoes and drugs in a plastic bag taped to the bottom of an ice cube tray. They also found a bottle of half-used brown hair dye and some dirty blond hair in the sink.

GIL dressed in his Sunday best for his date with his Sweetie. He even pressed his tan cotton slacks and a pale blue, short-sleeved open-collared shirt. He whistled as he combed the few cherished hairs on the top of his head. As he drove to Jeanette's house, he stopped and picked up a batch of fresh roses for his girl.

My bowl of puddin is gonna love these.

When he arrived at her home, Jeanette was sitting on her front porch on a white wooden porch swing. With the exception of her starched white collar, tiny rosebuds covered her entire dress.

Holy Moly – there's my gal!

Gil trotted up the porch steps, kissed his honey on the cheek and handed her the flowers. "Roses for my Rosebud," he said as his cheeks turned a blushing pink.

Jeanette fluttered her eyelashes and gave Gil a demure smile. His heart surged with pure euphoria.

"How's my handsome swabby this fine evening?"

Gil giggled, "Couldn't wait to see ya. Just knew you'd be all prettied up."

"This is going to be so nice. You know I don't get out to dinner much," Jeanette cooed as she kissed her blushing old salt on his lips.

Gil barely handled his intoxication and slapped his hands on his thighs. "My whole heart is thumpin away. I'm a man in love."

"Love? Do you mean that, Mr. Cliver?"

"Oh, I sure do. I love my Sweetie."

There was some more quivering of the eyelashes before Jeanette said, "You touched my soul, Gil. You make me feel like a pretty young girl again."

Gil beamed as he gallantly escorted Jeanette to his truck, opened the door and helped her inside. "I got us reservations for the Harbor View Seafood Restaurant."

"Oh my, we're going out in style tonight, sailor boy!"

Gil forced himself to let go of Jeanette's hand every time he had to shift the manual transmission in his old truck.

BOB Thompson picked up the warrant needed to search the Richard Coombs' property. He returned with it and the report on the wallet Charlie found. In the meantime, Chamaign had called for backup in case there would be any trouble if they found Roland.

She and Bob approached the front door. Bob knocked. Richard opened it.

"Mr. Coombs," Thompson said, "we have a warrant to search your property."

Richard dropped his head as he said, "Ro is not here. His stuff is in the barn."

"We will be searching the entire premise, Mr. Coombs," Chamaign said. "You might want to ask your wife to take your son out in the backyard to play. We're not here to scare the little guy."

Coombs left and spoke to his wife. She went to the toy chest and picked out a large orange ball and a short, oversized yellow plastic bat. She went out the rear door with her son. The little boy with the big brown eyes gave Chamaign a pinky-finger wave as he followed his mother. Chamaign reciprocated.

Chamaign and Bob made their way through the house checking closets, storage areas and under beds. Chamaign poked her head through the opening in the ceiling and inspected the blistering hot attic. Roland was not there. They inspected the yard, the bushes and the shed.

Once finished, they headed for the pole barn. Both officers drew their guns as they checked the perimeter of the building. They entered. The gray Chevy sedan sat off to one side. Once the officers were sure that Coombs was not in the building, Bob used a small forensics kit to swab the grill for blood. The swab was positive. He wiggled part way under the engine and could see several shreds of cloth caught on the axel. He bagged the blood-soaked pieces of clothing. One piece had a wad of hair stuck to it.

Inside the car, Chamaign found a small duffel bag stuffed with dirty clothes. She found an old flashlight at the bottom of the bag. She knew it was too light to have batteries inside. She unscrewed the end. The batteries had been removed and the cavity contained several small zippies filled with pot.

On her car radio, Chamaign called for a flatbed truck to haul the car out of the barn. She returned to the house.

"Mr. Coombs, we need to talk."

Coombs and Chamaign sat across from each other at his kitchen table while Bob looked around some more.

"Mr. Coombs, I expect the truth from you – the whole truth. Let's start with your brother's cell phone number," Chamaign said.

"Don't know it."

"Wrong answer. Let's try again or the three of us will head for the station."

Coombs shrugged his shoulders, but he answered the question.

"When did your brother leave here?"

Richard told them.

Chamaign asked a dozen more questions. Coombs answered all of them.

"Now for the most important question, Mr. Coombs. You have a three-car pole barn and there are only two cars inside it. Where is the other car?"

"Don't know."

"Wrong answer."

Chamaign picked up her handheld radio and asked Bob if he would dig a little deeper and empty all the bureaus and closets in the bedrooms.

"No, please don't do that. You won't find anything – no guns or drugs. Both my wife and I stopped the drugs cold turkey three years ago, and, I've never owned a gun."

"So the answer to the car question is …"

"My wife's car is parked on King Street somewhere. Ro took it to town. I have to pick it up."

"Why doesn't Ro, your bro, bring it back?"

"He called and I told him you were here. I told him my wife needed her car and he was on his own. Honest officer, my wife needs her car for work. She finished her associate's degree and finally found a half-decent job at the hospital. She can't afford to lose it. We need both incomes to keep going."

"Did you know your brother was involved in a murder last evening?" Chamaign asked.

"Figured he did something, but I didn't ask questions."

Bob entered, "I need to talk to you, Chamaign."

Chamaign slipped outside. He told her some of the things the officers found in Roland Coombs' trailer.

Bob and Chamaign returned to the kitchen where Richard was.

"Why did we find an open bottle of hair dye in your brother's trailer?" Chamaign asked.

"When he got here yesterday, Ro's hair was shorter and he had dyed it a light brown. He even wore a fake soul patch. He told me he needed to change his appearance. After he returned last night, he shaved his head and got rid of the soul patch."

"Where is he now?"

"A friend of his is stateside. Ro is using his apartment. I don't know its location and that is the truth. It is in Frederiksted – that's all I know."

"If something else comes to mind, it would be wise to tell us. We're overlooking the aiding and abetting for now, but we won't do it again. Officer Thompson will give you a ride to Frederiksted. Forensics will need to process your car before we can release it to you. Meanwhile, we'll call the sketch artist and have him make changes to our sketch. He can fax it to us and you will tell us how the sketch needs tweaking. After you sign a statement about this interview, you may come home to your wife and little boy. You will notify me if your brother tries to contact you. Agree?"

Richard nodded.

As Bob and Chamaign left the house, she told the little boy his daddy would be home in a couple of hours. She winked at the wife and mouthed a silent, "Thank you."

MANNY called Chief Hanneman. "I want you in this office for questioning."

"I'll be happy to comply. I'll call my lawyer and see how soon he can make it."

"You're going down, Hanneman."

"If that's a threat, I'll be sure to tell my lawyer."

"I'll pick you up in a half hour."

"My lawyer can't be here in a half hour."

"That's your problem," Powell said as he hung up.

The Chief called Murray Sedge. His lawyer told him to stay calm.

"Be sure not to answer any questions unless I'm there." Sedge also suggested that the Chief drive himself to the station. "Let him waste his time driving to your home and then back to the station. He only wants to see you humiliated in the back seat of his police vehicle. You take the initiative and piss him off. I'll catch the ferry; however, you need to give me a good two hours."

AS HE drove west on the main road, Pete Hummel saw a flatbed truck exit Richard Coombs' driveway.

That must be Ro's car.

Pete drove past Richard's property and saw no police around. He turned around and drove up to the house. Richard's wife came outside to greet him.

"Haven't seen you in years, Pete," she said.

"That only means your husband hasn't needed a good defense attorney. How's it going, Tess?"

"Ro's in trouble."

"Know why?"

"Two people are dead and the cops think he did it."

"Know where he's at?"

Tess shook her head.

"I'll be on my way then. I'll find him for you." Pete drove away.

I bet I know where my old buddy hunkered down.

Chapter 17

St. Croix Deputy Police Chief James Kingston sat at his desk and tapped the fingers of his right hand on the wood surface. After a few minutes, he picked up his phone and called his counterpart and best friend on St. Thomas, Deputy Police Chief Andre Johnson.

"How can I help you, buddy?" Andre asked.

"Tell me about Powell."

"He was in Internal Affairs while I headed the unit. He's arrogant, bombastic and cocky. It's all about him, unfortunately."

"He's not the nicest person I've ever met."

"James, I can assure you he isn't even a little bit nice. Once he makes up his mind someone is guilty, you can't change it. That's when he screws up – he never follows through, never covers his bases, and never dots his i's or crosses his t's."

"I'll make sure the Chief knows this."

"Did he get a lawyer?" Andre asked.

"Murray T. Sedge."

"Never liked defense attorneys, but at least he's a good one."

"It is rather bizarre, isn't it?" James said. "The only person every police officer hates is a good defense attorney. Now suddenly, a good defense attorney is our best hope for the Chief."

"Scuttlebutt has it the Chief's prints were all over the drugs. Is it true, James?"

"Afraid so."

"Ouch."

CHARLIE & Family arrived at the hillside restaurant. Charlie, Jake and the girls went inside. Jeremy led Laurie to the terrace so they could admire the exquisite scenery. The harbor town twinkled below as the ocean breezes gently fluttered tree limbs back and forth in front of the town's lights. The boardwalk's lights bounced off the water and appeared as a golden ribbon along the ocean's edge. The seas were so calm a dozen or so sailboats seem rooted in the water.

Laurie oohed and Jeremy aahed.

Molly wasn't interested in the astounding scenery. She had spotted a young teen around her age inside the restaurant. Annie noticed him, too. They both giggled as they stole peeks at the cute boy. Annie managed to snap a picture of him and send it to her friends in Indiana.

Gil and Jeanette arrived at the restaurant and joined Jeremy and Laurie on the terrace.

"Ya know, young fella," Gil said, "I've never noticed my little harbor before from this angle. I need my pad and pencils up here so I can sketch the town from a new perspective."

Laurie asked, "How and when did you do all those pictures in Jeremy's office."

"I started when I first owned the marina. Each day, I'd row *Petunia* around the harbor in the early morning. Then I'd let her drift while I drank my coffee and sketched as the sun came up. From here, I'll be able to doodle from the land looking out to the sea."

Jeremy assured Laurie that Gil was an artist and not a doodler. Jeanette watched Gil intently. She beamed with pride as he told his audience about his pictures of Christensted.

ROLAND Coombs found refuge in his friend's apartment in the

south end of Frederiksted. It was a small place with only one room and a midget-sized bath. The room contained a john and a small shower. The tiny sink in the kitchen performed double duty. The sink sat next to an under-the-counter fridge. A hotplate sat on top of the counter. Unfortunately, the place did not have air conditioning, so Ro had to rely on a ceiling fan and a small portable fan. He rooted through his friend's bureau drawer to find the car keys.

Before he left the apartment, he washed up and borrowed an almost clean shirt before he walked down a flight of steps to find his friend's car. His buddy had parked it on a side street two blocks away. Ro drove to the road in front of Charlie and Jeremy's house and parked in a neighbor's driveway. When he saw the Camry leave, he followed it at a safe distance. Going through Christensted, he had to drop back further since he would be easy to spot. At this time of night, the roads were empty except for tourists walking here and there. As the car left town, he had to speed to catch up. Once he saw the driver make a right onto Restaurant Hill, he kept going for half a mile, turned around and returned. He knew there was only one thing at the end of the steep, curvy road.

CHARLIE invited Gil and Jeanette to join them for dinner and the older couple did.

Roland sat at a table behind a panel of white slats designed in a crisscross pattern. Vines of silk ivy leaves provided the privacy. He sat with his back to the panel. He could hear every word spoken by the old hag with the gray hair. He heard Jake tell Gil and Jeanette about the locket watch, the etchings, the treasure and their visit to the King Street house.

"Holy Moly, is the treasure Spanish gold?" Gil asked as he slapped his thighs.

"Could be," Jeremy said, "but I'm betting its pirate's gold."

"Pirate's gold!" Annie said as her eyes bounced wide open. "Were pirate's around here?"

"Oh yeah," Gil said, "but it was before my great granddaddy got here."

"What about our four G?" Molly asked.

"Four G?"

"My great, great, great, great grandparents."

"Oh! The Pirates were around before their time, too," Gil told the girls.

Laurie asked, "How did the Pirate's Cove Marina get its name?"

Gil replied, "My own great grandfather built the very first private pier on this island and he named it. That was long before the funny looking man with all the eye makeup made them pirate movies."

"Don't talk about Johnny Depp that way – he's my hero!" Jeremy said as he winked at Laurie.

Everyone at the table laughed.

"Ms. Charlie," Laurie said, "both your sons are romantics at heart."

"All three of my sons are romantics. Jason called this morning from Indiana to check on Annie. I told him about the treasure hunt. He asked if he could come to help. Grandson David wants to come, too."

Jeremy and Jake looked at each other and then denied their mother's comments about their romantic side.

Do you think it is pirate's gold, Ms. Charlie?

Do you believe in Santa Claus?

I do ever since you wiggled into last year's slacks. I thought for sure you'd have to wear your Spanks tonight.

I won't be sharing my desert. You can go home now!

For the remainder of the evening, Gil told tales about the island in the old days. He spoke about his youth as the boy who always played hooky, and about his shenanigans in the Merchant Marines. Even Annie and Molly were captivated as Gil chronicled his epic and legendary adventures. As the evening ended, Gil, Jake, Jeremy and the girls agreed to find the treasure together. Roland remained at his table.

There couldn't really be pirate's gold, could there?

WHILE Charlie & Family were at dinner, the Chief followed his lawyer's advice and drove to the police station instead of waiting for Powell to show at the house. Just outside of Frederiksted, the Chief passed a police SUV and recognized Manny. He chuckled as he continued to drive.

He'll waste a good hour by the time he gets to my house, has a hissy fit, and then gets back to the police station.

Once the Chief parked, he entered the station and asked for James. When James arrived at the front desk, he welcomed the retired Chief.

Victor told him about passing Powell on the road. "I think his blood pressure will be up a bit by the time he gets back here. Let's slip over to the Danish Pastry Shoppe for a cup of coffee. We might as well relax before the fireworks start."

The two men had their coffees and covered the weather, sports and the new Christensted bypass, which slips natives and tourist from one end of the island to the other without having to drive through the quaint narrow streets in Christensted.

Once back at the station, James and the Chief went into the dull gray interrogation room. James said, "Chief, since Powell is going to be steamed anyway, let's do this right."

James left the table with a glint in his eyes and his gold incisor twinkling. He told his administrative assistant what he was going to do before he entered his office. He retrieved a deck of cards from the bottom drawer of his desk, returned, and the two men started to play poker.

Lynette giggled out loud when she told Bob Thompson about the game. Bob rounded up several volunteers. When Manny Powell returned to the station, six officers were in the interrogation room playing poker and anteing up paperclips. Each had a grin on their face.

ZEKE and Wizard hid in the woods behind their grandmother's house and discussed their situation.

"We got to do something, Zeke. Our drug suppliers will want to know why we're not buying. They'll figure out that something is wrong."

"Wizard, what do you expect me to do? Rob the evidence locker at the police station and then run out and sell the stuff?"

"What if the suppliers find out the police have the drugs? They'll shoot out our kneecaps or something. That's what they do on the crime shows I watch."

"They won't hurt us for not buying, but they will kill us for letting the cops get the drugs."

"We gotta get out of here, Zeke."

"How much cash do you have?"

Wizard checked his wallet. "Ninety-three."

"Between the two of us, we can make it to St. Thomas on the ferry and buy a little food."

POWELL seethed when he saw the officers in the interrogation room with Hanneman. He stormed through the door.

"I'm reporting everyone here to Chief Philippe!" he bellowed as spittle hit the far wall.

"On what grounds?" James asked. "Are you charging us for gambling with paperclips on our dinner break, Manny?"

"No, for aiding and abetting a criminal."

"What criminal? There are no convicted criminals here." James looked at each of his officers. Each man shook his head. James looked directly at the Chief, "Sir, have you ever been convicted of a crime?"

"Not yet, Chief Kingston."

"All of you get out of here!" Powell ordered.

All the men stood up and started to leave, including the Chief.

"Sit down, you buffoon!" Powell screamed as he slammed the Chief into the wall.

"Manny, five officers besides me witnessed what you just did. I suggest you be careful," James said.

Powell followed James into his office and slammed the door shut. James furtively put his hands in his pocket to turn on his small, but powerful, tape recorder.

Powell's nostrils flared as he yelled, "You undermined my

authority in front of those men. I won't let you get away with it."

"No, Manny, you undermined your own authority by acting like a jerk, pushing the Chief and shrieking at the top of your voice. You know damned well the Chief isn't a drug trafficker."

"The evidence tells me he is."

"Someone out there used his boat to store drugs. It's as simple as that," James said.

"Well," Manny huffed. "I'll see to it the evidence shows what I want it to show. You can't do a thing about it. I'm going for a conviction."

"The last time I looked, it was a crime to tamper with evidence, Manny."

"I don't care about you or your opinion."

James sat back in his chair, "This case is in your hands because the VIPD wants a fair and honest investigation. I will personally see to it that you are fair and honest."

"You've forgotten I'm in Internal Affairs now. We watch cops like you. I can destroy you and Hanneman any time I want for any reason."

Manny Powell stomped out of Chief Kingston's office. James turned off his tape recorder. He had an enigmatic smile planted on his face as he leaned back in his chair and put his feet on his desk. His gold incisor twinkled.

BOB Thompson entered Chamaign's office with a grin pasted on his round dark face. "You missed it, Chamaign. You should have seen the look on Manny's face when he saw us playing poker."

"What I want to know is why I wasn't invited to the game?" Chamaign said with a straight face. "Isn't that sex discrimination or something?"

"No, detective you weren't around."

"I was around, but I was working. I want to go home tonight on time."

Bob changed the topic. "Anything new on the murderer?"

"The car is titled to Roland Coombs. The dead couple's blood was found on the front grill, under the chassis and in the tire wells. Would you check your PC to see if the sketch artist revised our poster boy's mug shot?"

Bob left Chamaign's office, downloaded the image on his PC and returned to Chamaign's office. The officers hustled down the hall to a pint-size interview room where Richard Coombs sat.

"We have something for you to examine, Mr. Coombs," the detective said.

Richard looked at the picture and said, "Add a mole directly above the jaw on his left cheek and you have a mirror image."

Chamaign asked Bob to call forensics to see if they were ready to release Richard's car. They were. Richard returned home.

"I'll get the sketch out around here, St. Thomas, St. John and Puerto Rico," Bob said.

Chamaign added. "I'll ask James if he would approve posting someone at the airports. Then I'll contact the Coast Guard here and in Puerto Rico."

MANNY sat down at the table opposite the Chief. Before he even started to ask questions, Lynette tapped on the one-way window overlooking the interrogator and the suspect. The door opened and Murray Sedge entered. His thick white hair was halfway over his forehead.

"Good evening, Chief, and good evening, Manny," he said as he strolled in the door. He high-fived the Chief, set his briefcase on the table, sat and then leaned back in his chair. "How have you been, Manny? Your wife is fine, I hope."

Powell glanced at Sedge. Loathing registered on his face as his mouth twisted to the right.

The old lawyer brushed his hair off his face and bantered playfully. "Manny, since you've been in Internal Affairs, I haven't seen you around. How's it going?"

Powell kept his eyes riveted on the table. After a minute of silence, Sedge said, "Then it is down to business, I suppose." He patted his black leather attaché case, snapped it open and ceremoniously removed a pad of yellow paper. He picked up three pencils and eyeballed the tips. After a ten second pause, he chose the sharpest one.

"If you don't mind, Manny, I want a record of this conversation." He dug a black digital recorder out of his case and placed it in the middle of the table.

Powell immediately regretted he did not turn on the video recorder located outside the room. He smoldered.

Murray Sedge tested his recorder by having the Chief speak into it three different times. Sedge nodded to the Chief, "Now, remember what I told you on the phone."

The Chief nodded.

"Are we finally ready to start?" Powell growled.

Sedge directed his smile to the interrogator. "Certainly. You're up, Manny. First question?"

Powell was so agitated he had to clear his throat twice before he could speak. "Chief, how long was your boat in dry dock?"

Sedge replied, "Two years, three months and twelve days."

"I asked Hanneman, not you, Sedge."

"Manny, I get to decide when the Chief answers and when I answer."

Powell's jaw almost locked he was so indignant. He could barely be understood when he asked, "When and why did you decide to put your boat back in the water?"

Sedge answered the question. One hour and forty-two minutes later, Powell propelled his way through the door without discovering anything new or incriminating. The Chief smothered his grin behind the back of his hand while Sedge showed off his new white veneers with a clown-like smile.

ONCE the Chief and Sedge were alone, the attorney said, "Powell is out to get you on this one."

"Figured as much." The Chief told Murray about the low grades he gave Powell during his training.

"I'll have to keep that in mind. It could be grounds for a mistrial if we need it. Conflict of interest, you know. Ethically, he should have declined this assignment."

"What did your private investigator discover?"

"Kevin Michaels is my private investigator. I like to think I'm the Caribbean version of Perry Mason and Kevin is my Paul Drake. Remember that series?"

"Sure do. I was stateside for a few years while studying criminal justice in college. Perry never lost a case. Hope you're as good, as he was."

"I'll do my best. To answer your question, Kevin has been to Luther's shop and has a list of five men he has to interview."

After Sedge updated the Chief, he said, "Now friend, Lynette Speers said something about a poker game. Maybe you better tell me about that … and be sure to add why you didn't wait so I could play."

Chapter 18

After Charlie & Family returned, she left Jake, Annie and Molly talking in the kitchen. She went to her room wondering if the police had questioned Victor. She called his cell. He answered and told her about the interview.

"You're not in jail. Congratulations. Or did Mr. Powell allow you to keep your phone in your jail cell?"

"I did my best to get arrested, however, Sedge kept me out for another day or two." The Chief told Charlie about the poker game, Powell's reaction, and the meeting with Sedge.

"Sounds like James arranged a three-ring circus for Powell's entertainment. Why wasn't I invited?"

"Because we don't want you anywhere near the police station. Someone has to keep you out of trouble."

"You do understand, don't you, if the police don't solve this case and prove your innocence, I get to do it?"

"Charlie, I'm in enough trouble already. You steer clear of it."

"I don't make promises I can't keep, so let's change the subject. Do you still like Mr. Sedge?"

"I do. It's a shame I spent so many years disliking him because of his job. Sedge is a good man and he is doing his best to prove me innocent. Now, my lady, it's my turn to change the topic. How was your day?"

Charlie brought Victor up to date about her family's visit to their ancestor's home, the watch, the mystifying inscription, the cookhouse folly, the Spanish gold, and the sumptuous dinner. "Everyone will be dreaming of buried treasure tonight, Victor."

"The Spanish did occupy the island for a while. Whether or not they left any buried treasure is another matter."

After a few words of gooey endearment, Charlie and the Chief disconnected.

Wasn't that a tad too much schmaltz, Ms. Charlie?

Jealous?

Not me! I like my independence, Missy.

Me, too. But a bit of schmaltz here and there isn't so bad.

WHEN Roland returned from the restaurant, he sat in the tiny apartment and watched TV. His friend's set was old and the cable connection was poor. He soon drifted into sleep.

The next morning the television still blared. As he awoke, he glanced at the screen only to see a sketch of himself on the morning news. He was stunned to see his head was bald in the sketch.

How did the cops know I shaved my head?

He understood how easy he would be recognized now. He had to figure out how to get around town without raising any red flags.

I can't grow hair back overnight and I can't go buy a wig.

He went through his friend's dresser drawers and found a cotton skullcap in an American flag print.

This will cover my bald head but ...

Roland considered his dilemma for a few minutes before a solution surfaced. He had seen similar caps on patients undergoing chemo treatments.

I wonder if people lose their eyebrows and eyelashes with chemo.

He logged into his friend's computer and checked the Internet. He found some patients do lose their eyebrows and some lose their eyelashes. Some lose both. He took a pair of scissors to his lashes and shaved his eyebrows off. He put on the cap.

Why would anyone wear a cap in this heat unless he or she was self-conscious about hair loss due to cancer treatments?

Since the sketch on TV didn't show him wearing glasses, he put on his wire frames and flipped down the shades. He left the apartment and headed for a convenience store. He slowed his pace.

He saw several people stare at him for a second and then quickly look away.

The plan is working. People get embarrassed if you catch them staring at you.

Roland entered the convenience store and picked up cigarettes, beer, cereal, milk, chips and dip. As he checked out, the clerk said, "How's it going?"

"Not too bad."

"My mother has been getting sick with her chemo treatments. Have you?"

"Could be worse."

The clerk wished Roland good luck as he left the store to return to his apartment.

He felt so confident with his new disguise, he picked a pocket while a tourist snapped a picture.

Home free!

ZEKE and Wizard hitched a ride to Gallows Bay to take the ferry to St. Thomas. They stayed to themselves on a bench seat in the stern as it made its run between the islands.

"Zeke, what are we going to do once we get there?"

"We'll have to find some kind of work if we plan to survive."

"I've been fired from every job I've ever had, bro."

"You're going to keep one now if you want to eat," Zeke said. "We can trim bushes or something like that. Sure don't want to work in any kitchens."

"They'll feed us in a restaurant," Wizard replied.

"They would never hire you," Zeke joked. "One look at your waistline and they would want you as a customer and not as an employee."

"Are you sure going to St. Thomas will work, Zeke?"

"We can't take the chance that the cops or the drug supplier will find us here."

Forty minutes later, the brothers left the ferry in Charlotte Amalie. They stopped at a tourist's information booth and found a map showing all the hotels and resorts on the island.

"I'm hungry, Zeke."

"Look, bro, we don't have much money."

"Maybe we need to steal a purse," Wizard said.

"We can't take the chance of getting ourselves in trouble."

"But I'm hungry!"

Zeke checked the tourist map and found a grocery store in the area. They walked toward the edge of town to the store.

"How about we hit the deli so we can buy subs," Wizard said.

"How about we buy bread and butter."

Wizard grumbled as they entered the store.

After shopping, the two young brothers left with their white plastic bag. They stopped under the nearest tree and buttered two pieces of bread for each of them. After eating, they walked to the nearest resort with their plastic bag in tow.

AFTER Powell interviewed Laurie Glass, he didn't consider her or her boyfriend viable suspects. Neither Glass nor Bauer had a record of any kind – even speeding tickets. In addition, they had no prints on the bags of skag. Both had clean credit reports and their credit scores were in the high seven hundreds. Bauer had a credit card from his credit union, a local hardware store, and a liquor wholesaler. He paid his bills in full monthly and he never had a late payment on his car loan. Glass's report was essentially the same. Powell already knew the Chief had no police record. His financials were spotless and he owned his own home.

I could care less about his credit report. I'm going to get the Chief for those low grades he gave me. Those prints will do it.

Powell headed for Luther's to interrogate Joey Mills, George Tush, Tom Regis, Jeremiah Peale and Zeke Cort.

ZEKE and Wizard left the first resort together. There was only one job and that was for a kitchen helper. They hitched a ride to the next closest resort.

"Busboy – I don't want to be no busboy, Zeke. Are you mad at me for turning down the job?"

"For a man whose is hungry all the time, you certainly are particular. You take any job offered next time, hear me? We don't have time to fool around. Bread and butter isn't my idea of a meal."

The two brothers arrived at the second resort. The air was around eighty-two degrees. There were two jobs available. Zeke took the position of a bartender trainee for the pavilion's bar by the pool. He had had some training in the past and was pleased he could update his skills.

Wizard accepted the job of busboy.

While Zeke brushed up on his skills, Wizard cleaned tables and groused as he did. At the end of the lunch crowd, there was a large plate filled with uneaten food. He looked around, took the plate in the back hallway, and devoured the leftovers.

Much better than bread and butter ...

CHARLIE, Annie and Molly rose early the next morning. They each consumed a toasted whole-wheat muffin with a tad of butter and a sprinkle of cinnamon on it. They devoured a bowl of yogurt mixed with sliced bananas and fresh diced mangoes. Each drank eight ounces of water or guava juice.

You skipped the diet Pepsi and TastyKake doughnuts for breakfast, Ms. Charlie. Are you sick?

I'm not about to teach my granddaughters my poor eating habits. It's bad enough Molly inherited my addiction to sugar, and Annie inherited my obsession with chocolate.

Well, you ate a good breakfast – I'm proud of you.

Me, too. Now pass me the big, fat, sugar-glazed French cruller on the table.

Charlie and the teens left at nine to go to Elin's dress shop. A new shipment of merchandise had arrived. Charlie didn't want Elin lifting boxes in this stage of her pregnancy. She told her granddaughters about Elin's eclectic selection of jazzy sunhats and sunglasses. She promised to buy both of them something for helping with the boxes.

They hopped into her Camry, drove down the steep driveway, and made a left onto the main road. There was a car parked by the side of the road. Charlie glanced at it, wondered why it was there, but dismissed the thought and moved on.

ROLAND had parked under the overhanging branches of a walnut tree about one hundred feet from where Charlie's lane met the public road. He recognized her car when she pulled onto the asphalt.

Decision point: followed the hag with the kids or wait for the son?

Roland decided to follow the early risers. He didn't think the dad would go on a treasure hunt without the girls.

I can use gold to buy my way off this island. Saint Martin sounds like a nice place to live! And they have a lot more pockets to pick than around here.

CHARLIE pulled into the alley behind Island Elegant just as Elin unlocked the rear door of her shop. After a group hug and shared knuckle bumps, the ladies entered. The young teens cautiously stepped into a world designed for discriminating women obsessed with unique, high-quality fashions.

"Awesome!" Molly said. With an open mouth, her large brown eyes swelled with uncontained astonishment. She consumed the wonders before her.

"Whoa!" Annie uttered in one long expressive breath. She snapped a picture of the store and sent it to her BFFs in Indiana.

Like every other member of their sex, the girls delighted in their discovery of a collection of sophisticated, well-cut dresses, gowns and tops in a rainbow of tropical colors. Many tops were in bold prints with scenes of parrots, birds or seascapes. In sharp contrast, there was one whole wall dedicated to a black and white collection of blouses, skirts, slacks and sundresses.

With her mouth still open, Molly pivoted on her heels as she slowly cast her eyes around the room. "Grandmom, the bikinis!"

"You'll be old enough to wear one of Elin's wicked bikinis in ten or twenty years. Check out the sundresses."

Annie enthusiastically attacked the collection of sun hats and tried on each with undisguised glee as she skipped down the aisle. She took a selfie in each hat and sent them to Indiana.

Elin winked at Charlie as she went about opening boxes. She and Charlie removed the garments and separated them by style and size. Charlie entered the SKU number and other miscellaneous data into Elin's inventory software. After finishing the three boxes, Elin determined which garments required steaming. Charlie steamed white Elin tagged.

Molly racked the clothing, broke down boxes and trashed the empties. Annie separated each set of garments by size, and arranged size separators on each of the new display racks. Finally, she dressed a manikin in one of the new prints. She snapped another picture and sent it to her friends.

Both girls acted as gophers and went for mid-morning snacks at a small shop near the boardwalk. Molly finished her oozy and fruit before she tried on several sundresses. Annie didn't even sip her drink because she morphed into a costume jewelry junkie. With fun rings on each finger, her cheeks swelled into an excited grin.

After donning several delicious sundresses, Molly made her choice. The black and white polka dotted dress had an empire waistline and a bodice covered with tiny ruffles made from the same material as the dress. Both Elin and Charlie agreed Molly looked adorable, although Charlie thought her granddaughter looked a bit more sophisticated than adorable. Molly asked her grandmother to snap a cell picture so she could send it to her friends.

Annie, always demure, picked out a cute pair of teal shorts along with a sleeveless white blouse. The top had petite teal parrots embroidered around the collar. She picked out a straw sun hat with a brim that curled in the front to expose a dark teal silk flower.

The girls look so sweet, Ms. Charlie.

They take after me.

I wouldn't exactly describe you as sweet, Missy.

Oh?

Well you have been around the block a couple of times, you know.

And you've been with me. What's your point?

You're more ... let's say, worldly.

I don't exactly work the streets at night, Ding-a-ling. Let's simply say I'm cosmopolitan.

Is that another crossword puzzle word?

Elin said, "Girls did you see the raised ramp near the boardwalk when you went for snacks?"

"The thing that looked like a walkway that goes nowhere?" Annie asked.

Elin nodded, "It's for a fashion show. Every time we have a cruise ship in Frederiksted's port, I have a small fashion show near the boardwalk for the tourists. Would you two like to model for me tomorrow?"

"Awesome," Molly said. She immediately started to text her friends.

"I've never modeled before," Annie said.

"I'll show you how to walk," Elin said. "Molly, you're thick, long mane is spectacular and your ivory complexion is perfect. You'll do great."

Elin turned to Annie. "Those soft brown curls are lovely, but your smile is what makes you angelic. You're guaranteed to be a success."

Both teens beamed at the compliments and high-fived each other.

Elin picked out a pair of black sandals to match Molly's sundress. Then she examined a wall of straw handbags and chose a big black bag with a large white silk rose on the front. She chose a small, across-the-body teal purse and a delicate pair of mother of pearl earrings for Annie.

After Elin set the selection of clothing aside, Charlie, Elin and the teens left the store in the hands of Elin's manager, Carolyn Rodgers.

They walked the short distance to the catwalk. Elin stepped onto the ramp. She attempted to demonstrate how to do the model's stomp, but found she couldn't walk gracefully while she supported her extruded tummy with both hands. The girls clapped as she left and descended the runway ramp.

Not famous for her humility, Charlie decided she could do the model's swish. She clopped her way across the catwalk with one foot in front of the other while she led with her hips. When the teens saw their grandmother suck her cheeks into a cement-style pout, they both burst into shameless crackles. Annie grabbed her cell and took picture after picture. She sent them to Indiana.

Ms. Charlie, act your age.

Excuse me?

You embarrass me.

Tough munchies. At my age, if you've got it, you have a God-given right to flaunt it.

Next, Molly stepped onto the ramp and tried to imitate the one foot-in-front-of-the-other foot walk. It took her three trips down the runway, but she succeeded. Her hip thrust was exaggerated at first, but soon became natural and smooth.

Annie was self-conscious. As soon as she mastered the right gait, she seamlessly worked in the foot movements. "Grandmom, I feel like a Clydesdale horse!"

The teens hee-hawed as they practiced the required hallowed cheek pout.

Charlie showed her granddaughters how to pivot and turn at the end of the ramp. Both teens tried unsuccessfully. They promised to practice that evening. After a good forty-five minutes of tittering, mugging, and prancing, Molly and Annie were excited, Elin was exhausted, and Charlie was exuberant.

I don't remember you ever being as lean and trim as your granddaughters, Ms. Charlie.

Oh, I was indeed thin, but you weren't around then.

Why not?

Because I didn't need you then. I created you so I had someone to tell me when I had a chin hair. Remember, I now need a ten-X mirror to see them.

Chapter 19

Powell went to Luther's to meet with the employees. George Tush was an elderly mechanic who worked part-time to stay busy. He toiled over a Mercury outboard engine when Powell approached.

"Mr. Tush, some questions."

"Is this your Mercury engine, son?" Tush said as he looked up.

"No. I'm with the VIPD."

"Got a name?"

"Emmanuel Powell."

Tush stood with hands on his hips as he waited to see a badge. Reluctantly, Powell pulled out his leather ID case and presented his credentials.

"Is this visit about the Chief?"

Powell answered, "I ask the questions around here. Have you ever seen anyone on the Hanneman boat who shouldn't have been there?"

"I chased kids off of her a couple of times. Even seen dozens of customers invite themselves onboard for a peek."

"What about after hours?"

"I leave at three so I have no idea. Found beer cans on her during the week I had her engines apart."

"Hanneman ever try to sell you drugs?"

"Nope. Hadn't seen him for months until he decided to put *Gertie* back in the water."

Powell turned abruptly and left. On the way to the door, he stopped at a work table and took a clean rag out of a bin. After he wiped the dust off his shoes, he threw the rag on the gray cement floor and scraped the oil off the soles of his shoes. He gave Tush a disgusted look and walked out. Tush shrugged and went back to his engine repairs.

Powell looked at his notepad. Tom Regis worked in an open pole barn. Powell found him using an acetylene torch. He worked on the broken frame of a boat trailer. Regis didn't hear him approach, but did notice the shiny brown leather dress shoes when they appeared on the floor next to him. He turned off his torch and lifted his welder's shield.

Powell conducted a three minute Q&A, but no new information materialized.

After he was told that Zeke Cort wasn't at work, Powell found Jeremiah Peale. The man knew even less than Regis. He, too, offered no new information.

Joey Mills was next on the list. He was a sales clerk. He had found evidence someone had been near or on the vessel. He told Powell he noticed a slit in the canvas one morning. Luther told him to repair it.

"I will say this, Officer, the Chief cut the missus and me a break a couple of years ago when a neighbor called the cops during a loud argument. He could have canned us both, but didn't. He's a good man."

"Think so? I'm not so sure."

Mills was surprised with Powell's response. He was even more surprised when the officer stomped out the door without saying another word.

Powell didn't ask me the kind of questions that Kevin Michaels asked. I wonder if I should have told him about the night Luther's dogs went wild.

AS the ladies ambled back to the shop after their runway practice session, Charlie noticed a man with a cloth cap on his head. She smiled and nodded. She ignored the strange twitch in her brain.

Elin interrupted Charlie's thought process, "After laughing so much, Charlie, I have decided I want this baby to be a girl. They can be so much fun."

"I don't think James would mind if the baby was a girl since he already has two sons. I will tell you something to keep in mind – baby boys can capture the heart in a special way, too."

"I'll remember that. All we really want is a healthy baby to love and hold."

Once back at the shop, the girls hung up their runway clothes in Elin's office and left with their grandmother. Annie immediately called her father at work in Fort Wayne. She insisted he stop his press and look at her cell phone pictures. Afterward, Molly used her cousin's phone to send pictures to a mountain of her friends in Pennsylvania.

FIRED from their second jobs, Zeke and Wizard headed for town with enough money to buy food.

"You didn't have to push the kid into the pool, Wizard."

"He was asking me stupid questions."

"You should have given him stupid answers then!"

"I didn't like the place anyway, Zeke. The chef kept looking at me when I took a short break. And then he caught me eating left- over food."

Zeke didn't respond, but said, "I didn't like the place either. My boss told me to leave the water fountain for the guests. I was supposed to drink from the hose or something."

Tired, dirty and sweating, the brothers walked another half-mile under the searing sun along a dusty road. A beat-up white Honda stopped next to them.

"What are you two doing here?" the driver asked.

The brothers looked at the two men in the car and didn't know how to answer. The short, dark-featured men were Alberto and

Miguel, their drug suppliers. Alberto was lean with a superior demeanor; Miguel was all muscle – the enforcer.

"Why are you two on this island?" the kingpin asked.

"We got customers over here," Zeke replied as his eyes toggled back and forth between the two men.

Alberto frowned at Miguel and nodded. Both men got out of the car. Alberto stood toe to toe with Zeke; Miguel glared into Wizard's eyes. Zeke decided their aggressive behavior wasn't a good omen.

Alberto said, "This isn't your territory. I got men on this island already."

"Didn't know that. Sorry," Zeke said.

While Alberto interrogated Zeke, Miguel bunched Wizard's shirt up under his chin. He lifted him upward so only his toes touched the ground. So much sweat rolled down Wizard's cheeks, it made channels through the layer of dust coating them.

"What should we do with this one?" Miguel asked his brother.

Petrified, Wizard blurted, "Don't hurt me, please. It's okay, Alberto. The cops found the drugs but everything's cool. They don't know about us."

"The cops have the drugs? How did that happen?" Alberto screamed into Wizard's face.

Zeke answered, "The boat in dry dock isn't in dry dock anymore. The owner put her in the water and went for a spin. Water patrol stopped him."

"Are you sure the cops aren't after you two?"

"That's why it's okay," Wizard said, "the dumb cops don't know anything about either Zeke or me."

"Look stupid, now the dumb cops know there is organized drug traffic on the islands," Alberto barked. "You two numbskulls just put me out of business until the cops get tired of looking for me!"

With a throat full of cement, Zeke didn't try to respond.

"Tomorrow, you two be where you're supposed to be. Hear?"

Alberto and Miguel returned to their car and sped off. They discussed the latest developments as they rode.

"What will the cops do?" asked Miguel.

"By now, the cops know the drugs are from Mexico. They'll

notify the Coast Guard and the Coast Guard will monitor the sailing routes between Mexico and here. We're going to disappear for a while."

"And those two simpletons?"

"Gun loaded?"

"Always," said Miguel.

The brothers pulled to the side of the road, got out, and walked to the trunk. Alberto unlocked it. He opened a fake panel in the rear of the trunk and dug out two Glocks along with ammunition. "All we have to do is turn the car around and wipe them out."

MURRAY Sedge sat back in his chair and held his coffee mug with both hands a mere inch from his lips. Kevin Michaels, the private investigator, had his cup and saucer resting on a mahogany table next to his armchair.

"Tell me more about the dogs," Sedge asked.

"It happened earlier this week. Luther was on St. Thomas visiting his sister. A man named Joey Mills stayed at Luther's apartment on the second floor. He was there to keep an eye on the shop and Luther's boat yard. He heard the dogs put up a ruckus twice. Both times, he went outside and looked over the balcony. The first time he didn't see any movement. The second time he saw two men escaping through a hole in the fence."

"That introduces reasonable doubt, but it is still weak testimony, Kevin."

"There is a bit more. Mills told me he found some bones the next morning. He checked out the boats in dry dock, even the Chief's, but they all looked fine."

"Don't suppose he kept the bones, did he?"

"They went out with the trash."

"What about the other employees?"

"Talked to everyone except this Cort," Michaels said. "He hasn't been around since early in the week. Luther said he never called to quit or anything. Interesting coincidence, don't you think?"

"Very interesting. Did you go to his place and speak to him?"

"He lives with his grandmother and brother. I talked to her and she said the brothers left and didn't come back."

"Hum. Another element of doubt," Sedge said. "I wonder if the Chief can ask for a favor at headquarters and find out more about Cort."

"It's worth a try, Murray. There were no other locals with that name in the phone book or online."

"Good. I'll call the Chief and see what he can do."

The private investigator left the office. Murray Sedge started to outline a strategy. He also scribbled a paragraph about how Powell may or may not proceed with the case.

THE CHIEF worried about his predicament. He decided he needed a change of venue, so he took the light-weight canvas off of Rubee, his year-old red Mustang convertible.

After he folded and stored the cover in his garage, he filled a bucket with tepid water and suds to give his prized possession a bath. He gently cleaned her gleaming surface with a hand mitt. One section at a time, he rinsed, scrubbed and rinsed again as he systematically made his way around the car. The Chief took several squeegees and carefully dried his car. He cared for Rubee as he would a newborn baby.

The Chief went to a tall plastic cabinet kept in the garage. He removed several soft towels. He cleaned and polished the windows inside and out. A brush and hand vac cleaned the interior, which was already devoid of grit and gravel before he had even started. A soft cloth dusted the dash. He pulled Rubee into his garage and polished the supple black leather interior with a special leather wax. With his mind on automatic pilot, he waxed and polished the leather steering wheel three times. He used chrome polish on the rims until they sparkled.

Once *Rubee* passed his final inspection, he took his trophy out for a spin. He headed for the former sugar plantation known as Claudine's Quarters. The plantation was once owned and operated by Charlie's ancestors. The Chief turned into the driveway and drove up the gravel road slowly in order not to spit any gravel inside his wheel wells.

The Chief had purchased the abandoned plantation from the local government. He built a small dormitory with several classrooms attached. The facility served as an alternative to jail for teens. It accommodated young dropouts who had not yet decided to take responsibility for their actions. The boys planted and tended gardens to grow their own food in the early morning hours. The teens were able to sell leftover produce to earn spending money.

The Chief had written a number of grant proposals to finance the project and had actually received funding from the Federal government as well as from several private foundations.

He hired a married couple to oversee the teens. Two teachers from the school district were there in the afternoon so the students could obtain their GEDs. To date, the court had sent six young men to the facility in lieu of jail.

The Chief noticed the newest arrival. He was a fourteen year-old who had been caught stealing from several retail stores. After some one-on-one conversation with the young man, the Chief went to greet the other teens before he met with their counselor. He spent the rest of the day in his tiny office preparing more grant proposals for the following year. As hard as he tried to concentrate, he could not get past his own concerns. Despite all his hard work, *Rubee's* magic hadn't made him forget *Gertie.*

AFTER Alberto and Miguel drove off, Zeke and Wizard were so discombobulated that they left the road, went through some brush, and sat under a tree about fifteen yards from the road.

"I'm sorry I told them about the cops," Wizard sobbed. "I shoulda never mentioned what happened."

"We're okay for now. We're lucky they drove off."

"Bro, I ruined it for them and they'll take it out on me."

"Wizard, you got to keep it together. We'll get through this."

"What about the drugs? Can we get more?"

"Wizard, we're going to get jobs and we're going to keep those jobs. We are not going to quit and we're not going to get fired again. Got it?"

The brothers started to stand when they heard a car slow down on the road. Zeke pushed his brother on the ground, and he went down on his hands and knees. Through the brush, he saw the two brothers drive by, turn around, and drive by again.

Alberto had a gun pointed through the open window. After another drive-by, they drove off.

"I knew they'd come get me," Wizard said as he wiped the sweat off his face with his shirt.

"We better not go in town," the older brother said. "Let's head to the east end of the island. There are several resorts there. Maybe we can get a job in one of those resorts or in one of those restaurants in the back harbor."

"It's a long walk and I'm hungry. I'm scared, too."

"I know, Wizard, I know."

POWELL was anxious to finish the interviews so he drove to Zeke's house. The elderly grandmother answered the door.

"Mrs. Cort?"

"You a cop?"

"Yes."

"Your identification?"

Manny pulled out his ID and showed the woman.

"Does this concern my grandsons?"

"I'd like to speak with Zeke."

"Left with his brother." She told Manny about the missing money. "I have no idea where they went."

Manny gave Mrs. Cort his card and told her to have Zeke call him.

Mrs. Cort watched the officer drive away.

That cop didn't ask any important questions and he sure didn't care about my missing money. That nice young man was concerned about me and my boys.

THE CHIEF was still at his desk at the plantation when his cell vibrated. The ID said Murray Sedge.

"Hello, Murray. Anything new, counselor?"

"A couple of things." Murray proceeded to tell the Chief what Kevin Michaels had learned during his interviews. "Do you know Joey Mills?"

"I know he works for Luther. What about him?"

Murray told the Chief what Joey Mills said about the dogs barking, the unidentified men, and the meat bones.

"This is a good thing, right?"

"It helps when it comes to establishing reasonable doubt. Now I have a favor to ask. Is there anyone at the station who would do you a favor?"

"I can call in a favor or two. What do you need to know?"

"Run a background check on Zeke Cort and on any other Cort."

He told the Chief about the missing grandsons and the missing money.

"This has to be drug related, Murray. They probably paid their suppliers with the money and hoped to make some fast cash on the resale. Mexican black tar is bad news."

"See what you can find out, Chief."

Chapter 20

Deputy Police Chief Philippe of St. Thomas answered his phone on the second ring.

"It's Manny, Boss. I have only one interview left to go. Zeke Cort wasn't at work or at home. His grandmother answered the door. She said he took her savings and left with his brother. She has no idea where they went."

"And the other men that work for Luther?"

"Two had DUIs and the others were clean. Talked to all of them and no one had much to say."

"Recommendation?"

"Arrest Hanneman."

"You need to wait until I give my report to the police commissioner. Chief Farrow, Commissioner Dylan and I have a nine o'clock meeting tomorrow."

"Are you sure I have to wait, Chief?"

"Yes. Are you sure it's Hanneman, Manny?"

"Absolutely. The proof is in the fingerprints."

"What about all those other prints?"

"The interior prints have been run through the Fed's database systems and the National Crime Information Center. Everyone identified has been eliminated. The partial print belonged to a Willard

Cort. He is Zeke's brother."

"Have you taken under consideration that this Zeke and Willard committed the crime?"

"Actually, I have. If they are involved, they are working for Hanneman. Remember, Boss, only the Chief's prints were on the drugs. His story of touching the items as he cleaned the boat is a first class fairy tale."

"But this is Hanneman we are talking about. He was always above reproach. And here he started that teen thing on the old plantation. He paid for the land and the buildings himself."

"Well, Chief Philippe, now we know where he got the money to pay for it."

"Pull Hanneman in this evening. Go over everything again. Make sure you follow up on the Cort brothers. And check out those exterior prints."

PETE parked down the street from where he thought Roland Coombs might be hiding. He locked his car, walked to the middle of the block, and went up the steps to a second floor apartment.

He knocked. There was no answer. "Ro?" he said softly.

A few seconds later, Roland peeked out and allowed Pete to enter.

"I thought you might be here," Pete said.

"My loving brother kicked me out of his house."

"What's with the rag on the head? And where are your eyebrows?"

"Chemo treatments."

"Are you serious, Ro?"

Roland expelled a deep belly laugh. "Good disguise, huh? I can hide right out in the open."

"Fooled me."

"Want a beer?"

"Too early for me, man."

"You always were worried about your image even back in high school," Roland said.

"Well, buddy, my image got me through college and law school. It's part of my charm."

"Have much business?"

"I make my own business," Pete said.

"How do you do that?"

"I review all the arrests made and then speak with each man or woman."

"Isn't that like chasing ambulances?"

Pete tilted his head and he cackled, "I do that, too. It's not a bad way to make a living. I do okay. Have a nice car and boat. Good looking woman, too."

"You gonna charge me if I hire you?"

"Have to charge. I work for Sedge & Associates. This is a high profile case with those two murders and all. What made you kill them?"

"Competition. What else can I say, Pete? Those two pissed me off."

"Well, you won't find me hitchhiking when you're around."

JAMES Kingston answered the phone on his desk at the station. The Chief's name was on Caller ID.

"Hey, Chief, how are you doing?"

"I'm not in jail yet, James, but before Powell comes to my door with handcuffs, I need to ask a favor."

"Ask away."

"I need a report on an Ezekiel Cort and his brother Willard. Zeke works for Luther." Victor gave James the address. "Murray Sedge has his private investigator checking on everyone. Zeke Cort and his brother are nowhere to be found. According to their grandmother, he and his brother left and took most of her savings with them."

"I'll check on both men. Now I have a request. Write this number down." James gave the Chief a phone number.

"What's this number, James?"

"It's a prepaid cell I used when I was a detective. To make my informers feel safer, I told them to call it so our conversations were not recorded or traceable. I want you to buy a burn phone and give me a quick call with the number. That's how we can keep in contact without Manny Powell knowing about it."

ATTORNEY Pete Hummel had a hot date with St. Croix's prettiest dentist. He hummed as he combed his hair and applied his aftershave lotion. After he flexed his arm muscles a dozen times in the mirror, he smiled. He repeated the process again. Another smile.

Once he finished preening, Pete put on his skimpy Speedo and a pair of loafers. He went outside.

Might as well let the neighbors admire me. Every woman is entitled to a thrill once in a while.

He hooked his boat's trailer hitch onto his double cab black F350. Then he went into his garage, retrieved his water skis, a towline and a life jacket. He hummed as he set them inside his classy black speedboat.

He got in his truck and headed for a public ramp not far from the harbor in Christiansted. Alyse was to meet him there.

JAMES searched the police computer system for the name Cort. Both of the brothers had records. Zeke's name was on the list for several traffic tickets, a few old drug-related arrests, and a missed court appearance. Willard Cort, aka Wizard, lived at the same address. The younger Cort had a juvenile record and had done prison time for attempted robbery. He had no history of drug problems.

James paged Karl Lindstrom, the officer who currently worked undercover narcotics on St. Croix. Karl appeared in James' doorway dressed in dirty street clothes. He wore a worn gray and white plaid cotton shirt, beat-up kakis and scuffed casual shoes.

"Any increase in drug arrests, Karl?"

"There's been about a ten percent increase, but nothing specifically sticks out, Boss. I haven't raised a red flag yet."

"Black Tar?"

"More than I would normally expect."

"How about you examine the names and addresses of those arrested for the last three months. See if you can spot any trend."

"Right away. May I ask if this is about the Chief? I'd like to help."

"Don't ask and you can't help. Understood?"

"Understood. But if ..."

"Thanks, but no. Have a good evening, Karl."

EXHAUSTED, Zeke and Wizard reached the back harbor on St. Thomas. A ferry from St. John had just docked and most tourists and businessmen headed for taxis or parked cars.

Zeke and Wizard walked to the Blue Lagoon Restaurant. A cousin named Ray worked in the kitchen. The cousin quietly allowed the men in the back door. He showed them the restroom. Both brothers took off their sweat-laden cotton shirts. They used brown paper towels to wash their faces, necks and bodies. Both shaved. They each had a clean cotton shirt and a change of clothing is a blue gym bag Zeke had brought from home.

They dressed. Once done, both men washed their sweaty shirt and skivvies in hot water and hand soap. They couldn't wring all the water out of the shirts so Zeke opened the window and dropped their wet laundry on top of two big shrubs.

They carefully wiped down the restroom and left. They thanked their cousin as he gave them a bag of food. He also told them about a restaurant close by that was looking for help. The brothers left and retrieved their wet clothes. They walked to the shoreline. They laid their laundry on top of several rocks to dry in the searing afternoon sun. They sat on the beach and ate. Fifteen minutes later, they folded their sun-dried shirts and put them in the blue bag. The shorts took an extra fifteen minutes.

After their clothes were in the bag, Zeke and Wizard walked to the restaurant that needed help. Clean and presentable, the men entered the restaurant and asked for the manager. After a short interview, the manager hired Wizard as a busboy and Zeke as an assistant bartender. Zeke warned his brother not to eat the leftovers unless he asked permission.

The men worked for the rest of the day until late evening. Zeke earned a meager hourly wage but his tips were excellent. Wizard made less, but amassed a sizable bag of edibles. The owner paid the men under the table when their shift ended.

Before the brothers left for the evening, they washed their shirts and underwear in the employee bathroom, dropped them out the window, left the restaurant and retrieved their laundry again. They put their shirts on dripping wet and walked to the beach. The warm air and breeze dried the shirts in no time.

About a mile down the beach was a large resort. The brothers stealthily borrowed two chaise lounge chairs from the pool area, hid them in the brush, hung out there shorts, and bedded down for the night under the palm trees. They had full bellies and ninety-eight bucks between them. Life was good for the moment.

THE CHIEF left a convenience store with a pre-paid disposable cell in his pants pocket.

Burn phones, iPhones, iPads, iPods, Kindles, Wi-Fi, camera phones, apps! What could possibly be next?

He slid into Rubee, called James and gave him his new untraceable cell number. As he disconnected, his personal cell buzzed.

"Manny Powell here. I want you down at the station."

"Is this an interrogation?"

"I need some things clarified."

"My lawyer is not here and there are no more ferries between St. Thomas and St. Croix this evening."

"You were a big-boy cop. You can handle a few questions without having someone hold your hand, I'm sure. I'll pick you up."

"I'll call my lawyer. If he approves, I'll show at the station."

The Chief disconnected before Powell could reply. He called Murray Sedge. He agreed to the interview as long as he was on a speakerphone. The Chief drove home and picked up his tape recorder. He then programmed his new cell so he could speed-dial James. He tested the phone and James answered. The men arranged to keep the phone turned on during the interview so James could listen.

ANNIE giggled, "I'm so excited about the fashion show tomorrow, Grandmom. I hope I'll be able to sleep."

"Both of you did a good job perfecting your walk and pivots this evening. You'll be fine."

"You were awesome, Annie," Molly said as she consumed a big slice of pepperoni pizza.

"You're the one who has the height to be a real model," Annie replied.

"And I'm the one who will look like a big fool if I screw up!"

Grandmom said, "Neither of you will screw up. Get up on the catwalk like you own it. Show the audience you are there to have fun, and then strut your stuff up the kazoo!"

"It's time for you two to head for bed and get some rest," Jake said. "You've had a busy day and it will be even busier tomorrow."

"What time do we have to be at Elin's shop, Grandmom?"

"The show starts at eleven. We can do some of your makeup here, but wouldn't it be more fun to do it with the other models?"

"Yes!" Annie said. "That would be great. Are the models all pros?"

"They didn't start out as pros, but they are now. Elin uses her own salesladies. She had a makeup artist fly in from San Juan to instruct the staff as to how to use makeup to their best advantage. Then she hired an instructor from a modeling school for two days of training. In addition, she contracts for a hairstylist to be available on fashion show days. The models put up their own hair, but the stylist comes in to comb it out. She hasn't had one employee quit since she started her shows."

"There was one saleslady at the shop yesterday. She was on the heavy side. Is she a model?" Molly asked.

"Actually that lady is the larger-sized model. She is everyone's favorite. Many cruise ship tourists are not exactly svelte and they really appreciate seeing someone their size in the clothes because they know how the duds will look on them."

That includes you, Ms. Charlie.

Moi?

Well, you do have a couple extra po ...

Do you have a death wish?

Jake again reminded the girls it was time to hit the sack. They reluctantly agreed, but both hid their cells as they headed for bed. There was still enough time to do some serious texting.

JEREMY and Laurie strolled down the small boardwalk in an attempt to walk off some of those dinner calories. The moon was huge, the breeze was gentle, and the only sound either of them heard was the gentle lapping of the water against the rocky shoreline.

"You know, Laurie, we should do this every evening."

"Even when we're old and gray?"

"Even when I'm old and bald."

"That would require a commitment, wouldn't it?" Laurie asked.

"The M word comes to mind."

"And the M stands for ...?"

Chapter 21

In bed, but not asleep, two sets of teenage thumbs texted messages of madness about the fashion show the next day. Jake lounged in a hammock on the lanai with a Cruzan Cream in one hand and a plate of cheese and crackers in the other. Charlie sat on her bed and emptied her cranberry-red pumpkin-size purse by turning it upside down to discover what treasures were tucked inside its sacred depths. Buried within the volcano-shaped mass now displayed on her sheet, she found the security tape she had cloned from Luther's shop.

Let me get my detective raincoat, Ms. Charlie.

Get mine, too.

We can't let Jake know about this.

He has to know. I need his help. Watch and listen to see how a pro handles this ...

Jake was in a lounge chair on the lanai outside of Charlie's double doors. "Jake, I'm not trying to be a detective or anything, but I need your help," she said through the screen door.

Jake's eyebrows arched as he looked at his mother and waited for an explanation.

Charlie told him about the tape of the dry dock area next to Luther's shop. "This video was taken the night before Victor put *Gertie* back in the water. I want to see if anyone was around the boat that evening."

"I'll watch, but only to keep you out of trouble. If there is anything important on this video, there will be no action on your part. We will give it to the police pronto."

Jake faked a frown as he slid the tape in an old VCR Jeremy kept in his bedroom. Charlie grabbed a bag of potato chips, flopped on her son's bed, and put her head on the pillow. Jake, now an amateur gumshoe of sorts, sat on a chair. They watched the forty two-inch flat screen and studied the video. They quickly determined the security system was very old, very grainy, very black and white, and very boring. It also came with no sound. On the lower right corner of the screen was the time/date stamp. It was one fifty-two in the morning. After twenty-seven minutes of staring at the black and white screen, Charlie fell asleep.

Jake continued to watch. Unexpectedly, two dark figures appeared on the screen. Jake's body snapped into alert mode. He watched as two men climbed through a hole in the chain link fence. They proceeded directly to the dog run where two Rottweiler sentries stayed during the night. The taller of the men carried a plastic grocery-style bag and the squat man lugged two small gas cans. The tall trespasser took several items out of the bag and threw them near the dogs. Both animals rapidly attacked the objects as they discovered a feast of raw meat.

Jake turned to his mother and realized she was asleep with her open bag of chips rising and falling on her chest. He returned to the tape and watched as the men proceeded diagonally across the yard toward a boat. Only the stern of the vessel was visible, but Jake could read its name, *Gertie*. After the tall man climbed on board, the heavy set man handed him the gas cans. Then he climbed on top of two cement blocks acting as a ladder. He gingerly stepped onto the deck of the stern.

Jeremy's attention was riveted to the screen, but he didn't detect any other movement for the next six minutes. Then the men reappeared, exited the boat, threw the barking dogs two more pieces of meat, and left through the hole in the fence.

The cops found drugs in those two gas cans. Even mom would say this is not a coincidence. Those guys brought something to feed those dogs to shut them up. They had this whole thing planned. Sure bet those dealers didn't know Gertie would be launched the next day. This tape will get the Chief off the hook for sure.

The sound of a car on the driveway woke Charlie. She peeked out the window and recognized *Rubee.* She hopped off the bed, ran her hands through her hair, brushed her teeth, and headed for the front door. Jake savored the moment when he could tell the Chief and his mother what he had seen. He followed his mother outside.

Victor slid out of the car and said, "Charlie, we have to talk."

"What happened? Charlie asked as she leaned against *Rubee's* fender.

The Chief took Charlie's elbow and moved her away from *Rubee*. He paused for a second, grabbed a rag from under the front seat, and wiped non-existent dirt off the fender.

"I haven't sat in any dirt lately, so I didn't dirty your fender, Victor!"

"My girl smudges easily," he said.

Who is his girl, Ms. Charlie, you or the car?

Obviously the car!

The Chief was oblivious to the unintended slight and walked to the house. "I don't intend to worry any more, Charlie. With your help I plan to catch the guilty party."

"Me? Help? Did I hear you right? You want the help of a woman who just smudged Rubee?"

Go girl! Give it to him, Missy.

I would, but he looks so confused.

The Chief seemed baffled at Charlie's reaction and quickly looked to Jake for an explanation. Jake used his hand to demonstrate Victor wiping the car. Victor got it. "Oh, Charlie, I didn't mean to …"

"Chief," Jake said, "After you take your foot out of that large cavity in your face, tell us what you want my mom to do."

"I want your mother to have one of her Charlie Moments."

"Can you be a bit more precise? What is a Charlie Moment?" Jake asked.

"Jake," the Chief said, "a Charlie Moment is one of those unanticipated, unscripted, unimaginable, and incomprehensible moments in time and space when your mother solves a mystery. She says, 'Aha! I know who the bad guy is.' "

What do all those words mean, Ms. Charlie?

They mean he did two crossword puzzles this morning.

"To translate, Jake, Victor wants me to get involved in this drug case," Charlie said with a hint of sarcasm in her voice.

"No, it means I want you to have a Charlie Moment," the Chief said. "You let your mind prognosticate and then tell me the identity of the drug dealer. I'll go catch the man."

Prognosticate, Missy?

It's English. Trust me.

What does it mean?

I think it means I do the work and he goes home a free man.

The Chief told Charlie and Jake about the cell in his pocket and his tape recorder. "I've arranged for Charlie to get into the station and observe the interview through the one-way glass in the interrogation room. With any luck, she'll pick up on something she hears."

"Excuse me, Chief. I believe I had a Jake Moment less than two minutes ago." He grinned as he told the Chief and his mother about the security tape.

"Did I hear what I thought I heard?" Victor asked.

"I'll tell you what," Jake said, "if I can go with you, I'll show you the video right now."

"Jake, you most definitely inherited all your mother's best genes."

Let me see if I got this right, Ms. Charlie. You procured the tape and Jake is getting the credit. What about us, Missy? You and I should get some of the glory.

This is not the time to explain your existence to two hubristic men.

Hubristic! Ha, ha. I know that word and I haven't done any crossword puzzles.

AFTER watching the video, Charlie, Jake and Victor piled into *Rubee*. Jake squeezed into the cramped rear seat of the Mustang. He had to sit sideways to make his long legs fit.

Victor called James on the way to the station and told him about the tape. When the trio arrived, Victor let Charlie and Jake out in the rear of the station, and then he drove around front to park. Chamaign let Charlie and Jake inside and led them directly into her office.

AFTER a long, hot, boring day, Alyse Mikkelsen scooted out of Pete's car and entered her home without inviting Pete in or giving him the benefit of a good-night kiss. She shut and locked her front door. She had spent most of the afternoon and part of the evening with Pete on his boat.

Elin was right. He likes himself far more than he likes me. What a self-absorbed, egotistical, pompous, narcissist! I get to run the boat while he skis. Afterward, he hands me a beer so I can sit and listen to him talk about himself. Pete Hummel, you're officially dumped!

Pete stood outside of Elin's door for a second and then returned to his car.

She shut the door on me. Here I spent a whole day entertaining her and she isn't the least bit grateful. Women! Must be her time of the month.

GIL stood on Jeanette's front porch as he said good night. "Oh Sweetie, I had such a nice evening." He tenderly kissed her cheek.

"Sailor boy, you are so dear to me." Jeanette stood on her toes and placed a soft, loving hand on each side of Gil's face. With tears in her eyes, she gave Gil a long, gentle kiss.

Gil recovered after a minute of serious heart thumpin. "I've wanted to talk to you about something …"

Gil removed a bit of non-existent lint from his pants, shuffled his feet, loosened his already loose collar, scratched his neck, studied the moon, and then said, "Do you think we're too old to get serious about each other?"

Jeanette fluttered her eyelashes a few times before she asked, "How serious is serious, Gil?"

Gil's heart palpitated faster. He made a conscious effort to control his breathing. He looked to his right and studied the fuzz on the leaves of the potted African violet in the window. Then he turned his head to the left and meditated on the affect the moonlight had on the color of the bougainvillea bush in the yard. After he evaluated the shine on his shoes and checked the porch ceiling for peeling paint, he cocked his head and glanced at Jeanette. "Like the two of us gittin married. Would you be my wife?"

"Gil, I'm eighty-one years old and the best description of an old maid there is."

"Don't matter none to me. I never got married either."

"You had a girl in every port, I bet."

Gil moved his foot left and right like an Argentinean soccer pro. His Adam's apple toggled up and down a few more times before he said, "A few maybe. If it makes you feel any better, I haven't had an honest-to-goodness lady friend since I left the Merchant Marines forty years ago."

"Gil, you're the sweetest man I have ever met. I've cared for you since the moment I first saw you. I'd love to be your wife." Jeanette began to weep as happy tears flowed.

Gil pulled a stray thread from the hem of his shirt and tied the thread around Jeanette's ring finger on her left hand. "Tomorrow we'll go looking for a proper ring."

THE CHIEF entered the station. Before he went to the interrogation room, he called Sedge on his cell and James on his burn phone. He walked into the room feeling empowered.

"Good evening, Manny," the Chief said as he extended his hand to shake Manny's.

Manny had anticipated a worried, distressed, and nervous man walking into the room. The Chief's spirited stride and robust greeting confused him. He stood up and shook Victor's hand.

Not waiting for Manny to point him to his seat that faced the one-way window, Victor seated himself at the table with his back to the window. He pulled his chair close to the table and stretched his torso so his back was straight, but angled slightly toward his antagonist. "Well, Manny, what do we need to discuss?"

With the interviewer's seat occupied by the interviewee, Manny sat facing the Chief and the window. He hesitated to answer the question as he watched the Chief set a cell on the table and punch the speakerphone button.

"Manny, Mr. Sedge is on the phone."

"Greetings, Lieutenant Powell. I'm anxious to learn what you've discovered," the attorney said.

Manny had not yet realized that the Chief had again assumed the role of interrogator, and he would be the one on the defensive. With his train of thought interrupted, he sputtered, "The drug … the drugs in your boat – where did they come from?"

"I didn't put the drugs there, and I don't believe for one minute Jeremy or Laurie did either. Have you eliminated all possible suspects?"

Manny remain flustered and still didn't realize the Chief was in control of the interview. "Chief, there are no other suspects."

The Chief put his hands on the table in front of Manny. He leaned toward his adversary and into the officer's personal space.

"Tell me about the other fingerprints."

Manny wiped the sweat from his forehead with his hand. His torso slumped and his legs became antsy. He unconsciously tapped his right foot. "There were your prints, Jeremy Bauer's and his girlfriend's."

The Chief remained in Manny space. "Now tell me about the others."

Chapter 22

Charlie, Chamaign and Jake were in the room abutting the interrogation room. It had the one-way window plus the video and recording devices.

Ms. Charlie, what's going on in that room?

Victor took charge and charged the charger!

Huh?

"Mom, isn't Powell supposed to be interviewing the Chief?" Jake asked. "The Chief seems to be interviewing him."

"Victor maneuvered himself into the catbird seat. Powell isn't exactly making a good impression, is he?"

"The Chief is being smart, too," Chamaign said. "He isn't letting Powell know he has received inside information. Instead, he knows what questions to ask so Powell tells him everything." Chamaign stifled a laugh. "At the rate the Chief is going, Manny will confess he put the drugs on the boat."

THE CHIEF asked Manny about the prints. The officer told him what he knew. The Chief stood and slowly paced. His left arm crossed his waist and the hand supported the elbow of his folded right arm. He touched the bottom of his chin with his pointer finger and his thumb.

He resembled an astute scientist pondering the depths of the universe.

"So there were other prints, you say. I figured there had to be. Thank you. I'm glad you eliminated Luther and almost all of his employees. You mentioned a Willard Cort. Who is he?"

"I couldn't find him."

"Do we know where he lives, Manny?"

"Yeah. He and his brother live with their grandmother. She said they packed and left with some of her money."

"The brothers left together?"

"Yeah."

"So this Willard Cort works for Luther?"

"No, his brother Zeke does."

"And they both left together. Interesting."

"Couldn't find Zeke either, so the two of them must be together."

"As I said, interesting." The Chief continued his absent-minded professor routine. "I wonder why this Willard's prints were inside my boat when he doesn't work for Luther. Now, Manny, things are getting more interesting, aren't they?"

Manny nodded as he looked at the floor.

JAMES stood on the porch of his home as he listened to the interrogation over his burn phone. As planned, the Chief kept his disposable phone turned on and hid in his pocket. James smiled as he pictured Manny squirming in his seat.

THE CHIEF returned to his seat. He leaned back in his chair, with his elbows on the armrest and steepled his fingers. The look on his face was one of somber contemplation as he pretended to study the bare light bulb on the ceiling. Finally, he said, "Manny, you didn't happen to notice a security camera at Luther's shop, did you?"

"Didn't see one."

"Check it out for me. Would you do that, Manny? Check for one in the boat yard, too."

Powell nodded.

The Chief stood. “Good night, Manny. Let me know if there is a tape and we can watch it together.”

As the Chief left the room, he put his arm around Manny’s shoulders. “Son, do you know what half of a zwei is?”

THE CHIEF plowed out of the room at the same time Charlie, Jake and Chamaign disappeared back into Chamaign’s office. Victor walked out the police station’s front door and folded into Rubee. His call to Sedge was still connected, so he told him about the security tape.

“Excellent detective work,” Sedge said. “I think I will give Chief Philippe a call and offer him a private viewing. Pack up the tape and send it to me on the first seaplane flight tomorrow.”

The Chief grinned, “Not a problem.”

“I’ll draw up a request to review the tapes from the security cameras at the ferry dock and the airports. Kevin Michaels can review those tapes. I want to stay one step ahead of Powell, possibly two or even three.”

Murray and the Chief disconnected. Then the Chief and James did the same. James stood on his front porch and stared at the stars.

Zwei? What was the Chief talking about?

THE CHIEF drove around the back of the station and picked up Charlie and Jake.

“I’m impressed, Chief,” Jake said. “That didn’t resemble any interrogation I’ve ever seen on any television show.”

“It’s all about control,” Charlie said. “Victor displayed a confident air the second he walked into the room. When he sat with his back to the one-way window, he forced Powell to sit in the seat facing the window. Powell didn’t protest. Victor hijacked the role of the interrogator and assumed complete ascendancy over the interview.”

The Chief chuckled as he said, “When I leaned closer to him, I could actually see the sweat in his pores. Can we have a celebratory drink as we watch the tape again?"

"Only if the drink is Cruzan Cream," Charlie said.

MANNY had a sleepless night as he tried to figure out why his interrogation didn't go well.

What happened? I felt I was the one interviewed. And what the hell is a zwei?

The first thing the next morning, Manny called Chief Philippe. "I'm not going to arrest Hanneman yet, Chief. I came up with another idea and need to check the boat yard to see if it has a security system. I don't want to do anything rash. It may make the police department look bad."

ZEKE and Wizard rose early, returned the lounge chairs, and finished off the rolls and butter left in the plastic bag.

Wizard said, "I'm thirsty. Let's walk down to the harbor and see if we can find someplace where we can get some coffee. We have a couple of hours before we go to work."

"Wizard, while we have the money, let's head home. I don't want the Rodriguez brothers to find us here."

At the back harbor, the two worried man found a small shop open. Both ordered a coffee and a big bottle of water. They took a Vitran, an inexpensive open-air bus, to Charlotte Amalie. They had to walk two blocks to the ferry dock. On the way, they stopped at a small store. Zeke ordered a breakfast sandwich and Wizard bought four doughnuts. After the ferry left, they ate their breakfast.

"We spent most of our money on the ferry tickets," Wizard said. "Think we can get a job back home?"

"Since we're not exactly the hoighty-toighty type, maybe Bert the Bartender will give us a job. If not, we'll head for the area around the pier in Frederiksted. With those cruise ships, we should be able to find something."

Once docked, they left the ferry and walked to a small store. Both men bought a second cup of coffee. They returned to the dock and sat on the end of the pier with their feet dangling over the water. Zeke and Wizard were so engrossed in their conversation that they didn't notice a dark, dusty car pull into the parking lot. Both men felt a piercing pain. A bullet pierced Zeke's shoulder and a second shot hit him in the stomach. A single shot passed right through a fat roll hanging over Wizard's belt.

Without hesitation, Wizard jumped into the water. Zeke lost his balance and fell forward into the harbor. When Wizard surfaced, he saw his brother struggling to stay afloat. He swam to Zeke and pulled him over to the edge of the pier. He held onto the piling with one hand and held onto his brother with the other.

The clerk in the coffee shop saw what happened and called nine-one-one. When the EMTs arrived, the clerk helped the medics pull the brothers out of the water.

WHEN Gil woke, he wore an expansive smile on his gray stubbly face. A love-struck glaze covered his still sleepy eyes as he listened to the birds tweet outside his open window. He lay in bed and remembered Jeanette's kiss and the string of blue thread made into an impromptu engagement ring.

I proposed. Holy Moly! I got me a cutie whose gonna be my wife. What will my buddies say?

Jeanette woke with an equally wide smile on her face. She immediately checked her finger to ensure the little string of dark blue thread was still there.

Whom should I call first? What will James and Elin say? Since I'm the only auntie James has, I'll ask him to give me away. And every lady in my Red Hat group will be a bridesmaid. Oh Gil, you dear sailor boy, you make me so happy.

JAMES had left for work before Elin struggled to pull herself out of bed. She rubbed her back with both hands.

Why does my back hurt like this? I don't have time for a backache today. I have a fashion show to run.

JEREMY sat on the edge of his bed and stared at the wall for a second before his mind focused.

I proposed. I can't believe I did it. I'm getting married.

With a Clem Kadiddlehopper grin spread from ear to ear, he speed-dialed Laurie's number and a sleepy voice answered.

"Sorry to bother you, ma'am, but can I speak to the fiancée of one Jeremy Bauer?"

Using her hometown Savannah drawl, she said, "Why, sir, that's me, I believe."

"What do you say we formalize our engagement and go ring shopping? Between St. Thomas and St. Croix, we have about a hundred jewelry stores to choose from."

CHARLIE made her early morning call to Victor. They rehashed the conversation they had the night before about the interview. After she disconnected she watched the tape again.

One man is tall and thin and the other short and broad. Both are black. I wonder where Willard Cort's prints were located. The gas can? Stern? Seat? I wonder if Luther heard the dogs bark? I need to do a little bit of digging.

JAKE sat at Charlie's kitchen counter and ate his morning bowl of Kashi decorated with dried cranberries, almonds and soy milk. While he digested his food, he studied the sketch the police had of the man who stole the locket and murdered two people.

I'm going to solve this case one way or another. Oh God, help me. I sound like my mother!

THE CHIEF had made a copy of the tape before he left Charlie's the night before. He packaged it and drove to the location of Sky High Seaplanes. He paid to have it transported to St. Thomas and told the pilot someone would pick it up at the dock office. Then he called Murray Sedge's office, told him about the tape, and asked to have the tape retrieved.

Sedge said, "Chief, there's no doubt I can win this case now if it goes to trial. But I can't see it getting that far."

"Murray, knowing how Manny Powell dislikes me, he could claim I hired these two men. The police may go overboard to cover their keisters so no one can scream favoritism."

"I suppose it's possible, but I wouldn't worry if I were you," Sedge said. The two men enjoyed fifteen minutes of banter before they disconnected.

ROLAND Coombs sat on the edge of the bed and felt the stubble on his face and head. He smiled.

I wonder if anyone will go for a treasure hunt today.

He showered, shaved his face and head, and dressed in a loose fitting tan plaid shirt and khaki cargo pants. He made coffee and toast, and spread mango jelly on the top of his bread. He wrapped his flag-print rag around his head. With several bottles of water in his arms, he went to the car and drove to the first intersection from Charlie's driveway.

EMERGENCY Management Services took Zeke and Wizard to the hospital. Zeke underwent immediate surgery. The bullet bypassed his clavicle, but lodged under the shoulder blade. A surgeon extricated the bullet. The second bullet passed through the stomach and exited through his back. Fortunately, a gastrointestinal surgeon had been at the hospital for an early-morning appendectomy, and he repaired Zeke's damaged intestines. The patient was placed on a heavy duty antibiotic IV drip to prevent infection.

Wizard had his tummy wound cleaned and stitched at both the entrance and exit sites of the bullet. The doctor told Wizard his brother would be hospitalized for an undetermined amount of time. The young man sat nervously in a room off the emergency room. Tears rolled down his cheeks. He shivered when he recognized the light blue shirt and dark blue pants of a VIPD officer.

ROOKIE Rand Brownstone entered the room and introduced himself. The short but solid officer with light tan skin sat next to Wizard.

"Mr. Cort, I need your full name and address."

Wizard gave his name and his grandmother's address. Brownstone wrote down the information. He had no idea that the two injured men were wanted by the USVI police. He asked Wizard about his brother and Wizard gave the officer his brother's personal info.

"Tell me everything as it occurred, Mr. Cort."

Wizard described sitting on the pier drinking coffee. He didn't mention anything about the drugs.

"Why would someone do this to you and your brother, Mr. Cort?"

"It musta been a random shooting, I guess. Don't know any reason."

"What were you doing at the dock?"

Wizard explained he and his brother had jobs on St. Thomas, but decided to come home and find work. The officer continued to ask questions for over an hour. He knew very little more than he did when he first started to question Wizard. The officer told him he would return later to interview his brother once his anesthetic wore off. He also wanted to talk to both of them together. He gave Wizard his card as he left.

ON THE way to his office, Pete Hummel drove past Roland's car sitting on the side of the road. He pulled over, stopped, and walked toward his client. "Do I want to know why you are sitting here?"

"I doubt it."

"I take it the police haven't stopped by yet?"

"Either they're too stupid or I'm too smart."

"Did you see this morning's paper?"

"Don't have time to read the paper. Nothing in it."

Pete handed Ro and article written by reporter Terry Mitchell for the Virgin Island Press, also known as the VIP.

ROAD KILL

The St. Croix police are still looking for the man who ran over and killed two visitors from St. Thomas. The couple was returning from the Three Kings Day Parade. The massacre occurred near the Palm Shack, just off Centerville Road.

The young couple had stopped for food. As they tried to hitchhike back to Christensted, the suspect ran over the couple. The police feel the action was deliberate.

The alleged suspect, Roland Coombs, lives on St. Croix. Coombs is five feet eleven, and approximately one-sixty pounds. The police believe the suspect may have shaved his head. Anyone seeing the alleged murderer should call the police department immediately. Citizens are asked not to approach the subject.

Ro looked at Pete, "I'm famous. It's about time."

"They'll catch up to you sooner or later. I can get you a better deal if you turn yourself in."

"Not me. I'll be off this island soon. I need a bit more time to handle a few loose ends."

"If these loose ends are illegal, I don't want to know about them."

Roland glanced at his former high school buddy and said, "Let's say I'm coming into some money and leave it at that."

DETECTIVE Chamaign Benton and Officer Bob Thompson had an early morning meeting to go over their notes about the double homicide.

"I've checked all the airport videos for the past week as well as the video from the security cameras down at the ferry dock and Sky High Seaplanes. Nada," Bob said. "This guy is still around."

"We've papered both Frederiksted and Christensted with Wanted posters. We now have officers posted at the airport, ferry and Sky High. Sooner or later, we'll get him."

"And he has to eat," Bob said.

"We need to ask the stores to post pictures at the registers."

"What about our smaller mom and pop stores and gas stations?"

"Go for it, Bob. I'll take the post office, the hospital, the Social Security and IRS offices, plus our local government building. Let's avoid the tourist shops, but I do want to leave posters with the restaurant managers."

Both Chamaign and Bob grabbed a fistful of posters and vamoosed.

AS ELIN walked to her closet to get dressed, she felt her first labor pain. She called her obstetrician's office and described the pain to the nurse.

"Mrs. Kingston, it sure sounds like a labor pain. The doctor will be in shortly. You stay home, walk around the house as much as you can. If you are in labor, walking will speed things up. Call me back in an hour."

Elin called Charlie. "I'm in labor, I think. What am I going to do about the fashion show?"

"Carolyn Rogers is a good manager. She can handle the store and I can orchestrate the fashion show. We'll be fine. Did the doctor give you an idea of when you should go to the hospital?"

Elin relayed what the nurse said.

"Then you do as told. If you are in labor, you'll soon know for sure. With an eight-pounder preparing to launch, you'll be holding your belly all day. Is James with you?"

"He's left for work. I don't want to worry him until I know for sure."

"Oh, go ahead and worry him. That's what husbands are for during labor!"

Elin managed to smile as she felt a second contraction. "Ohhh."

Ms. Charlie, my tummy hurts, too.

Well huff and puff then!

Chapter 23

Powell duplicated Luther's tape, took it to the station and watched it. He saw the two men climb on the boat.

I will get my conviction. Now I only have to prove those men work for him.

Powell sat back in his seat and grinned as he mentally patted himself on the back.

THE two teens taunted each other playfully.

"It's Tony," Molly said.

"No, it's Timmy," Annie replied. "He has such pretty eyes. And besides, he likes Abby."

Charlie stood in the doorway and listened for a few minutes. "Are you two still arguing about who is the cutest man on *NCI S*?"

The girls looked at each other before they nodded and grinned.

"You both are wrong. Gibbs is the hunk. End of story."

The teens rolled their eyes and gave their grandmother a give-me-a-break look. Then they pursed their lips to hide their giggles.

Molly said, "Shouldn't we get ready for the fashion show?"

"Shower and eat breakfast first. Then dress. Elin may be in labor, so I will coordinate the show today. I'm going to run to her house for fifteen minutes and then come right back."

The girls headed for the showers while Charlie grabbed her car keys and her tent-size purple and yellow canvas tote. She headed up the road.

Upon arrival, she tapped on the partially opened door and stepped inside. She saw Elin standing in a puddle of water.

"Is that what I think it is?" Charlie asked.

"Think so."

"Congratulations. Now that your water broke, you are officially in labor."

Elin picked up the phone and called the doctor's office. The nurse paged the doctor at the hospital. He asked Elin to come in.

"Charlie, can you close my suitcase and carry it?"

"Sure. I'll also clean this up. Right now I need a thick towel so you can sit on it in the car. Where can I get one?"

Elin told her where two beach towels were in the linen closet. Charlie grabbed them and then held Elin's arm as they walked to the car. Charlie returned, cleaned up the floor, and grabbed the valise. Once she arranged the seat belt around Elin, she drove to the hospital.

Elin registered and Charlie pushed her to the birthing room in a wheelchair. "After you undress and the nurse does her thing, I'll return to harass you. You might also want to let your husband know where you are."

Charlie left and entered the waiting room to get bottle of water. The room had one long bench for seating. She sat next to a young heavyset man. His hands trembled and tears streamed down his cheeks. She probed her tote for a packet of tissues. She shoved the banana, makeup bag, and cell aside to find them. She handed the tissues to the young man.

"Is there anything I can do?" she asked.

"No, thank you, ma'am. My brother just got out of surgery. I'm really worried."

"If I may ask, what kind of surgery?"

Wizard told Charlie about the harbor and the bullets. He lifted his shirt and showed her his dressing.

"Did you call your family?"

"Nah. Our Nana is mad at us. She would say we got what we deserved."

"What did you do to deserve being shot?"

"It's a long story, but those guys are gonna kill us sooner or later."

"The police will protect you. Did you tell them about the guys?"

"I can't tell them anything," Wizard said as he broke into a sweat. His tears turned into a flood and he bawled, "They'll kill us."

"For your own protection, you need to tell the police."

"Can't do that. See, I'm on parole and if the cops knew I know these guys, I'd end up right back in a cell. My brother and I tried to get some money ahead – that's all."

Wizard stood and started to leave. Before he got to the door, he turned and said, "Thanks for the tissues, ma'am."

JEANETTE called her nephew's house. No answer.

I have to tell someone my wonderful news!

She called the police station to reach James. Lynette Speers took the call.

"Miss Kingston, you'll be happy to know your nephew just left for the hospital. Elin's in labor but she has a way to go."

"Oh my goodness, I'm going to be a great aunt."

"I know Chief Kingston will be busy today, so will you give me a call when you know something about the baby. Everyone at the station is anxious to know."

After Jeanette promised she would call, she hung up and called her new fiancé. "Gil, guess what?"

Jeanette told him about Elin. Gil said he would pick her up when she was ready to go to the hospital. They disconnected after a few minutes.

Oh my goodness. I still haven't told anyone about Gil!

Jeanette headed for her small walnut desk and dug for her private phone book. She grabbed the phone and called every one of her Red Hat friends. After that, she tackled her church directory.

CHARLIE said good-bye to Elin when James arrived. She returned to the girls.

"Molly, your eyes look beautiful. When we get to the shop, put a touch of gloss on those lips and you're good to go."

"But Grandmom, look at this zit on my cheek."

"I have cover-up makeup in my handbag. The only difference between you and me is that I cover age spots, not zits!"

Ms. Charlie, what would we do without our cover-up makeup?

Everyone would know our deepest, darkest secrets.

Not me! I don't have any age spots.

Remember, you're in my head. If I have them, so do you.

Annie broke Charlie's chain of thought when she asked, "What about me?"

"You can darken the lashes a bit and add a touch of blush. Your hair is perfect. Ask the models for help if you need it."

Charlie and granddaughters climbed into her Camry. Before she left the driveway, she reminded Jake not forget the camcorder when he came to the fashion show. She wanted him to film the girls as they pranced down the catwalk.

Charlie flew toward Christensted and fifteen minutes later she parked in Elin's parking space behind Island Elegant. She entered the shop from the rear. Carolyn Rodgers was there so Charlie told her about Elin.

"I wondered how much longer Elin could hold her tummy up," the store manager laughed.

"Or stand without supporting her back," Charlie chuckled. "Carolyn, I'll tend to the fashion show if you tend to the shop. Elin will have to huff and puff on her own."

What was the huff and puff like, Ms. Charlie?

I don't remember. Back in the good old Fifties and Sixties, doctors put mothers to sleep. Not one huff or one puff.

A few of the models were at the shop and had started on their makeup. The ladies helped the teens perfect their faces and slip into the clothes they were going to model.

BEFORE Jeremy left the house, he told Jake about his engagement. "I'm not telling mom until Laurie has her ring."

"That's smart. If she knew about you two, she'd want to go ring shopping with you."

Jeremy told his brother he would take his scooter to town so Jake could use the truck. "I didn't offer you my scooter because I didn't want to spend the rest of my life listening to you compare my little blue scooter to your Harley," he said as he grinned. Before Jake could reply, Jeremy dashed out of the house with his heels clicking. He drove to Laurie's hotel.

He found Laurie waiting for him outside.

"Shall we start with the stores in town?" she said.

A few minutes later, the couple entered Rings and Things. There were a few tourist milling around, however, the owner recognized Jeremy and came over. Jeremy introduced Laurie.

"Engagement ring! Congratulations. Let's start at this counter over here," the manager said.

One hour and seventeen minutes later, they left the shop. "Honey, I've never seen a sapphire and diamond engagement ring before," he said. "Are you sure you want that ring?"

"That or a pearl and diamond ring. We need to look around some more."

As they left Gems Galore, Jeremy said, "Are you sure you want a Burmese *Rubee*? I thought you said sapphires or pearls …"

"Let's try Gems by Jewellers," Laurie said. "They design their own jewelry."

MANNY Powell called Chief Philippe on St. Thomas. "Chief, I discovered there was a security video at the dry dock yard at Ole Luther's Marine Repair Shop.

Powell told Philippe about the men and the dogs.

Philippe didn't tell Powell that Sedge had given him a copy an hour earlier.

"I have a theory, Chief. Hanneman hired these two guys to hide the drugs in the boat so he wouldn't be seen. He is one cagey drug dealer – he thinks of everything."

"Find those two men," Philippe said as he disconnected. He stood and looked out the window.

I find it amazing that Sedge and Hanneman came up with the tape before Powell.

COOMBS did not follow the woman and the teenagers or the other man who left on a blue scooter. Instead, he waited for the tall man who had chased him out of the harbor's restaurant. It was mid-morning before his prey left the driveway in a small truck. Coombs followed Jake to Christensted.

Maybe our treasure hunt starts now.

Once in town, Roland lost sight of the truck, so he parked and started to canvass the area. He was surprised when he found the truck parked behind a dress shop. When he walked around the front, he saw that a crowd had congregated down by the water. He strolled in that direction. He noted the raised platform, but had no idea why it was there. The tall man had perched himself on a stone retaining wall around a shrub bed. He was testing a camcorder.

Ro adjusted the red, white and blue cotton scarf around his bald skull.

So far, so good. People are so gullible. Their glances of pity are pathetic.

A woman stopped him. "Best of luck, young man. I've gone through chemo and I'm now cancer free."

"Thank you ma'am, I need to hear things like that. You give me hope."

People can be so unbelievably stupid.

CHARLIE monitored the models while Carolyn Rodgers tended the store. Charlie went over Elin's checklist: no tags showing, no bra straps showing, camisole straps in place, and no see-through skirts without half-slips. She placed the models in order of appearance. Then she double-checked her index cards to ensure they were in the same order as the models.

She inspected Annie and her cute little shorts and top.

She looks so adorable, Ms. Charlie.

She takes after her grandmother.

Since when?

Charlie kissed Annie on the cheek. When she went to wipe the imprint of her lipstick off her granddaughter's cheek, she stopped. She dug in her purse for a tube of lipstick and then proceeded to draw a big red heart on Annie's cheek. "Perfecto."

"This looks so silly, Grandmom," Annie protested.

"No it doesn't. Just make sure you smile instead of pout!"

Annie shrugged her shoulders and glanced at Molly with a typical teenage roll of the eyes. She texted her best friend in Indiana about the ridiculous thing her grandmother did.

Charlie scanned Molly's outfit. Grandmom preferred Molly's long straight hair back from her face. Molly liked it half in front of her shoulders and half in the back. Molly twisted her lips, when her grandmother adjusted the hair from the front to the back.

"There is a reason for this. The neckline of your sundress is its best feature so we don't want to hide it."

There was a second roll of the eyes and a text to Pennsylvania.

JEREMY and Laurie left the sixth jewelry store.

"Laurie, you know how many jewelry stores we've visited?"

"Let's go to St. Thomas. There are hundreds over there."

"You haven't even decided what kind of stone you want."

"I've narrowed it down to pearls, diamonds or aquamarines. I love your mother's aquamarine surrounded by diamonds."

"That ring was my grandmother's. My granddad gave it to her the day my mother was born. Now it's mom's."

"Oh, Jeremy, that is so romantic. Let's see if we can find one in Charlotte Amalie."

Jeremy silently groused.

"Jeremy, don't you want me to be happy?"

"I want something to eat and a beer."

JEANETTE called the hospital and spoke with Elin. She told the mother to be about her engagement. "Should I come to the hospital to be with you, or do I have time to go ring shopping with Gil?"

Elin assured Jeanette her delivery wouldn't be any time soon and encouraged her to go ring shopping. After a few more minutes of chit chat, they hung up. Jeannette called Gil and he drove to her house. The couple headed for the ferry dock and boarded the next ferry from Christensted to Charlotte Amalie. They visited a multitude of jewelry stores. Jeanette had difficulty deciding if she wanted a marquis cut or a square cut diamond. She noticed an oval cut surrounded with baguettes.

"Gil, darling, this is so exquisite. It speaks perfectly of our love."

Gil, not prepared for a philosophical discussion about diamonds and love, simply answered, "Sure does, Sweetie. It's perfect."

"Tell me how this ring makes you feel."

Jeanette's expectations of Gil's answer were stratospheric. She anticipated a profound explanation about how the ring embodied his passion for her.

"Sweetie, I would, but it's time for my afternoon nap. Can we go home now?"

Jeanette's eyes filled with tears. Her mouth went into the same pout she perfected as a three-year old. "Gil Cliver, you don't love me!" She stomped out of the store.

JAKE was primed to capture Molly and Annie on his camcorder for all posterity to enjoy. He continued to stand on top of the stone retaining wall in his orange and black Harley tee and tan khaki shorts. He grinned as he mindlessly watched the crowd. For some reason his eyes stopped on the man with his head wrapped in a red, white and blue cap.

That's the guy on the snorkeling trip. Why on earth would he be here?

WIZARD touched his brother's arm. "Zeke, wake up. We gotta get outta here."

"Let me sleep," Zeke said.

"You're fine. The doc says you'll be okay. Now wake up, we gotta leave."

"Go away."

Wizard started to weep again. "Wake up, bro. The cops are around."

Zeke forced his eyes open. "Did you talk with them?"

"I didn't tell them anything important. Just told them we were shot. Told them we don't know nothin else. His name was Brownstone. He gave me his card and said he would be back."

"Did they take fingerprints?"

Wizard shook his head.

Zeke said a silent "Good."

"But Alberto and Miguel must know we're here. What are we going to do?"

"Leave. Where are my clothes?"

"They are in a bag on the table."

"Get me dressed."

Wizard wrestled his brother into his blood-stained shirt and fed each leg into a pant hole. Zeke stood. His fingers fumbled as he tried to zip and button. He fainted. Wizard panicked and ran into the hall. He called for the nurse, sat on the bed, and bawled as the nurse scolded him for trying to dress his brother.

Chapter 24

Charlie came out of Elin's shop with a portable mike in one hand and her index cards in the other. On each card, she had the name of the model and a complete description of what the model would be wearing.

Jake filmed his mother and waved. She responded with a smile.

Roland's eyes toggled back and forth as if he watched a tennis match. He sensed the tall man watching him, but he needed to keep an eye on the old hag, too.

The waiting audience greeted the first model with a round of applause as she stepped onto the catwalk. She appeared in an aqua linen skirt with an aqua and white linen tailored blouse. Charlie read the complete description from her index card as the model stomped down the catwalk, whirled, and posed with one shoulder raised. After of five-second pose, she continued to the center of the walkway, twirled, posed and re-created the shoulder action. She pranced off the catwalk.

Charlie clapped vigorously and the audience mimicked her cue. As the second model appeared, the crowd became silent. She wore one of Elin's most sophisticated bikinis. The women gawked; the husbands drooled. Comments filled the air – *awww, ohmagosh,* and *lookatthat.*

The shapely slim model had a combination half-smile and half-pout on her face.

As another model emerged in a luxurious orange silk gown with a brown sash flowing down her side, Charlie began reading the description. As the model performed, there were loud oohs and a few awestruck wows. The crowd's animation steadily built. They responded with gusto when they applauded.

Next, Annie appeared. Instead of the pout and the model's stomp, the audience watched the teen with the dancing cheerleader curls prance across the stage. She stopped and posed mid-catwalk. Instead of suction-cup cheeks, and she gave the audience one gargantuan smile. The prominent fire engine-red heart on her cheek inflated. The essence of her personality bloomed. Annie executed a perfect pivot, returned down the walkway, and waved to the crowd. The audience responded with applause, and every synonym for *cute* and *adorable* was heard among the crowd.

Jake filmed Annie's every step. As he panned the crowd for their reaction to his niece, his camera stopped on the man in the cap. The neurons in his skull issued an SOS code.

What am I missing here?

As she watched the audience embrace Annie, Charlie grinned with pleasure. She clapped energetically and pride oozed through her pores. Her gaze traversed the crowd to gauge their reaction.

Look, Ms. Charlie, I've seen that man before. See him, the one with the flag wrapped around his head?

Yeah. He was sitting in a car on the road next to our driveway. I've seen him elsewhere, too. Where?

Find that refrigerator sticky inside your head and do it fast. I don't like this.

A plus-size woman in a chocolate brown one-piece bathing suit walked up the ramp. The audience did not respond immediately, as they were not expecting a heavy-set woman to be in the show. Once their surprise registered, a whopping ovation followed.

The model glided down the runway with grace. She stopped at the center and pointed to the slimming features of the suit as Charlie read from her cue cards. The model wrapped a matching-colored cover-up around her torso. Applause exploded from the crowd.

Then Molly stepped on the ramp leading to the catwalk. Her thick brown mane swayed gently across her back as she began her strut. Her skin was flawless, her makeup minimal, and her lengthy gams galumphed in perfect rhythm to the beat of the background music. The self-confident teen in the black and white polka-dotted sundress sucked in her cheeks. In mid-strut, she started to laugh and the crowd laughed with her. She stopped, flipped the skirt of her dress, posed, and then pivoted with another flip of the skirt. With the aplomb of a pro, she navigated the catwalk flawlessly and melted her daddy's heart to its core. As with Annie, she rated a perfect ten. Her proud daddy filmed it all.

Just before the last model walked down the runway, Jake glanced at the man with the do-rag. He got it. He finally got it.

That's the bastard who stole the watch and murdered the two people.

Jake made his way to the end of the catwalk where his mother stood. He handed her the camcorder, whispered in her ear, and made his way through the crowd toward the thief.

Oh Miss Charlie! What are we going to do?

I'll call James. No, I can't call him. He's with Elin.

Charlie grabbed her cell and called police headquarters instead. Chamaign was in the Frederiksted police station at her desk. Her phone buzzed when the call transferred.

"In Christensted! And Jake followed him? I'll be right there. And Charlie, if you possibly can, tell Jake to halt."

Once Chamaign disconnected, she called for all available backup to go to the harbor area in Christensted. She asked everyone to take the sketch of the wanted man and informed them about the flag headwear.

GIL glanced at Jeanette, "Sweetie, can we go back now? I think we've been to nine or ten jewelry stores. I kinda lost count."

"We've done enough for one day, Sailor Boy. There's always tomorrow."

Gil was grateful Jeanette agreed to head home. He was too tired to worry about the engagement ring. He and Jeanette headed for the ferry to return to St. Croix.

"We'll find the perfect ring tomorrow. There are still dozens of shops on St. Thomas we haven't visited. I know we will find exactly what we want," Jeanette said.

Gil snuck a peek at his Sweetie.

I wish I knew what we wanted.

Once off the ferry, Gil said, "What you say we have lunch on the boardwalk? We'll both feel better."

After Gil and Jeanette decided on the restaurant and were seated, the bride-to-be said, "Pookums, I made a list of who I want to be my bridesmaids."

Pookums? What's a Pookums?

Gil patted the three hairs crossing his scalp, but didn't have time to ponder the meaning of Pookums before Jeanette spoke again.

"Sweetheart, there will be only eight."

"Eight what?"

"Turtledove, you weren't listening. Eight bridesmaids."

Turtledove?

Gil felt panic grasp each nerve in his body. He had thought in terms of a small wedding with a few of his buddies, friends like Charlie, Jeremy and Laurie, plus James and Elin. The only response he could muster was, "Oh."

"And my list of guests is now over two hundred. Can you believe that, Luvvie?"

Luvvie?

Gil put his menu in front of his face so Jeanette couldn't see the trepidation in his eyes. "That's a lot, isn't it, Sweetie?" Gil said as he peeked over the top of the menu.

"Why Gil, my love, I haven't got to my church group yet."

Gil's right knee started to vacillate and sweat appeared on his brow. "Have you thought about a quiet small wedding?"

"Oh my dear Pookie, I waited eighty-two years to plan the wedding of my dreams. You want me to be happy, don't you?"

"Sure. I want you to be happy." Gil wiped his brow with his

napkin. His bright blue eyes read the menu, but his mind refused to compute.

The server appeared and took the lunch order. Gil pointed to something on the menu. He had no idea what he had ordered.

"Gil, are you all right? You look a bit flushed, Honeykins."

What's a Honeykins?

"Jist a bit hot, I guess." Gil picked up the dessert list and fanned himself.

"Oh, my poor Snookums. You really look warm. You don't have a fever, do you?"

"Nah. Jist a wee bit tired." Now both of Gil's knees jerked in unison and the back of his cotton shirt was soaked.

"Hug Bunny, I've been thinking I'd like to have our wedding reception at the main facility of the Botanical Gardens. How does that sound?"

"That's a big place, isn't it?"

"It will hold four hundred guests easily. That many of my friends will come, I'm sure."

Gil cringed.

Ohmagosh, now what do I do?

Finally, Gil asked, "Who pays for the wedding, Sweetie?"

"Oh, Pooh Bear, I just love it when you call me Sweetie." Jeanette batted her eyes. "I have some money saved and I thought you would help me with the rest. We are a little old to expect anyone to help us, aren't we?"

"I suppose," Gil said. The fan movement of the dessert menu accelerated from a slight breeze to hurricane force.

"Oh Gil, my darling, this is the one and only wedding in my lifetime. I've been going to weddings for years. Now it is my turn to be the bride. I'm the happiest person in the world, my Honeypoo."

"I made some money when I sold my marina to Jeremy. I guess I have enough to pay for a big wedding."

"I knew you'd be a Cuddle Muffin about this. I can spend my money on my wedding gown. I saw this incredible gown with this elaborate bustle and a beautiful long train in *Bride's Magazine*."

Gil thought he'd better not gag in front of his gal. His throat became so dry he couldn't even swallow his beer.

JAMES sat quietly next to Elin. He had an uncertain smile on his face as he patted her hand. His silent encouragement wasn't helping the exasperated mother-to-be.

"James, this having a baby hurts more than I expected."

"Stay calm. You're doing just fine."

"When your sons were born, did your wife go through all of this?"

"No, back then the doctors gave mothers a spinal."

"Then why am I having natural childbirth?"

"I thought your doctor told you this was better for the baby."

"He did. But your sons turned out just fine. I'll kill the doctor right after I kill you for not telling me about the spinal!"

"Honey, this must be a safer way to give birth or the doctor would not have recommended it."

"Stop being rational, James. I don't want to hear rational right now."

Alyse entered the room. "How are we doing, Sis?"

"How are we doing? How are WE doing? I don't see you doing anything. It's only me and a bowling ball in this bed."

Alyse said, "James, why don't you go downstairs for some coffee while I sit with Elin?"

James didn't require any urging on Alyse's part. He kissed Elin's forehead and darted out of the room.

THE CHIEF used his disposable cell phone to call James on his private cell.

"James, have you heard anything?"

James explained where he was and why.

"Then you concentrate on Elin and don't worry about me." The Chief gave James a quick update about Powell.

"Manny knows your tape will cause reasonable doubt, Chief. He'll try to get something else out of you so he can arrest you. Be prepared."

"I'm working on a new offensive strategy now."

LAURIE said to Jeremy, "Honey, if we get the afternoon ferry to St. Thomas now, we will still have several hours of shopping."

Jeremy decided to avoid any more tears. He suggested they order takeout to eat on the ferry. He ordered a BLT and two beers. Laurie ordered a turkey on rye and a giant soda. They headed for the dock.

"We'll miss the last ferry for sure, you know," Jeremy said.

"We can stay over and get the first ferry out in the morning. That way, neither of us will miss too much work."

Less than an hour later, the two young lovers left the ferry in St. Thomas. They walked hand-in-hand up an alley to Main Street to the heart of the jewelry section. They strolled from one store to another.

"Laurie, we better stick with the better stores if we want a decent stone."

Six stores later, the two entered a small shop outside the jewelry district. It had its own goldsmith onsite. Most of the jewelry was handmade gold and silver. Laurie stopped dead in her tracks at the rear counter. "That's it! That's it, Jeremy! That's the ring."

The jeweler saw the look on Laurie's face and knew he had a sale. He went for the kill. "May I show you the ring," he said as he unlocked the case. It took extra effort to hide his priggish smile.

"What do you think, Jeremy? How do you like this ring? It's so gorgeous!"

"Isn't it a bit big for your hand?"

The manager interceded. "Each ring has its own aura and ambience, you understand, and a ring looks different on each and every hand."

Laurie looked at Jeremy and silently pleaded.

"Can she try it on?" he asked the manager.

The jeweler already had the black velvet display box in his hand. A plush, inverted cone held the ring in place. He handed the bauble to Jeremy and said, "Put it on your lady's finger. Let's see how it looks and feels."

Jeremy's hand trembled as he gingerly picked up the ring with his thumb and forefinger. As he turned toward Laurie, he fumbled.

The jeweler caught the ring in mid-air. "I understand this is a big moment, sir. Try again."

Jeremy slipped the ring on Laurie's finger. It was eighteen karat white gold with a two-caret oval diamond in the center. The gem was surrounded with deep aquamarine rounds.

"It makes a perfect engagement ring," the jeweler said as he watched the glow on the bride-to-be's face. "I can have a wedding band made to match."

The manager motioned for the goldsmith to join the conversation.

Jeremy was unnerved. "About the price …"

"Sir, we can make this affordable. May I introduce you to Gilberto?"

Heads nodded. The jeweler continued the sales pitch. "Gilberto designed the shank, and he handpicked the gems for this one-of-a-kind ring."

Gilberto said, "It is a large center stone, but the gentle substance of the lady's hand makes it fit so well. For a wedding band, I would recommend two bands connected at the sides. I would put enough room between the bands so the engagement ring can slip between them. Then I can put a small triangle of three aquamarines on each side of the band. Nothing should compete with the main diamond – it takes center stage."

Laurie looked at Jeremy. "Do you like it?"

Jeremy thought of his bank account and all the money he borrowed to improve the marina.

The jeweler continued, "The diamond is almost perfect in every way. The color is the best you can buy. There is one small inclusion on one side, but it would take a jeweler's loupe to see it. The cut is excellent. Sir, let's look at the stone through my gemological microscope."

Jeremy did what the jeweler said. He couldn't see the inclusion primarily because he had no idea what an inclusion was.

Laurie asked, "Does it come with papers?"

"Of course, miss. The Gemological Institute of America, known as GIA, graded the stone. And, may I add, it is not a blood diamond. We deal with a very ethical wholesaler."

"Jeremy," Laurie said. "It's so perfect. I would never want a blood diamond."

"Miss, may I offer you a seat and a refreshing glass of iced tea. Your fiancé and I need to speak privately."

The jeweler and Jeremy discussed the price for fifteen minutes. Jeremy bargained for a twenty percent discount. The manager agreed after five minutes, but with an indulging smile. He knew the ring had been marked up over one hundred percent. Profits would still be mighty good.

Jeremy waived Laurie back to the counter. She skipped over to him. "Big ring; small wedding. Agree?" he said.

"Agree!"

The goldsmith took a few more measurements for the wedding band. The two lovebirds left the store beaming. Laurie looked at Jeremy, "How small is a small wedding?"

Chapter 25

Jake left the catwalk area and followed Coombs past Elin's shop to Strand Street. Strand ran parallel to the harbor. When he reached the corner, he swiveled his head to the right and then to the left. He spied Coombs as he ran down the street toward Fort Christiansvaern. The fort sat between the downtown area and the ferry dock.

Jake picked up his pace and spotted Coombs duck to the left onto the Pan Am Pavilion. The area catered to tourist. It was a wide pathway paved with fancy brickwork. It had large stone planters in various places. The larger planters were filled with palm trees and deep green topical plants. Stores, casual restaurants, and a few offices were located on each side of the walkway.

Jake paused as he stood at the entrance of the Pavilion. He peered through the thick green palm trees. Coombs was mid-way down the block when Jake spotted him again.

Well, Mr. Coombs, ready or not, here I come.

Jake escalated his pace and dodged several strolling shoppers as he navigated around the stone planters. To his dismay, Coombs disappeared in the crowd.

Jake proceeded down the Pavilion and peered into each shop or office on the way. He spotted Coombs at the end of the passageway.

The man was on the boardwalk adjacent to a restaurant with outside tables and chairs. He disappeared into the hungry hordes.

By the time Jake got to the area, Coombs had slipped away. Jake stopped and scanned the restaurant crowd, but didn't see him. He checked the boardwalk to his left as it headed toward the seaplane pier. There was no one except a few tourists examining an old armless windmill. He turned right toward the King Christian Hotel located at the far end of the boardwalk.

The hotel had been a three-story army barracks housing troops in the days of colonialism. Over the course of the years, it metamorphosed into a forty-room hotel. A series of graceful arches decorated the front of the hotel and provided a covered walkway.

Jake studied the area. He could see no tall men with headgear or a bald head. He scrutinized the plush green lawn between him and the fort. He did not see Coombs, so he walked through the covered passageway and checked behind each pillar of each arch. Again, Jake detected nothing red, white, blue or bald. Finally, he noticed movement of some kind as he neared King Street. He dashed in that direction.

As Jake reached King, he halted to reassess the situation. There was a continuous stream of cars and cabs coming toward him on the one-way street. He yelled to a taxi driver and asked if he'd seen a tall man running. The driver shook his head.

Jake crossed the street and walked toward the grounds surrounding Fort Christiansvaern. There were tourists milling around, but no evidence of Roland Coombs.

JEREMY and Laurie checked into a small hotel in Charlotte Amalie on Blackbeard's Hill. The site had a beautiful courtyard and the young couple had a magnificent harbor view.

They stood and admired the stately white floating hotels at the piers. One ship blew its deep bellowing horn beckoning its five thousand guests to return onboard so it could set sail.

"This is so romantic, isn't it, Jeremy?"

"Romantic it is. How is your ring doing?"

Laurie flashed the diamond so it would catch the rays of the waning sun. "I love my ring. I know it cost a lot, but it's the only engagement ring I'll ever have."

"You're worth it," he said as he stole a kiss.

JAKE was determined to find the bald-headed Coombs. The closest building to him was the Old Danish Scale House. It was open so he cautiously peeked inside. He saw the old scales once used to weigh the barrels and casks of sugar, rum, molasses and cotton for shipment to Denmark. Part of the structure was a gift shop run by the National Park Service. There were numerous tourists inside looking at materials about the island's historic sites. Several people perused history books about the island's multiple plantations and slave labor. Jake was confident his thief was not among the islands visitors.

Thief? This man murdered two people on purpose. He could murder me.

CHARLIE rushed into Island Elegant and put Jake's camcorder under the counter. The girls were in the back reliving their first modeling adventure.

"Ladies, you stay in the store until I return. Okay?"

"Grandmom," Annie said, "how did we do?"

"You were both great. Now, I have to leave for a few minutes. You are to stay right here until I get back. Agree?"

"What's up, Grandmom?" Molly asked. "You look like you're worried."

"I'm fine. I only need to find your father. I'll explain later."

The teens agreed to wait as they watched their grandmother dash out the rear door.

Charlie climbed in her car, turned the key and headed in the direction Jake had gone. Since Strand Street was one-way heading in the wrong direction, she turned on King. As she proceeded down King, she checked each alley and road leading back to the boardwalk. When she got to the corner of King and Church streets, she pulled in front of the taxi pick-up sign, stepped out of the car, and carefully surveyed the area.

Where's Jake, Ms. Charlie?

Don't know. We need to find him and make sure he's okay.

We are really back in the detective business, aren't we, Missy?

As the Fonz would say, "Exactamundo!"

GIL escorted Jeanette home. His stomach seemed a bit edgy so instead of sitting on her swing, he told his girl he had to get to the marina to perform the late afternoon inspection. "I promised I'd help Jeremy, you know. You call when it is time to go to the hospital."

"That would be fine, my love. I'll make a quick call to James to see how things are going. If I have time, I'll take a quick nap."

"Okay," Gil said as he kissed her ruby red lips.

Gil drove to the marina and used his own key to open Jeremy's office. He took the clipboard down from its nail and walked around the marina doing the inspection. All was well.

Holy Moly, I know what I need to do. *Petunia* and me need a quiet ride. She'll help me understand why I'm so jumpy inside.

Gil returned to Jeremy's office and made coffee. He filled a thermos that he stored in Jeremy's cabinet. He walked to the end of the pier and climbed down the ladder. It gave Gil access to his rowboat and Jeremy access to his jet skis.

Gil untied *Petunia's* ropes and rowed out of the marina. When he passed the flotilla of anchored sailboats, he put his oars down.

Petunia, you been my best gal since the day I bought you. But another girl named Jeanette has come into the picture. You're still the best rowboat any man on earth could have and I still love you, but I got me a real live girl now. I know you two will like each other. I just want you to know you and I will still go rowing every morning, and I'll still draw sketches of our little town while you and me talk things over. Now, let's get to some important stuff right now. Petunia, I got this situation on my hands ...

GIL talked and *Petunia* listened. For over an hour, he discussed his discomfort about a big fancy wedding in front of a lot of people. Feeling better after his long discourse, he returned to the pier and secured *Petunia* for the night. He went to his friend's house.

WILLY Wilson was a heavy set man with a full head of white hair and larger than usual ears. He had his arms tattooed from his shoulders to his fingertips. He wore a black tee so he could roll up the short sleeves with his pack of cigarettes in the fold – a habit he practiced since the early Fifties. Only his wife and a few old Merchant Marine buddies had ever seen the tats on his chest, back and rump. He had more ink on his skin than the Virgin Island Press used for its papers in one week.

"Willy, got a few minutes?"

"Sure do," Willy said as he opened a can of beer and handed it to Gil. They both seated themselves on the top step of Willy's small house on the outskirts of Christensted.

"You know my gal?"

"Jeanette, right?"

"Yeah. We're getting married and all."

"I'm happy for you, Gil. Every fellow needs a nice gal like her."

"She really is a sweetheart, you know. But this getting married stuff makes me nervous."

"Don't follow you. You don't want a wife?"

"Oh yeah, I do want a wife. It's this getting married and all."

"Let me see if I understand you. You love Jeanette and you want a wife, but you don't want to get married. Right?"

"No. I do want to get married. I just don't want to get married in front of four hundred people."

"Gil, you don't even know four hundred people."

"Jeanette does."

"Oh. Did you tell her you don't feel comfortable?"

"I'm a bit afraid to do that. She's having so much fun planning her wedding. I don't want to make her unhappy."

"That's a tough one, Gil. Lila and I ran away and got hitched.

You could do the same thing. Ask Jeanette to elope."

"Elope? I'm a little old to climb down a ladder with Jeanette in my arms. I'm not sure I can even carry Jeanette over the threshold. She's a little plump, you know."

"Elope, Gil, elope. You just take Jeanette's hand and walk to your truck. Let the preacher know ahead of time, though."

"Sounds perfect to me. Thanks for being such a good friend, Willie. You always did have good ideas."

JEREMY and Laurie heard the cruise ship put its engines in reverse. They watched it back away from the pier. They could even hear its engines rev as it slowly turned one hundred-eighty degrees and faced seaward. The cruise ship still at the pier was pulling its ropes off the bollards and preparing to sail.

"That ring looks good on your hand," Jeremy said as he stole another kiss.

"I think so, too. When are you going to answer my question?"

"What question?"

"How small is small? Fifty, one hundred, two hundred?"

"Fifty."

"How about one hundred?" Laurie said quietly.

"Why don't we compromise and have seventy-five guests."

"Seventy-five wouldn't even include my mother's list."

"Laurie, I don't care about your mother's friends."

"My sisters all had big weddings."

"And did your dad pay for them?"

"We had a choice to make. Daddy would pay for either a big wedding or college. I chose college."

"That sounds to me like you made the choice to have a small wedding. So, since we're footing the bill, seventy-five guests sounds fine to me. We can have a casual wedding and get married barefoot in the sand if you want."

"I think my mother would want the wedding in Savannah."

"Honey, I don't care where we have the wedding. All I know is it will take me eighteen months to pay for the ring. I do not intend to pay for a fancy wedding reception for the rest of my life. Big diamond; small wedding. Remember?"

Laurie didn't bring the wedding up for the next forty-five minutes.

AS JAKE walked around the end of the gift shop, movement caught his eye. He saw a tall man run onto the narrow gravel path leading to the fort.

That's him!

Jake scampered with ease across the grass and up a slight incline. What looked like a narrow gravel path from a distance turned out to be a recently built brick walkway. Some foundry somewhere made the new bricks to resemble the hundreds of thousands of bricks used to build the old fort. Jake approached the two thick green wooden gates that led to a brick courtyard inside the fort. A decorative red sentry post stood on the right side of the gate.

The fort gates were ten or eleven feet high and had nasty green spikes across the curved tops. Massive black hinges secured the gates to the wall. Jake was hesitant to enter because he couldn't see who or what was behind the high walls surrounding the courtyard.

Jake noticed a number of square holes in the wall about chest height. A plaque near one hole explained how soldiers in the courtyard use the holes to fire upon anyone trying to break into the fort. Jake decided to make them his own personal peep holes. He went to each one to check for Coombs in the courtyard. Nada.

ONCE home from Willy's house, Gil picked up the phone and dialed Jeanette. He thought Willie had the perfect solution to a big wedding. "Jeanette my sweet …"

Thirty seconds later Jeanette slammed down the phone, ran to her bedroom, and started to wail.

He doesn't love me. Gil doesn't love me. And I've already ordered my dress, bustle and all!

Gil was stupefied. He had no idea why his Sweetie was so upset.

He had no idea what he did wrong.

I don't care if she has a big fancy wedding dress and all, we could still elope.

Gil felt sure he had solved the problem so he dialed Jeanette's number again. Thirty seconds later, Jeanette dropped the phone to the floor. All Gil could hear was Jeanette sobbing as she cried, "I've waited eighty-two years for my man, and he wants me to elope!"

Gil decided Willie Wilson wasn't the best person to go to for advice about gittin married.

WITH caution, Jake went through the dark green gates and entered the courtyard. Bricks laid in a herringbone pattern formed the base.

Stop admiring the architecture. Concentrate on the man ready to ambush you!

To the right Jake saw an open door next to a barred window. There was no one in the courtyard, so Jake entered the dark doorway with exterior walls at least two feet thick. With his body firmly planted against the wall, he sidestepped into the room. He breathed a sigh of relief when he spotted a park ranger behind a counter.

"Excuse me, did you seen a tall, bald man enter the fort?"

"I heard footsteps go through the courtyard a few minutes ago but no one came in here." Jake nodded and exited the room. There were two open doors a couple steps from where he stood. He looked inside.

This was probably a carriage room or something like that.

The cave-like room was empty. He quickly explored the remaining openings – all had Hunter Green arched gates built with slats of wood – stables. All were empty.

Since Jake had entered the courtyard, he had seen neither tourist nor his murderer. There was only one place left to go. Jake went up the steps through a massive arched entrance with thick concrete pillars. The cross piece above the door was intricately carved in a fancy pattern.

GIL walked back to the marina.

That young fella is in love, too. I'll ask him what I should do.

He called Jeremy's cell.

"Howdy, young fella. Got a few minutes?"

"It's been a long and frustrating day for me, Gil. How about you?"

"Me, too. I really botched it." Gil told Jeremy about his day, Jeanette's wedding plans, Willy's suggestion, and Jeanette's reaction.

"Wow, your day was worse than mine." Jeremy proceeded to tell Gil about Laurie's expectations.

"What are we going to do, young fella?"

"I don't have a choice. I can't borrow any more money, and most of the money I have is in reserve for a bad hurricane. I can come up with six grand, but not a cent more."

"I can pay for a wedding. I just don't want all those people looking at me."

Jeremy and Gil spent fifteen minutes talking, twiddling their thumbs, and commiserating with each other. Neither one of them knew what to do as they disconnected.

AT THE top of the five brick steps leading to the interior of the fort, Jake stood for a second. The entry had arched iron gates that were opened. Inside was a long, dark, tunnel-like entryway.

Looking through the tunnel, he could see a large green interior courtyard at the far end.

With body pressed tight against the wall, Jake crept through the dark tunnel leading inside the fort. At the end, he found the entry area to the courtyard. To his right and left were long covered outdoor walkways.

He went to his right and immediately found a locked door on one wall. The bolting mechanism was on the outside so he was not worried Coombs could be inside. Next, he found a heavy short door on the left. It had a small barred window set in the door. Some person, long ago, had built the room under a stairway. The door was ajar.

When Jake opened it, he realized what it was. The tiny space was no more than four feet high from the floor to the top of the arched ceiling and at least ten feet long. The air was close and damp. At the end of the room was a barred window much too small for any human to squeeze through. There were carvings in the wood floor – most likely done by captured run-away slaves housed there.

Chapter 26

The Chief called Charlie as she stood next to her car parked near the fort.

"What's up, Victor?"

"As soon as Murray Sedge gets here, he and I will meet with Manny Powell down at the main station."

"Are you still concerned?"

"I'm uncomfortable. He wants to pin this on me."

"Now I have two of you to worry about. Jake and I spotted the thief who stole part of our locket. He was at the fashion show. In case you forgot, he is the man who also ran over those two people near the Palm Shack. This Roland Coombs realized Jake recognized him, so he took off. Jake followed. Now I'm following Jake. I just saw him enter the fort."

"Let me call headquarters, Charlie. This man is dangerous and I don't want you to follow."

"I called Chamaign. She's on her way and is bringing plenty of backup."

"Please don't go in, Charlie. I don't want you anywhere near another murderer."

"It's not me I'm worried about this time, Victor. It's my son. I've got to go."

The Chief started to say something, but realized Charlie had disconnected.

She had started up the path toward the green gates.

We're in trouble with the Chief, Ms. Charlie.

My son is in more trouble.

You won't get us killed if we go in, will you?

If I go, you go. Non-negotiable.

Charlie reached the exterior courtyard of the fort about five minutes after Jake disappeared into the arched entrance room. She couldn't see or hear anyone. She gingerly made her way around the courtyard.

JAKE continued down the hall. Locks were on the remaining doors. The National Park Service secured each door with either bolts or bars. Some rooms had glass instead of walls. The glass allowed visitors to see the rooms. Displays showed how the soldiers lived two hundred years earlier. At the end of the walkway, Jake retraced his steps and returned to the entrance. He needed to explore the other half of the first floor hallway.

AFTER Jeremy finished talking with Gil, he walked outside into the hotel's courtyard. He found Laurie sitting next to a flower garden.

"Maybe if we pool our cash we can have what you want," he said.

"I have about four thousand in savings, but half of it will go for my gown."

"I can put up six grand, so we have a total of eight to spend. What will that buy us?"

"A few flowers, the hall, a DJ, a half-dozen wedding pictures, and catering for thirty guests," she said.

"Where can we cut back?" Jeremy said.

The dam broke.

JAKE proceeded down the left side of the fort. He saw another cell for prisoners and a room showing how five artillery men shared quarters. There was one small, narrow hallway leading to a small room. A plaque on the wall said it was called the Black Hole, a dungeon reserved for slaves convicted of serious crimes. Its low ceiling would have required Jake to bend at the waist if he tried to stand. He shuddered.

After taking a gulp of fresh air into his lungs to calm down, he headed for the second floor located above the rooms he just inspected. He quickly ran through the rooms that had been reserved for the Commandant and other brass. All were empty. From the balcony, he scanned the large, grassy interior courtyard below.

Behind the grass was the gunpowder magazine. It was located partially below the grade of the green rectangle. On top of the magazine was the battery. There sat four large freshly-painted black cannons smugly facing seaward.

Jake carefully made his way down the left staircase to the courtyard and took the left walkway. He headed for the brick steps leading to the deck over the magazine. A small sign on the wall announced that the original builders constructed the outer wall of the magazine thirteen feet thick to withstand a naval bombardment. Jake paused a half second to reflect upon that fact.

Concentrate, man. Concentrate.

As he crept up the steps, he noted there were cannonballs back along the bright yellow front of the magazine. The Park Service built a green slatted fence in front of the balls so the balls could withstand a tourist bombardment.

After Jake scrutinized every shadow on the front of the magazine, he continued up the steps to the battery.

JEANETTE telephoned James.

"James, Gil wants me to elope."

"Congratulations, Aunt Jeanette. I'm so happy he finally proposed."

"You don't understand. He doesn't want me to have a wedding!"

"Aunt Jeanette, this isn't a good time for me to talk. Elin is in labor and her pains are getting closer. Can I call you back?"

"Why does he want to buy me a ring if he doesn't want a wedding?"

"Did he say why he doesn't want a wedding?"

"No. He simply called and suggested we should elope."

James held the phone away from his ear as Jeanette boohooed on the other end.

"Aunt Jeanette, did you tell him you wanted a nice wedding?"

"Of course I did. I saw this one gown with a bustle and a long train. I fell in love with it, James. I simply have to have it. That didn't upset him nearly as much as the reception with a few guests at the Botanical Gardens."

James began to get the picture. "Aunt Jeanette, how many guests do you plan to invite?"

"All of my Red Hat friends and almost everyone in the church directory. And then there are the ladies in the women's club."

"How many people altogether?"

"James! This is the first and only wedding I'll ever have," she howled. "Can't I invite who I want?"

"How many, Aunt Jeanette?"

"A little over four hundred, I guess."

"My dear aunt, that's a lot of guests. I think you scared Gil. That's a pretty shy fella you have."

Jeanette bawled louder. "You don't want your aunt to have a beautiful wedding either!" Jeanette's entire house rattled when she slammed the phone down.

CHARLIE advanced up the fort's steps to the long tunnel-like entrance way. Each of her steps was slow, soundless and deliberate.

Why aren't we running, Ms. Charlie?

Because I clop, not run.

Why are we whispering?

So no one can hear us.

How can anyone hear us, Missy? I'm in your head.

That's your problem, not mine.

She padded her way to the exterior covered walkway. She peeked right and then left and saw nothing. She had to squint to look at the courtyard area because the sunlight was so intense. The midday sun caused creepy, razor-sharp shadows throughout the entire courtyard. Every crevice in the walls appeared sinister and foreboding.

Ms. Charlie, this place is spooky.

And the shadows are macabre.

Is that another crossw ...

Shut up!

After her eyes adjusted to the blinding light, Charlie scrutinized each crevice around the large courtyard.

I see something, Ms. Charlie.

Me, too.

Is the man Coombs or Jake?

We need to figure that one out fast.

THE CHIEF grabbed his car keys as soon as Charlie disconnected. He went into his bedroom and unlocked the small gun safe holding the Glock he used while he was on the police force.

Powell can wait. I have to get to Charlie and Jake before Roland Coombs does.

JAKE bounded up the steps leading to the battery. The Danish had built the battery to protect shipping in the Christensted harbor from pirates and privateers. The four eighteen-pound cannons were evenly spaced across the top. Large wooden carriages, painted a dark green, supported the heavy, glossy black cannons. The massive wooden wheels allowed for movement when the cannons recoiled.

Jake walked to the edge of the battery facing the water. If Coombs had jumped from there, it would have been instant suicide. The embankment fell some thirty feet and abutted large jagged wave-worn rocks. Jake walked to the inside edge of the battery looking down upon the courtyard. That is when he noticed an ever so slight movement. He could see Roland Coombs standing in a shadow almost directly under him.

JEREMY paced for a few minutes and then walked up behind Laurie. He put his arms around her and kissed her on the cheek again. "Honey, if we put the wedding off for a year, we both could save like crazy and pay off our bills. What do you think?"

"I don't want to wait so long, but I have a thought. My sister designs clothing and she's an excellent seamstress. I wonder if she would make my gown."

"If she did, it could be her wedding gift."

"She'd do it, I'm sure. You know what else. If we had the wedding down here, not as many people could come so it would be cheaper."

"Jeanette wants to be married in the Botanical Gardens," Jeremy said. "Gil says there are several places there to hold a reception. That shouldn't be too expensive. We'd have to bring in a caterer."

"It might work, Jeremy."

"It will work if we make it. I'll have to tell the Chief I can't buy *Gertie*. I'm sure he'll understand. Who knows – maybe he'll lend it to us to motor to St. John. We can drop anchor in the bay and honeymoon on it."

"That sounds delicious!"

CHARLIE spotted Jake when he ran up the steps to the battery.

Ms. Charlie, I see Jake.

Me, too.

What are we going to do?

Prognosticate.

Oh give me a break!

JAKE saw his mother and used hand signals for her to stay where she was. She nodded. He decided there was only one way to catch Coombs. And that would be from the air.

I'll make him my cushion.

Jake made of flying Superman motioned with his arms for the benefit of his mother. She studied him for a second and then nodded behind her oversized sunglasses.

Missy, what's he doing?

He's reliving Halloween as a nine-year-old when he wore a Superman costume. I knew I should have burned that cape!

COOMBS spotted Charlie as she stepped to the edge of the grass. He assumed she was nodding her head because she had spotted him.

Charlie chose that moment to step onto the grass in the courtyard. She stood tall and decided to bait Coombs to show himself.

What are we going to do?

Watch me dare him.

Charlie put her thumbs in her ears and waved at Coombs with her fingers. She yelled, "Nah, nah, na, nah, nah!"

Have you gone nuts, Ms. Charlie? You look like a child and sound like an idiot.

Exactly.

Coombs took the bait and headed for Charlie. Jake saw him take his first step. On the third step, he plunged off the edge of the battery and aimed for Coombs' back. Both men went down. Jake's two hundred ten pound frame pasted the one hundred-sixty pounder into the sod.

Despite the cushioning, Jake's body bounced off his foe. He hit the ground hard on his left shoulder. Jake made it to his feet poised to strike again despite the shoulder pain.

Stunned, Coombs hesitated a second and then stood.

Before his prey was fully upright, Jake rammed his good shoulder into his opponent's chest. Coombs fell again, but rolled so there was a distance between them. He stood ready to fight.

Like her son, Charlie didn't pussyfoot around. She scooted toward Coombs. As she approached him for a rear assault, she swung her boulder-size chartreuse and orange cloth purse filled with three bottles of water, a Diet Pepsi, a bulging wallet, and a zippy stuffed with mini-doughnuts. On the down arc of the swing, the purse bounced off the crown of his head.

Not expecting a rear attack, Coombs took two faltering steps toward Jake. Jake responded with an uppercut with his right arm that rearranged the murderer's face.

Coombs landed on his back. Jake turned him over and pulled the man's arm back and crossed them at the wrist. Before Jake could look up, he saw two hands slap handcuffs on the killer.

Detective Chamaign and Officer Bob had run through the entrance to the courtyard just as Jake took his Superman plunge wearing his orange and black Harley tee under his make believe cape.

"That's enough Jake. You got our man."

Jake chuckled, "I can catch murderers, too, Chamaign. Of course, my mom helped a little bit."

Bob radioed for the EMTs.

Jake won, Ms. Charlie. He's almost as good as you!

That's because he's my progeny.

What about me, Missy?

You're a figment of my imagination. Remember?

"You okay, Jake?" Chamaign asked.

"Fine, except for my shoulder. It might be displaced. And my knuckles are a bit raw."

Jake took pleasure as he described his dive from the battery and his tussle with Coombs. After his saga ended, Jake bent over the handcuffed Coombs and patted his rear pockets. Not finding what he was looking for, he patted Coombs' right side pocket. He felt the rear casing of the watch.

"I know it's considered evidence, Chamaign, but he has the casing of our watch in his pocket. I guess you can't give it to me, can you?"

"Not anytime soon, Jake. You'll get it back after the trial. That's a promise."

THE EMTs arrived as did a half-dozen dark blue police SUV's. The Chief was thirty seconds behind them.

While Jake answered Chamaign's questions, the Chief walked over to Charlie.

"Are you all right?"

"Jake did it, not me. I just used my purse."

"Jake still took a big chance. What if Coombs had carried a gun? He didn't hesitate to kill two people before, and he would have done it again if he had had a weapon."

"I thought of that as I watched them fight," she conceded.

The Chief hugged Charlie, "You did a good job, my lady."

Charlie told Victor she was going to stay with Jake until another EMT van appeared.

"That fine. I need to get to the station to see my interrogator as soon as Murray Sedge arrives."

When the second van appeared, Charlie said, "Jake, I'll get the girls, take them home, and then come to the hospital to pick you up."

Jake nodded. As soon as the truck left, Charlie went to find her illegally parked car. Fortunately, the officer writing the ticket saw the police arrive en masse at the fort and ran over to help. He never finished the ticket.

Charlie was able to maneuver her car between the police vehicles and return to Elin's shop.

AS SOON as Charlie entered the rear door of the shop, the teens descended upon her.

"How did I do?" Annie asked for a second time. "I almost slipped once – did you notice? What about my posture?"

Molly asked, "How did my hair look in the ocean breeze? Were my teeth white enough? Did I look stupid when I sorta lost my model's pout?"

Charlie led both girls into Elin's office since tourists still occupied the shop.

"You were both magnificent. No, Annie, I did not notice any slip and your posture was perfect. The crowd went wild when you smiled, and the heart on your cheek grew as big as your own heart."

"And Molly, your gorgeous tresses were beautiful. The crowd loved it when you lost your pout and gave a big smile instead. Young ladies, you were a hit!"

The teens prattled for another twenty minutes. Charlie tried hard to absorb their excitement, but her mind returned to Jake. She retrieved her cell and called. He didn't answer.

He must be in the emergency room getting his shoulder checked.

A few minutes later, Charlie reached Jake.

"How bad is it?" she asked.

"I dislocated my shoulder. Being a hero will do that sometimes."

"I'm not amused. I need to take the girls back to the house. How soon can I pick you up?"

"I will be at least two hours. Terry Mitchell from the newspaper is interviewing me. I'll give you a call."

"That's fine. I'm coming to the hospital to check on Elin, so I'll be around when you're ready.

Chapter 27

Terry Mitchell, the reporter, asked, "You jumped off the building?"

"I was on top of the battery when I saw Coombs. He was hiding in the shadows in the courtyard. I figure if Superman can do it, I could, too. I aimed for his back, but when I rolled off of him, I injured my shoulder."

"How far was the jump?"

"Ten feet, maybe. Remember, I had a soft cushion."

"Was Coombs in the first EMS van to leave the fort?" Chamaign overheard Terry's question and answered, "Coombs is headed for surgery to get his jaw wired shut and his nose reset."

"I hope he is handcuffed to the hospital bed," Jake said.

Chamaign responded with an explosive grin, "I wouldn't have it any other way."

ON THE ride back to the house, Charlie said to the teens, "Do you to remember the man who robbed us?"

Both teens immediately stopped texting and looked up.

"He was hard to forget," said Molly.

"I agree," said Annie. "He was not only a thief, but a smelly thief."

"Did you realize he was with us on our snorkeling trip?"

"I didn't see him," Molly said. "There was a weird man who kept looking at us, but he was bald."

"That was him," Charlie said.

Annie said, "So he shaved his head so we wouldn't recognize him?"

"Actually, shaving his head was one of several disguises. His name is Roland Coombs. His real occupation is picking pockets. I saw him do it at a parade. I even worked with the sketch artist to build a computerized picture. When I first saw him, he had long blond hair. Yesterday, I found out he murdered two people. To go undetected, he cut and dyed his hair. This is when he grabbed our watch and ran. Later he shaved his head."

"Gross!" Molly said.

Charlie continued, "To make matters worse, he's been following us around. I don't know why."

"That's awful," Annie said as her lips and chin tightened into a frown. "Is he still following us?"

Charlie shook her head.

"I need to text my friends! I can't believe we actually snorkeled with a murderer," Molly said.

"Don't text yet. There is more – a lot more." Both teens sat riveted to their seats with eyes alert and fixed on their grandmother.

Annie asked, "Was he going to murder us?"

"I don't think so. Molly, did you notice that your father disappeared toward the end of the show? He saw the man in the crowd and recognized him as the thief. Your dad left the camcorder with me and went after him." Charlie told the girls how Jake dashed after the man, followed him to the fort, and captured him.

"Awesome" Molly said. "My dad is a certified hero!"

"Awesome squared," Annie added.

Charlie continued the story about how she followed Jake, the Superman leap and the wrestling match. The girls were spellbound. Fingers snapped into instantaneous action. Texts traveled around the world.

After a second, Molly stopped. Her eyelids opened wider and her brow creased with concern.

"Dad's okay, it isn't he, Grandmom?"

Charlie explained how he hurt his shoulder. "I'm taking both of you to the house. Afterward, I'll pick up the camcorder and then go get my oldest son.

MURRAY Sedge was on the last ferry headed for Saint Croix. He knew the retired deputy police chief would be there to pick him up. He sat on a metal bench during the ride and wondered what Manny Powell planned.

Surely, the tape would exonerate the Chief, or at the very least produce enough reasonable doubt that the Chief wouldn't be charged with a crime. But, how do I explain the fingerprints? Is the truth as simple as what the Chief told me?

Murray spent his time musing over all the Chief's personnel files from the USVI Police Department. His career was stellar. There was not one discipline during his thirty plus year career. Several disgruntled criminals filed charges of rough treatment. Internal Affairs hearings vindicated the Chief's veracity each time. A dozen commendations also spoke of his commitment to the force.

Murray reviewed all of the Chief's financials from his early days as a rookie to the present.

His finances are above reproach. How could anyone think a man who would buy an old plantation, pay to build a special school for teens, and deal drugs at the same time? This school alone is a testament to the man's integrity.

JEANETTE called Gil. She told him about Elin's progress and asked him to pick her up.

"Holy Moly. I'll be right there, Sweetie."

"You and I can watch the baby being born. Won't that be wonderful?"

Luckily, Jeanette couldn't see the look of aversion on Gil's face over the phone.

"Sweetie, I don't feel comfortable even thinking about it. It's sort of a lady thing."

"If I was young enough to have a baby, you'd want to be there with me, wouldn't you?"

Gil shoved some non-existent dirt from side to side with his right foot, winced and said, "It's hard to say, Sweetie. I'm a mariner at heart. One time when I was young, I saw some kittens born. I kinda excused myself and ran to the outhouse."

"But you'd do it if it was me having the baby, wouldn't you?"

Gil decided he couldn't get into too much trouble if he agreed with Jeanette. He figured a little white lie wouldn't hurt since babies and similar stuff wouldn't happen to Jeanette and him.

"Of course, Sweetie."

"Oh, Gil, you do love me."

Gil nodded his head as he disconnected.

I love you, but this getting married is a bit more than I thought.

CHARLIE arrived at the hospital. After parking, she headed for the emergency room. She inquired about her son at the desk. The receptionist disappeared into a cloud of billowy white curtains to check on Jake.

When the lady returned, she told Charlie that Jake was getting additional x-rays.

Charlie called Molly and told her that her father was fine, but he wasn't ready to leave the hospital yet.

Charlie decided to check Elin's progress. As she reached Elin's door, she heard her cousin growl, "James, I'm moving to the spare bedroom when I get home.

Charlie rapped lightly on the doorframe and said, "Is it safe to come in?"

James stood immediately and offered Charlie his seat. He excused himself and disappeared down the hall.

"You scared your husband."

"Charlie, I decided to take a lifetime vow of chastity."

"That should make for an interesting marriage."

Ms. Charlie, did you ever do that?

That falls under my Don't Ask, Don't Tell policy!

"When will this be over, Charlie?"

"What did your doctor say?"

"I'm a little more than halfway there."

"The second half will go faster than the first, I assure you."

"Why can't I be one of those women who have their babies in a car or in the hospital elevator?"

"If it makes you feel better, I wasn't one of those women, either. Are your mother and Alyse going to watch?"

"Of course. James invited the whole world to the viewing!"

Ms. Charlie, isn't a viewing for when you're dead?

I believe Elin means Alyse and her mother want to be here to see the baby born.

Did anyone watch you?

In my birthing days, even the doctors weren't allowed to look.

"Jeanette and Gil want to come, and he agreed to that, too. I know James is proud of this baby, but I don't want an audience."

"Then you have to tell everyone how you feel. This is your baby and you're the one having it. Be adamant. Tell James it is just him, the doctor and the nurse. Everyone will understand."

THE CHIEF worked on a crossword puzzle while he waited for Murray's ferry.

What starts with an X and end with a U? Where on earth is this place of contentment? How does Charlie do these things?

JEREMY and Laurie snuggled on the beach at Megan's Bay in St. Thomas.

"Honey, I'm worried about using the money I have in reserve for the wedding. It might be best to wait until we get out from under our current debt."

"We could borrow the money. With me working, I can pay off

my loans."

"Laurie, it's not as simple as that. I own my house with my mother. We both pay on the mortgage. She's not into house-sharing. She agreed to share with me because it was her way of helping me with my finances when I bought the marina."

"I was wondering about that. Your mother lives life by her own rules, doesn't she?"

Jeremy nodded. "Does she ever! She wears me out."

"Would she buy you out so we can get our own house?"

"Honey, I'm making it now because I'm only paying on half a mortgage. If we get a house, I'm paying on a full mortgage."

"Oh Jeremy," Laurie said as her mouth tightened. "I just started my job, and I'm at the bottom of my pay scale. I can't make a car payment, a credit card payment, and a mortgage payment, too."

Jeremy said nothing.

Laurie and I were so happy before we became engaged. What happened?

Chapter 28

Powell paced in the interrogation room at the police station. *Where is that crook? I won't tolerate his delay tactics any longer. He'll be behind bars before the night is over. I'll be the shiny new star of the Virgin Islands PD.*

THE CHIEF greeted Murray Sedge as he walked down the gangway from the ferry. "Thanks for coming."

"My pleasure. I find it hard to believe he would arrest you, but I can assure you I can convince any juror who is awake that you are innocent. I have never met anyone who has served his community so well for so long."

"Thank you for the compliment. I told Charlie I wasn't going to worry anymore, but I can't seem to stop fretting. I outmaneuvered Powell the last time. It may not be so easy this time."

"I'm not sure if Powell sees the whole picture – especially the part concerning the dogs. Plus, no one has seen the brothers as far as I know. I have Kevin working on that loose end. He spoke with the grandmother again and got several pictures we can use to identify the men."

"How do we handle this interview, Murray?"

"What if we pound on him for not finding the brothers? It would put him back on the defensive."

"I like the way you think."

TERRY Mitchell finished his newspaper article about Roland Coombs after he interviewed Officer Benton at the station. As he was leaving, he also spoke to Rookie Rand Brownstone in the parking lot.

Terry headed to the hospital to speak to the Cort brothers. At the hospital's reception desk, he asked for Ezekiel Cort. The volunteer directed him to the proper nurses' station. After arriving, the nurse told him Cort could have no visitors, but the second man injured was in the waiting room. Mitchell headed there.

"Excuse me, are you Mr. Willard Cort?" Terry asked as he opened the door.

Wizard nodded. "Are you a doctor?"

"No, I'm Terry Mitchell with the VIP. I'd like to ask you a few questions."

Wizard wiggled in his seat.

"How were you injured, sir?"

"In the stomach. The bullet went in and out. It didn't hurt nothin. Stings though."

"How about your brother?"

"He's bad. He took two bullets and could end up with a serious infection."

"Your brother is Ezekiel Cort, age twenty-four. Right?"

"Yeah."

"Your age?"

"Nineteen."

"Do you know who shot you?"

"Course not. How would I know that?"

"Anyone mad with you or your brother?" Terry asked.

"Course not. We didn't do nothin."

"Then why were you shot?"

"Probably some random shooting or something. My brother and I were just sitting on the edge of the dock when someone got us. We were sittin ducks."

"What did the police tell you?"

"Those dummies don't know nothin much."

"Do you have any theories?"

"Don't know nothin about nothin."

Terry thanked Wizard and walked to the door. Wizard looked down at the floor. Terry aimed his camera at the injured man and snapped a photo without using the flash. Wizard was so worried about Zeke he didn't even notice.

PETE Hummel drove to the police station to speak to the duty officer. He was doing more thinking than paying attention to his driving.

Why did Alyse hang up on me this morning? Called me supercilious. She'll never do better than me – I'm the best thing around these parts. I'll show her. Once I get to St. Thomas, I'll get me one of those Brown twins I always see in the paper. They keep winning beauty contests right and left. I'm so good I bet I can get them both at one time. A little ménage a trois.

Pete parked and entered the station. He went directly to the duty officer's desk.

Private Celeste Parker asked, "What do you need, Mr. Hummel?"

"Just thought I'd stop by to see you, honey."

"I'm not your honey. I'm Private Parker."

"Fine, Private Parker. I'm here to do my daily check on arrests. What's been happening?"

"You did know that Roland Coombs was arrested, didn't you?"

"So, they finally caught up with Ro. Took them long enough. I'm his lawyer. Why wasn't I notified?"

"You better talk to Detective Benton about that." Celeste picked up the phone and called Chamaign. The detective told her to send Hummel back to her desk.

When Pete got there, he said, "Where's my client?"

"Who is your client?"

"Don't act dumb with me. You know Roland Coombs is my

client."

"Actually, Mr. Hummel, I didn't know he was your client. I hope you are a good lawyer because we have all kinds of signed statements from him."

"Are you telling me he signed statements without me present?"

"Coombs said he didn't need a lawyer. After he signed the confession, he changed his mind. He asked for Murray Sedge. I called Sedge, but he was out, so I left a message."

"Why Sedge?"

"I didn't ask. It sounds to me that you're not his lawyer."

Irate, Pete dashed out the door of the station only to bump into Sedge and the Chief. Without thinking the situation through, he said, "Murray, Roland Coombs is my client, not yours."

"Roland Coombs?" Sedge said. "I don't know anything about him."

"I was told he asked for you."

"If he asked for me, how does that make him your client?"

"Murray, I've known the man since high school. I was talking to him just the other day."

"If you two are so close, why did he ask for me?"

"He was probably flustered. The cops forced him into signing a couple statements."

The Chief was standing next to Sedge and heard the conversation. "Murray, I know about this case. Coombs picks pockets for a living. He ran into some competition at the parade the other day. He handled it by running over the two people and killing them with his car. He also stole an heirloom locket watch from my lady friend, Charlie. Her son Jake spotted him and captured him for the police. He's now in the hospital."

"Sounds like an interesting case."

"He is a murderer, Murray. He ran over the two people with his car – and not once, but three times to make sure they were dead."

"He still deserves a good defense lawyer, Chief. If the police have their ducks in order, he'll be convicted with or without me."

"I guess there are things you and I will never agree upon, Murray."

"Yes there is. But I will work as hard for him as I am for you."

Murray turned to Pete, "If he asked for me, he's my client. Now if you will excuse me, the Chief and I have business to take care of."

Pete seethed and felt his wallet deflate.

WIZARD sat quietly in the hospital waiting room wondering if he should call his grandmother. He didn't know if the police knew Zeke and he had been involved in drugs. He knew there should be something he should do, but he didn't know what.

AFTER Charlie left Elin in her husband's hands, she went to find Jake. The receptionist told her Jake had not been released yet.

She went to the waiting room to buy a pack of peanut butter crackers. She noticed the young man she had seen earlier. He was again sitting in the corner with tears rolling down his face.

"Is your brother any better?" she asked as she sat next to him.

"About the same, ma'am."

"Did the bullet in the stomach do any permanent damage?"

Wizard lowered his head. "I'm not sure. I didn't understand what the doctor was saying, but he did say something about an infection."

"I think the doctor meant your brother's wound may have leaked bacteria into his stomach cavity."

Wizard looked up at Charlie. "That sounds something like it. Said my brother had to stay in the hospital until they were sure there was no infection. He won't die, will he?"

"I don't think so. The doctor probably has him on antibiotics already. Did you talk to the police about the shooter?"

"No. Zeke tells me what to do."

"You need to explain everything to the police."

"Can't do that, ma'am. I have to talk to my brother first. Thank you for being so nice, ma'am."

Charlie smiled as she rose and left the room.

Poor kid. He's so worried. Wish I could help him.

MURRAY tapped on the door of the interrogation room. Powell opened the door and angry words spewed from his mouth. Finally, he ended his diatribe with, "… and that was two hours ago!"

"Manny, you know unless the Chief agrees, you can't speak to him without me present. Now don't blame the Chief for exercising his rights and don't blame me for doing my job."

Murray and the Chief walked past Manny. The Chief immediately sat with his back to the one-way mirror. Murray sat next to him. The defense attorney immediately slid a batch of folders on the table in the direction of the Chief. Victor reached for one.

Manny realized he was outmaneuvered again. The only place for him to sit was facing the window. He bellowed, "I'm the interrogator, Chief. You sit in the other seat."

"Powell, I didn't come here this evening to play musical chairs. Let's get this interview over with so I can head home."

Murray quickly interjected, "Lieutenant, I assume the Cort brothers are in custody?"

"I'm not ready to arrest them yet."

"Then you have spoken to them?"

Powell ignored Sedge's question and looked at the Chief. "When do you …"

Sedge used his let's-not-play-games voice, "Excuse me, please. Lieutenant, did you or did you not locate the Cort brothers?"

Powell glared at Sedge but didn't answer.

"All right," the lawyer said, "I assume you haven't found them. You do admit two men boarded the Chief's boat. Right?"

"I saw what was on the security tape. I even had the grandmother come in and watch it. She identified the men."

"That's progress," the Chief said. "Excellent job, Manny."

Powell almost smiled at the compliment until Sedge asked, "And did Joey Mills tell you any more about the dogs and bones?"

Powell's blank expression spoke volumes. "Joey Mills?"

"Yes, Manny," the Chief said, "Joey covered for Luther the night the men visited the boat."

Manny looked from Sedge to the Chief. "What?"

"Manny, Manny, Manny," Sedge said, "You haven't done all

your homework, son."

Powell slammed his fist on the table. "I'm running this investigation and I'll ask the questions. You address me as Lieutenant."

"Didn't mean to upset you, Lieutenant. However, I do get the feeling the Chief and I are doing your investigating for you."

Powell's face turned a purplish red. His hands fisted so tight his tan knuckles went white. He managed a deep breath to control his rage. As he started to reply, he saw Sedge look over the top of his glasses and say to the Chief, "Do you think the two of us can find the Cort brothers for the good Lieutenant?"

"If we can't find them, I'm sure my Charlie can. She's good at catching crooks."

"You two stay out of this case. I know how to do my job."

"Manny," the Chief said in a slow and deliberate manner, "You are ravaging my reputation, and I don't appreciate it. If you continue, I will file a formal complaint with your superior."

Powell made the mistake of challenging the Chief, "And the grounds for that complaint would be?"

"You should not have accepted this assignment. You cannot be objective in this case because you did not like the grades I gave you as a rookie. If I speak to the Commissioner, we will see whose reputation is ruined."

The Chief and Murray stood and quietly walked out the door. Manny stood at the table and cursed. As he watched the two men walk down the hall, he yelled, "You can't threaten me!"

Chamaign stayed inside the little room with the viewing window. She stopped the tape of the interview after Powell's response. She made a copy for herself and slipped it in her pocket. As soon as Manny left, she returned to her office.

JEANETTE kissed her nephew. "Oh James, your mother would be so happy for you if she was here."

Gil stood next to her and tapped the four corners of a tan floor tile with the tip of his left shoe.

"Aunt Jeanette, I know only one thing for sure right now – I'll be happy for me when this is over."

"What about me?" Elin bellowed. "I'm the one ready to implode if this bowling ball doesn't budge!"

Jeanette went to Elin's bedside and took her hand. "Honey, how can I help?"

"You can't, Aunt Jeanette. I have to do this myself. I don't want company right now. Would you please wait in another room?"

"But Gil and I want to see the baby born, dear."

Gil quickly corrected his Sweetie, "Not me, Miss Elin. I'm going to wait down the hall. I'll say some prayers for ya though."

"Thanks, Gil," James said. "We would appreciate your kind thoughts."

James inhaled and faced Jeanette, "Elin needs her privacy right now. Would you mind waiting down the hall?"

"James, this is my grandniece or nephew we're talking about. Can't I stay? I'm family."

"Let me walk you and Gil to the waiting room." James took his aunt's elbow and firmly led her out of the birthing room. "Elin wants this to be a private time for us. I'm asking you to respect her wishes."

Jeanette held back her tears for the moment and asked, "Is Elin's mother and sister allowed to be with her?"

"No, Only the medical staff and me," James said with non-negotiable firmness in his voice. "I haven't told Mrs. Mikkelsen and Alyse yet. I'm sure they will be disappointed, too."

The moment Jeanette and Gil entered the waiting room, she turned to Gil, "James doesn't love me and neither do you. I don't want to marry you!"

CHARLIE called to check on the girls. They were fine and were watching videos on YouTube. She went to check on Jake. She found him speaking with the doctor. She went upstairs to see Elin. She encountered James in the hallway.

"Elin has just about had it. She keeps calling our baby a bowling ball."

"That's an accurate description for her situation right now. You need to go in there and huff and puff with her through this. It will help her concentrate on getting that ball down the alley of life."

Corny, Ms. Charlie.

Then you think of something clever for once.

James almost smiled and then his forehead wrinkled again. "She's so angry at me. Why, Charlie?"

"She's not angry at you. She is in a ton of pain and can't do a thing about it. Go be her coach and mentor. Rah, rah, rah her through this. It won't go on forever and the end product is priceless."

"Everyone will be upset with me by the end of the day. Elin doesn't want anyone present when the baby is born. Aunt Jeanette is bawling, and Grace and Alyse will be, too, as soon as I tell them."

"Your only job is to keep Elin content. Now, go in there."

James nodded and obediently returned to the birthing room. The expression on his face was of a scared puppy dog. His gold incisor was not twinkling.

Ms. Charlie, a bowling ball?

Yep, a ten-pin bowling ball, no less.

That's sounds gross.

No, it's not. Once the baby is born, everyone will immediately forget they were upset.

AS CHARLIE walked down the hall, she noticed Jeanette and Gil in the waiting room. Jeanette dabbed at her tears. She tiptoed past the room and headed for the waiting room with the vending machines. She had finished her crackers and craved something sweet. When she entered, she saw the young man still in the corner.

She sat down. "Would you like to talk?"

"I'm so scared."

"Your brother will be fine, I'm sure."

"Hope so. Zeke looks after me. There are so many things I can't understand and I can't do."

"Zeke must be a good brother. You're lucky to have him."

"I won't be so lucky if they send me back to jail."

"What's your name?"

"Wizard. It's short for Willard." He looked at Charlie with his huge brown teary eyes.

"I know jail must not be pleasant. I understand why you don't want to return."

"They will kill me even if I'm in jail. They have their inside guys who will do their dirty work for them for nothing more than a carton of cigarettes."

"Shouldn't they be in jail – you know – the persons who want to kill you?"

"They are the really bad guys. Zeke and me are only the small stuff."

"What do you mean by big time?" Charlie asked.

"Big time drug distributers."

Charlie's antenna made a rapid ascent.

Ms. Charlie, are you thinking what I'm thinking?

Sure am.

We're going to get some action again. Whoopee.

Don't whoopee yet. We have to help this young man first.

"What have you done, Wizard?"

Wizard started to sob again, "They'll put me back in jail for what I did."

"What have you done?"

"Zeke and me bought a lot of drugs so we could sell the stuff on the street and make some cash."

"Why do the distributers want to kill you? Now that the drugs are sold, they can sell you more."

"I slipped up and told them about the cops."

"So you were caught selling?"

"No. Zeke and me separated some of the tar in little packets and hid them. The cops found our stash. Now the distributors want us dead. They know the cops will be looking for them now."

"You have to tell the police about this, Wizard."

"I'm scared of jail."

"It will be better for you to tell the police instead of the police figuring out what happened and find you. It will go better for you if you cooperate."

"I'm scared."

"Where did you get the money to buy the drugs?"

Wizard told Charlie about his grandmother's money, the Rodriguez brothers, and the boat in dry dock.

Charlie's heart started to pound. She decided it was her duty to probe deeper. "Let me clarify something, Wizard. You said you bought the drugs, divided the powder into small packets, and hid the drugs in a boat. Where was the boat?"

"The dry dock near that Pirate's Cove Marina."

"And the name of the boat?"

"It had a stupid name like *Bert* or *Gert* or *Gertie*. Like I said, a stupid name."

"I want you to be specific for me. Where did you hide the drugs on the boat?"

Wizard told Charlie the hiding places.

"Do you know who Victor Hanneman is?"

"Isn't he that old cop who owns the boat?"

Charlie nodded. "Have you ever met him before?"

Wizard shook his head.

"Did he have anything to do with the drugs?"

"No way. I don't make friends with cops."

"Wizard, look at me. Look me in the eye. I know the man who owns *Gertie*. He is a retired police officer and very respected. The police have been interrogating him all evening. They think he is the drug dealer. Are you going to let him go to jail for something you and your brother did?"

Wizard averted his eyes and stared at the floor.

"Wizard, you were very honest with me. I won't call the police unless you tell me I can."

"I can't go back to jail."

"If you go to the police first, the jury would see you tried to do the right thing."

"Would they lock me up?"

"I don't know. I do know it would be better for you."

"And Zeke?"

“I don’t know about Zeke.”

JEREMY and Laurie walked the beach on Megan’s Bay.

“Do you still love me, Jeremy? I need to hear you say it.”

“Yes, and I still want to marry you.”

“What are we going to do then?”

“Can’t we just be together for now and talk about marriage when we’re in a better financial situation?”

“That’s probably best since we haven’t been together all that long. What about my ring?”

“We’ll save the ring for down the road. The next time I put it back on your finger, it will be paid for.”

Laurie smiled and put her head on Jeremy’s shoulder. She tried her best not to cry.

Chapter 29

Greta Mikkelsen and her daughter Alyse joined Jeanette in the waiting room.

"Why is my sister acting like this?" Alyse asked. "I don't understand why she doesn't want us with her when the baby is born."

"I tried to talk to James," Jeanette said, "but instead of understanding, he escorted me out of the room. I can't believe my James did that to his only aunt."

"Ladies," Greta said, "neither of you has had a baby. Elin has very little control over her world right now. But, she can control her privacy since that's important to her. I don't want to hear another word from either of you."

Jeanette fired back, "I am part of this family, you know! I was with my sister Grace when James was born. She didn't mind."

"Jeanette, this is Elin's decision. It is nothing personal. My own daughter doesn't want me with her right now. I have to respect her wishes. If I can do that, you can, too."

CHARLIE sat with Wizard for a few minutes before saying, "I may know a way we can keep you out of jail. I'm not sure, but I think it may work."

"No jail? How can that be?"

"Like I said, I don't know for sure. Let me try something. Before I do anything though, would you be willing to identify the drug dealers and tell the police where they can be found?"

"If I do that, the brothers will have me killed in jail."

"Wizard, if what I have in mind works, you will have to identify them to stay out of jail."

"I'll do that if you're sure I won't go back to prison."

"Will you stay here while I try to arrange something?"

Wizard nodded. The look on his face was almost hopeful.

"Ma'am, the cop who talked to me gave me his card. Do you want it?"

Charlie looked at the card.

Rand Brownstone. Hum. Very strange.

What's strange, Missy.

An officer already interviewed Wizard.

So?

Why didn't he recognize the Cort name?

I guess he didn't know they were wanted men.

But Officer Rand Brownstone should have known.

Charlie asked Wizard for Zeke's room number and left the room.

CHARLIE went to find James. She started to poke her head in Elin's room when she heard the doctor say, "We're real close now."

Charlie left and walked down the hall. When she passed the waiting room, she saw Alyse and Mrs. Mikkelsen speaking with Jeanette. Gil sat in the corner. His head was cocked sideways, his eyes were cast downward, and his shoulders were slouched. He was the picture of a man who had no idea why his Sweetie was upset.

Charlie went into an empty birthing room and called Victor. Her call went to voice mail.

Now what, Ms. Charlie?

I have to be creative.

That's why I'm here. What are we creating?

A way to keep Willard out of jail.

Can we do that?

We can try, but we better have some fancy crossword puzzle words first!

Charlie headed for Zeke's room. When she found it, she rapped on the door before she peeked inside.

"Are you Zeke Cort?"

The man in bed nodded. "You're not going to take more blood, are you?"

"No. I was talking to your brother a few minutes ago, Zeke. He's worried about you."

"I'm good. It will take me a while to get better though."

"I'm Charlie Mikkelsen. Can we talk about Wizard for a few minutes?"

"He's okay, isn't he? Has he been arrested?"

"He has not been arrested yet, but he is frightened. He said he is scared to go back to jail."

Zeke pressed a button to put the top of his bed up. "What did he tell you?"

"He told me what happened – the distributors, the drugs and the boat."

"You're no cop, right?"

Charlie smiled. "I'm a little old to be a cop. The bulge at my waist is a cute little fat roll, not a gun."

Zeke's face relaxed a little. "I can take care of myself in jail, but Wizard can't."

"What put him in prison before?"

Zeke told Charlie about his brother's attempt to rob a bank because a friend dared him to do it. "He can't make good decisions. He may not be too bright, but inside he is a good kid. My little brother will always be a good kid, you know what I mean? I got him into this mess. I will take the fall for the drugs."

"What happened to him when he was in prison?"

"He got beat up almost every day. He's big, but his reflexes are slow, probably because he's so heavy. I went to see him every visiting day. Each time, at least one of his eyes was swollen shut. He even lost a kidney while in there. When parole time came, even the warden recommended his release."

"How did you two get involved in the current situation?"

"I got us involved. I know it is no excuse, but I was frustrated. There aren't many jobs around here except for waiting on tables, cleaning hotel rooms, or driving tourists around. Sorry I said it that way, but it is true. I wanted to open a car repair shop. I even had my eye on one little shop. Then this recession came and the tourists didn't. I lost all my savings and my car."

"Zeke, did the man who owned the boat have anything to do with the drugs?"

Zeke shook his head. "It was just me and Wizard."

Charlie considered what Zeke had told her before she replied. "I really should tell the police about this, but I promised Wizard I wouldn't. The officer in charge of this investigation believes the boat owner is the drug distributor. The owner can end up in jail for something you and your brother did."

"Tell them about me, but don't say a word about Wizard. Would you do that?"

"The police have both of you on video from the dry dock yard. They already know about Wizard. I do think I know a way to keep Wizard out of jail. No promises though."

"If you'll try, I'll write you a confession right now."

Charlie dug into the vast cavities of her prodigious purse for her notepad and pen. She handed both to Zeke and slid his portable table in place.

"In this confession, please say something about the owner not being involved in any way."

Zeke struggled to write, but did get the paragraph written. He showed it to Charlie and she read it.

"Good job. Thank you. Zeke, we need an outsider to witness your signature." Charlie went into the hall and flagged down a nurse. After telling her what she needed, the nursed stepped into the room and witnessed the signature.

Zeke signed and dated the document. Then the nurse signed and dated her signature.

After the nurse left the room, Charlie said, "You did a good thing, Zeke. But, there is something else. Are you willing to identify the drug distributors and tell the police how to find them?"

"Sure. I don't need either of them shooting at me again."

"I can't guarantee I can keep Wizard out of jail, but I'll try."

Zeke thanked Charlie profusely. She promised him she would return. She left and headed for Elin's room. She saw Greta Mikkelsen, Alyse, Jeanette and Gil in the hall congratulating each other on a job well done.

"Boy or girl?" she asked Grace.

"I have a granddaughter. Elin and James named her Greta Grace after James' mother and me. I'm ready to burst I'm so happy."

"Have you seen her yet?"

"In a few minutes."

Does this make you feel good, Ms. Charlie?

Very good. I'm so happy for James and Elin.

Does it make you feel like you want another baby?

Not me. At my age, any diapers I buy will be for myself!

"Where is Greta Grace?" Charlie asked.

"The nurse took her to clean her up." Jeanette said. "James is helping Elin get herself together."

"I'll see you later," Charlie said. "We'll have to celebrate."

Charlie walked into an empty room and called Victor again. This time he answered.

CHARLIE was hyped. She started her conversation with "News Flash Alert."

"I'm listening, Charlie," the Chief said. "What's up?"

"I know where the men are who put the drugs on your boat. I even have a signed confession from one of them!"

"You know where they are? And you have a signed confession? You did it – you had your Charlie Moment."

"I guess you can say that. One of the men wrote a short confession. He even stated you had nothing to do with the drugs. And, get this, this detective even had a nurse witness his signature and date it. She signed and dated it, too."

"Who knows about this?"

"So far, only you and me. The nurse didn't get to read the confession."

"Hold on, Charlie. Murray Sedge is here."

Charlie heard muffled voices and then the Chief came back on the line. "Where are they? I'll call headquarters."

"Since Murray is there, put your cell on speaker phone."

The Chief did so after Murray showed him which button to press.

"Now Charlie, where are the men and this signed confession?" Sedge asked.

"I need a favor first before I tell you. I want a plea bargain for one of the men or you get no signed confession from me."

"Now Ms. Charlie," Murray said. "You better tell me about this plea bargain."

That's not fair, Ms. Charlie. He's calling you Ms. Charlie and that's my line.

Life isn't always fair.

It should be.

If life was fair, we would always be in Xanadu.

Do I have time to puke?

Charlie gave Murray a sense of Wizard's intellectual abilities, how he got to prison, what happened when he was there, and how he and his brother got involved with drug distributers. She even told him about the shooting earlier in the morning.

"Now let me see if I got this right. You want me to get Wizard a reduced sentence?"

"No, Murray. I want more than that for Wizard." She told the two men what she had in mind. "And there is a good reason why Zeke Cort should get a reduced sentence, too. He is willing to identify the distributors and to tell the police where to find the men."

The Chief spoke and agreed to Charlie's conditions for Wizard.

"You drive a hard bargain, Ms. Charlie," Murray said.

"That's what a real detective like me has to do. Now a question for you. How do I proceed?"

"I was hoping you would allow me to take over," Sedge said. "I can use the information as a bargaining tool."

"What would you do?"

"I would call Chief Philippe and explain the situation. If he agrees, he could order Powell to arrest Willard and put him in lockup or put an ankle bracelet on him and hand him over to his grandmother. Zeke would be arrested and go to jail until the trial."

"Zeke's in the hospital." Charlie explained about the shooting.

"Then Zeke would get a bracelet that will attach him to his hospital bed. Powell would have to arrest the two drug distributors. I can file the paperwork for a plea bargain on behalf of Willard and Zeke, clear the Chief's name, and talk to the judge myself about your recommendations. Wizard might end up with a bracelet or go to lockup for a couple of nights, but no prison."

"Sounds like a good plan to me providing Wizard and the distributors are not in the same cell. You know, Murray, Officer Brownstone interviewed Willard this morning about the shooting. The officer obviously didn't recognize Zeke or Wizard's names. Why not? Wasn't an APB issued?"

"Interesting point, Ms. Charlie. An All-Points Bulletin is standard procedure in a situation like this. I'll tell Chief Philippe about that, too. I'm sure he'll ask Manny Powell the same question."

"Another thing, Murray. Do you ever do pro bono work?"

"On occasion. If these two men admit their involvement and identify the distributors, they can consider my services free."

"Now would you please tell your client that his lady friend is a really good detective?"

AS CHARLIE returned to Zeke's room, she passed the Kingston-Mikkelsen family outside of Elin's room.

"Charlie," Jeanette said, "we can go see the baby and Elin now."

"May I come?"

"Of course," Greta said.

James opened the door to Elin's room. "Ladies and Gil, may I present Mrs. Elin Kingston and Miss Greta Grace Kingston."

All the ladies had happy tears on their faces. Even Gil had a few although he wasn't sniffling like the ladies.

Jeanette exclaimed, “I forgot my camera.”

“I didn’t,” Charlie said as she extracted her large digital Canon from the depths of the titanic blue tank hanging from her shoulder. “I’m always prepared.” She snapped picture after picture of the baby, Elin and the baby, James, Elin and the baby, Grace and the baby, Alyse and the baby, Jeanette and the baby, and Jeanette, Gil and the baby.

“I think my memory card just died, she laughed.”

After a few more minutes filled with admiration and a heated discussion about who the baby looked like, Charlie excused herself and went to Zeke’s room.

MURRY punched numbers into his cell. “Chief Philippe, please. This is Attorney Murray Sedge calling in regard to the drug case involving Chief Hanneman. We have a signed confession from one of the Cort brothers.”

Dwayne Philippe did not hesitate to take the call. “Mr. Sedge, you have my attention.”

“Chief, I sent you a copy of the video showing two men boarding the Hanneman boat while it was in dry dock. I assume you’ve seen it.”

“I have. Lieutenant Powell has identified the two men.”

“Chief, Officer Rand Brownstone interviewed one of the two men in the video this morning for a shooting. The officer didn’t recognize the man or the name. Was an APB issued?”

Philippe hesitated a second to control his response, “I’ll check into it, Mr. Sedge. Where are these men?”

“Chief, I need to explain something to you first. Do you happen to know Charlie Mikkelsen?”

“You’re going to tell me she is involved in this case, aren’t you?”

“She is very much involved and has been from the beginning. She is the one who checked to see if Luther had a security camera. He did. Her son viewed the tape, duplicated it, gave a copy to the Victor, the Chief gave it to me, and I sent it to you. Charlie is also the one who initially talked to Willard Cort and figured out the connection with this case."

Murray filled in most of the details Charlie had told him, including the signed and witnessed confession. "I realize the police will want their own signed confession from Zeke Cort, but it shouldn't be a problem since he's already signed one."

Philippe mouthed a silent *Unbelievable* as he shook his head. "Another thing, Chief Philippe, the men are requesting a plea bargain and Zeke Cort agreed to identify the distributors and give the police their address."

"When are you going to tell me where they are, Mr. Sedge?"

"I have agreed to represent these men. I will bring the younger man to the Frederiksted police station. I need time to get to him and drive him to town. Will you allow me to bring him in?"

"What about the other brother?"

"I'll tell you where you can find him when I bring Willard to the station."

"You have a half hour, Sedge."

"An hour would be better since I also want some time to question the brothers together."

"If everything you tell me is true, there should be no problem with plea bargains. Understand that I can make no promises and there may still be a sentence. Needless to say our prosecuting attorney will need to agree, as well as a judge."

CHARLIE headed for the waiting room where Wizard sat. On the way, she saw Jake come down the hall with his arm in a splint.

"How serious is the shoulder?"

"Displaced. The Doc put it back in place. There was no nerve or soft tissue damage – that's the good news. I'll be in the splint for a while so I hope you have bags of frozen foods I can put on my shoulder to keep the swelling down."

"Not a problem. Any prescriptions?"

"A pain killer. I just picked it up at the hospital's pharmacy."

"Help yourself to the frozen peas. Do you mind grabbing a cab and heading home?"

"What are you up to?"

"I just identified the two drug dealers that kept their stash on *Gertie*."

"You did what?"

"You heard me. I had to do something while I waited for you. So, I solved the case."

"Is this what the Chief called a Charlie Moment?"

"I suppose. He is tap dancing right now, but I'm sure he would agree. I'll fill in the blanks later when I get home, okay?"

"Okay. I'm going back to the house. I need one of those pills."

Ms. Charlie, we're a good team, aren't we?

Extremely good.

We're smart, too.

We need to feel smart once in a while. Those refrigerator sticky notes don't always work because we forget to look at them.

CHIEF Dwayne Philippe dialed Police Commissioner Dylan's number to update him.

"It looks like the drug case is solved. Defense Attorney Murray Sedge will bring in one of the two men. Once Sedge does that, he will tell us the location of the second man. Hanneman is cleared of any involvement."

"Good for Manny. How did he do that?"

"Powell had nothing to do with it. I haven't even told him yet." Dwayne told his boss about Sedge's call, what part Charlie Mikkelsen played in the drama, the signed confession, and the plea bargain.

"Commissioner, what angers me is that we could have arrested these men ourselves. An officer spoke to one of them about a shooting this morning. He didn't recognize the man's names because Powell did not put out an APB."

Commissioner Dylan expelled an angry breath. "Did I make a bad decision appointing him to the case?"

"Both of us made a poor decision, sir. Belatedly, I went through Powell's records. It appears Hanneman pounded Powell's performance as a rookie. Low grades across the board. I believe Powell spent his time trying to make Hanneman look guilty instead of evaluating all possibilities. He was prejudiced from the beginning."

CHARLIE found Wizard still sitting in his corner. "Wizard, have you had anything to eat?"

The young man shook his head. "Don't have no money."

Charlie fed some dollar bills into the vending machines and had Wizard pick out what he wanted.

"We're going to Zeke's room to talk about what is going to happen."

They went down the hallway and into Zeke's room. He was dozing. He woke as soon as his visitors entered the room.

"Are the cops coming to put me in jail?" Wizard asked his brother.

Charlie said, "Let me tell you what I know so far. The police know about the two of you now. From what I've been told, Murray Sedge is the best defense attorney in the U.S. Virgin Islands. He has agreed to represent both of you free of charge. He will be here in a few minutes. Mr. Sedge will be questioning both of you. Afterward he will take you, Wizard, to the police station in Frederiksted."

Wizard panicked. "But I'll go to jail."

"Let the lady finish, Bro. She's trying to help us."

"As I said, Mr. Sedge will take you to the station so you won't have to leave in handcuffs. You may have to stay in lockup for a few days or you may be sent to your grandmother's with an ankle bracelet. The police will arrest the distributors and finish the investigation. Everyone has agreed to consider your plea bargain."

"Will I end up in prison?"

"Mr. Sedge doesn't know anything for sure, but you can help him and yourself. Answer every question he asks truthfully. Do not answer an officer's questions unless Mr. Sedge is present."

"That's really important," Zeke said. "Don't let those cops try to fool you. You answer no question unless Mr. Sedge says to answer it. Now you repeat what I just said."

Wizard did so correctly and beamed as he saw pride in his brother's eyes. Zeke grinned.

"Ms. Mikkelsen," Zeke said, "did you tell Mr. Sedge I talked Wizard into buying the drugs. I led and he followed."

"You tell him that, Zeke. I've already requested a reduced sentence for you, too. No guarantees, of course."

CHIEF Philippe picked up the phone again. This time he dialed Manny Powell.

"Manny, what do you have on the drug situation?"

"It's Hanneman, Chief. No question about it."

"I just checked and there was no APB issued on the Cort brothers. Why not?"

"That's next on my to-do list, Chief."

"Did you know one of our St. Croix officers actually interviewed one of the Cort brothers this morning for a shooting?"

"That shows how stupid the cops are on this island, Chief. He should have brought the man in."

"Manny, do I need to draw you a picture? The officer didn't know about the Cort brothers because there was no APB issued!"

"I'll pick up Hanneman. He'll have to tell me where the Cort brothers are."

"You're a little late, Manny. We have a signed confession from one of the Cort brothers, and the confession clears Hanneman completely. Your smear campaign didn't work."

Manny sat speechless as Chief Philippe dismissed him from his assignment and ordered him to return to St. Thomas for disciplinary purposes.

Chapter 30

The man with a thick white head of hair entered Zeke's hospital room.

"I'm Murray Sedge, defense attorney, gentlemen. You must be Zeke and Willard Cort."

Murray smiled as he shook the men's hands. "Where is our Ms. Charlie Mikkelsen?"

"She went to see some lady who just had a baby," Zeke said.

Murray started to ask Zeke questions. By the time Charlie returned, Murray was almost finished talking to the men.

"Good to finally meet you, Charlie," Murray said. "Victor has told me a lot about you."

"Good to finally meet you, Murray," Charlie said. "Victor has told me a lot about you, too."

"All good, I hope."

"He now has a more positive opinion of defense attorneys."

"I can't ask for any more than that, now can I?"

"I guess not."

"When do I have to leave, Mr. Sedge," Wizard asked.

"I promised Chief Philippe you would be at the station within an hour. We must leave now. We can talk in the car."

"Will you stay on St. Croix tonight?" Charlie asked.

"Yes, as soon as the police finish questioning these two young men. The Chief offered me free room and board for the night."

CHIEF Philippe called James at his office. Lynette Spears referred the call to James' cell.

"James, its Chief Philippe. Murray Sedge – you know him?"

"He's Chief Hanneman's attorney. I've seen him down at the station on several occasions."

"He's on his way in with one of the drug dealers in the dry dock video. He has a signed confession from the older brother, courtesy of one Charlie Mikkelsen. The brothers want a plea bargain and they are willing to identify the distributors and tell us where we can pick them up."

"I guess I owe Manny an apology. I didn't think he'd get anywhere on this drug case."

"You don't owe Manny a thing. He didn't locate the Cort brothers – your wannabe detective did. She's the one who got a confession in writing, cleared Hanneman, suggested a plea bargain, and talked Sedge into representing the brothers."

"Charlie solved this case?"

"Yep! She met one of the brothers in the hospital and figured it all out. Manny is on his way back here. He's been recalled. Would you assign this case to your Detective Benton?"

"Absolutely. Does this mean Chief Hanneman is completely cleared?"

"If everything Sedge told me is true, Victor is cleared."

A grin came over James' face and his gold tooth twinkled. "Well, I'll be. Charlie did it again."

"I heard that Chamaign also has your murderer in custody now."

"He's in the hospital. Charlie's son tackled him and broke a few bones."

"It must run in the family. I understand Charlie is the one who discovered the video at the dry dock place, too."

"That she did. Now Chief, I have some good news of my own. Elin had our baby a little while ago and I'm as exhausted as she is."

"Congratulations. Boy or girl?"

"Greta Grace Kingston is an eight pound seven ounce beautiful, healthy baby girl."

"That's wonderful, James," he said.

The two men spoke for a few more minutes before Philippe hung up.

CHARLIE arrived home.

So much happened in one day, Ms. Charlie.

You're right. No bugaboos will keep us from our bed tonight.

Bug-a-what?

Bugaboo. Someone or something that gets in your way – like a flat tire on the way to work or a visit from the bogey man when you're trying to sleep.

Bogey man? Your brain has been invaded, Missy.

"Grandmom," Molly said, "Annie took pictures of me on her cell and I took some of her on mine. We emailed them to our friends and they thought we did great in the fashion show."

"Mom," Jake said, "I edited the footage of the show from my cam. We're just about to watch it on the computer."

"I have an idea, Uncle Jake. Can we put parts of the show on *YouTube*?" Annie asked.

"I need to think about that, Annie. And we need to get approval from your dad first."

"Let's see the show first," Grandmom said. Charlie & Family sat down and watched the video. "You two did super great!" she said between mini-donut number four and five.

"I think the part where I flubbed up is pretty funny," Molly said. "Pleeeze, pleeeze, pleeeze, Dad, can we put it on the internet? Maybe some famous fashion dress designer will want Annie and me as models."

Jake said, "What do you think, Mom?"

"It will be okay as long as you don't identity the girls."

"Annie," Jake said, "call your dad. Get his approval."

While Annie called home, Jake tweaked his editing. Charlie

went into her bathroom to wash the makeup and cover-up off her face.

You have a half dozen new age spots, Ms. Charlie.

As long as I can afford to cover them up, no one ever has to know.

Missy, the Shadow knows.

Oh, what evil lurks in the hearts of alter egos!

Charlie returned to the living room in her PJ's just as Jeremy came in the door. "What have you been doing for the past two days?"

"Did you get my message about staying overnight on St. Thomas?" Jeremy asked.

Charlie nodded.

"Laurie and I sorta got engaged."

Like you sorta have a gentleman friend, Ms. Charlie. Like mother, like son.

Shut your trap, Nit wit!

Annie ran in the room and started to speak. When she heard the word engaged, she stopped abruptly. "That's so romantic, Uncle Jeremy! Can I be in the wedding and wear a beautiful pink gown?"

"I want a lavender one," Molly added.

"The wedding won't be for a long time, ladies. In fact, you two might end up married before me."

"Are you or are you not engaged?" Charlie asked.

"Laurie has her ring, but she put it back in the box for now."

"Uncle Jeremy, what happened?" Annie said. "You didn't break her heart, did you?"

"No, Annie. We decided we couldn't afford to get married yet. Laurie wants a nice wedding. We both need to save. I also need to pay off the ring and save for a house. And, I won't be buying the Chief's boat."

Ms. Charlie, Jeremy is as bad as you – can't make a decision about marriage.

I've made my decision. I'd drive Victor so crazy he'd run. At least our relationship is a solid one now.

That's not it at all. You have a bugbear in your head somewhere.

Since when did you start doing crossword puzzles?

After everyone commiserated with Jeremy, Annie switched

subjects. "Dad says we can put the fashion show on *YouTube*. He wants to watch it."

Jeremy helped Jake edit the show for the next twenty minutes. After he uploaded the ninety-seven second video, the whole family watched it on *YouTube* eleven times.

THE Chief made his regular late night phone call to Charlie. "You do understand, don't you, that I'll be eternally grateful for what you did today?"

"I'll cash in my chips one of these days. Never fear, Charlie is here."

Couldn't you think of anything more intelligent to say, Ms. Charlie?

Mind your own business.

You are my business. Remember?

"James called me a little while ago." Victor said. "He told me about Greta Grace."

"I should have called from the hospital, but there was so much going on with Zeke and Wizard."

"No problem. James also told me he and Chamaign are convinced I had nothing to do with the brothers or the drugs. I think they know Manny tried to prove I was involved with the drugs despite what evidence he found. Dwayne Philippe also called and told me he verified the bad blood between Manny and me. Chamaign had played him portions of a tape James made of a private conversation in his office. Manny had said that he was going for a conviction regardless of what any evidence showed."

"How will this impact Manny's job?"

"He'll get nailed for not getting the APB issued, and he will probably be transferred out of Internal Affairs. Don't know about any pink slips."

"How did Murray make out this evening?"

"He said he did well. He wants to negotiate sending Willard home for now under the custody of his grandmother. I suspect that young man is as scared of her as he is of jail."

"I don't think of Wizard as a hardened criminal. He's more like a small child who is easily led."

"Your suggestion about his immediate future is a good one. I'll talk to the right people tomorrow."

JEANETTE called her nephew. "James, I'm sure Gil doesn't want to marry me."

"What's happened now?"

"I know he doesn't want me to have a big wedding."

"Aunt Jeanette, start at the beginning. Do you still want four hundred people?"

"I thought something at the Botanical Gardens would be nice. I would want it catered and would invite a few guests."

"Aunt Jeanette, how many guests is a few?"

"A few hundred."

"How many hundreds is a few? You wanted four hundred last time we spoke about this."

"It still comes to about four."

"Aunt Jeanette, no man Gil's age wants to get married in front of four hundred people. I'm half Gil's age and I wouldn't want to do it."

"Oh, James!"

"Aunt Jeanette, think about Gil for a minute. He's not a loud, noisy person. I bet Gil would love to see you in a beautiful white gown with a bustle and a train. I also bet he wouldn't mind being married in the Botanical Gardens. I think if you kept your guest list small, he'd want to get married tomorrow."

"This is the one and only wedding I'll ever have, James. I deserve this."

"You do indeed deserve this, Aunt Jeanette. I don't deny that. However, Gil deserves what he wants, too. If you compromise and take Gil's wishes into consideration, you'll both be happy. Tomorrow, you and Gil and I can talk this out."

Chapter 31

When Charlie entered the kitchen, Jeremy had finished breakfast and was putting his plates in the dishwasher.

"Did you sleep well?" Charlie asked.

"Not really. I kept waking up and thinking about Laurie."

"You really don't need to worry about buying another house. I have plenty of space in my new wing to put in a small kitchen. I'm also here only part of the year."

"You wouldn't mind?"

"No, but you would want to update the kitchen for Laurie and probably build a master suite like I did."

"I really like our little house. Our view on the hill is great and the lot is big enough to build an extension, too. Unfortunately, expanding the house costs money, too. I really do need to pay off a few bills and save a bit."

"Wise decision. Marriage can be difficult enough without being in serious debt. I'm proud of you and Laurie."

"Thanks, Mom. I need to get out of here and head for the marina. I have two days of work to make up. Let me know what everyone is doing this afternoon and I'll try to join you."

Charlie finished stacking the dishwasher.

Ms. Charlie, you're cleaning.

Did you forget we have guests? I'm only a slob some of the time.

CHARLIE heard Jake moving around so she circled the living room, picked up a few dirty glasses, and put them in the dishwasher. She straightened up the couch, blew dust off of a couple of tables, and stood back and admired her accomplishments.

What a difference, Ms. Charlie.

I'm the champion of sixty-second makeovers.

"Morning, Mom," Jake said as he made his first appearance of the day. "Do you have anything planned?"

"I was thinking we should take the girls to see the plantation once owned by my great, great grandparents. You won't recognize Claudine's Quarters. Victor did so much with the land after he bought it."

"So he still owns it?"

"He does, but things have changed. He built the small dormitory and an educational wing is attached. There are now five or six teens living there. Soon he'll rent the facility to the local government for one dollar a year. You heard all about Zeke and Wizard Cort yesterday. I asked the attorney, Murray Sedge, to negotiate terms so Wizard could go to Claudine's Quarters instead of jail. He's nineteen and a little slow. He could get his GED while serving his time. So far, Victor has managed to get all the teens housed there part-time work."

"What about the other brother?"

"Zeke will serve some time in prison. He may get a plea bargain since he and Wizard identified the drug distributors. I suspect Chamaign and Bob will go after those two guys today if they haven't already done it."

"So the Chief is completely in the clear?"

"Yep!"

Molly entered the hallway. She had not yet brushed her thick mane, and she still wore one of her father's old gray tee shirts that reached to her knees. "What are we going to do today?"

Before Charlie could answer, Annie appeared. She was showered, dressed and smiling. "Are we going to have as much fun as yesterday?"

Charlie told the girls about the planned excursion to the plantation.

"Sounds good," Molly said. "Dad, when are we going to get back to the treasure hunt?"

"Molly!" Annie shrieked, "Would you believe we've had 37,542 hits on *YouTube*!" Annie's soft curls bounced as she jumped up and down in her lime green shorts and tan halter top.

"Whoa! And I haven't even texted all my friends yet!" Molly whooped.

Both girls dashed back to their bedroom to find their cells.

"That's a lot of hits," Jake said. "I guess I'm not as attached to my computer as the rest of the world."

Charlie grabbed the high-back office chair at the computer desk before Jake took it. "Mothers first!" she said. Jake leaned over her shoulder and they watched the video again.

After it finished playing, Jake noted the number of hits. "They are up to 41,147! They just might get a modeling job out of this."

Both girls were wired as they texted and walked into the kitchen.

How can they text and see where to walk at the same time, Ms. Charlie?

It's beyond me. I have enough trouble remembering where I'm going after I get up to go someplace.

"I'll give Victor a call and see if it's okay to tour the plantation today," Charlie said.

Jake tapped into his email account and sent two global emails – one to his personal contact list and one to everyone at work.

GIL and his buddy Willy Wilson sat in a booth in the Ole Danish Pastry Shoppe in Frederiksted.

"What do you think I should do about this wedding? I love my little Sweetie, but all those people looking at me give me the heebie-jeebies."

"No doubt about it, Gil, you got yourself a bad case of the willies. Would it help if you explained this to Jeanette?"

"Don't know. She really wants a big wedding. Another thing bothers me, too. Since she is going to get so gussied up, she'll probably want me to wear one of them tuxedos. Never wore one of them in my life. Holy Moly, Willy, the only time I wear a dress shirt and a tie anymore is when I go to a funeral. And here we done buried almost all of our friends!"

Willy threw his head back and roared with laughter. "Seeing you in a tux would be a sight to see, you ole swabby. I'd even pay to see that. You are gonna invite Lil and me, aren't you?"

"Course I am. With this guest list up to four hundred, what's two more?"

Gil sat back in the booth and studied the napkin in his lap. "Chief Kingston wants to talk to me. I guess I was supposed to ask his permission to marry his aunt, or something like that. I wonder if he would understand my predicament."

"It's worth a try, buddy."

Gil and Willy said good-bye and Gil headed for the station. He hesitated before going inside, but willed himself to open the door.

The duty officer asked if she could help him. He stammered as he asked for Chief Kingston.

"May I ask your name, sir?"

Gil answered the question.

"May I ask what this is about?"

Gil closed his eyes and tried to disappear. When he opened them the officer was still in front of him. He lowered his head, tilted it sideways, looked up and said, "I'm supposed to marry his aunt."

The officer hid her smile as she escorted Gil down the hall.

LAURIE rapped on the door of Jeremy's office. Her face showed evidence of recent tears.

"Can we talk?"

"Sure." Jeremy rose from his desk, embraced Laurie and held her tight.

"I called home. My dad said we made the right decision."

"My mom said practically the same thing," Jeremy said.

"How long do we wait?"

"Your ring will be paid off in eighteen months. By that time, I should be some money ahead."

"My car loan and credit cards will be paid by then, too. My mother said most of our relatives won't have the money to fly down here, so we shouldn't expect too many guests."

"This is beginning to sound like a wedding we can afford."

"It definitely means it won't cost as much. I do want a beautiful gown through – maybe one with a lot of lace and a long train. You know – a traditional Southern gown."

"I want you to have a beautiful Southern gown. Your sister didn't by any chance offer to make it, did she?"

"She can't wait. I had another thought, too. Most of my weekends are free, so I can freelance. Since I have all my own video and editing equipment, I can video weddings and make some extra money."

"Maybe you should put the engagement ring back on,"

"Why do you think I brought it with me? Would you do me the honor, sir?"

WHEN Gil entered James Kingston's office, he saw Jeanette sitting across the desk from her nephew.

"Good timing, Gil. Have a seat," he said.

Gil looked at his Sweetie, "Hi, Jeanette."

Jeanette peeked at her fiancée, "Hi, Gil."

James looked from one to the other. "What can we do to get this wedding planned? At the rate you two are going, one of you is bound to croak before you make it up the aisle."

Jeanette giggled; Gil grinned.

"I would love to have a beautiful wedding dress and a big bustle and a long flowing train," she said.

Gil pictured his Sweetie all fancied up and smiling blissfully. "You'll be so pretty. I can't wait."

"Gil, you don't mind?"

"Course not. I'll have the most angelic bride in the world."

"Oh Gil, you're so sweet to say that. I'll go ahead with our plans."

"Not so quick, Aunt Jeanette. It's Gil's turn to tell us what he wants."

Gil squirmed in his seat as he looked at Jeanette, "I would prefer a small wedding."

"How small is small?" Jeanette asked.

"Bout a hundred, maybe."

Jeanette jumped on the negotiating bandwagon. "One hundred and fifty?"

Gil cleared his throat. "One hundred and one."

James said "Gil, buddy. Help me here. Could we compromise at one hundred and twenty-five?"

"I suppose."

Jeanette jumped up at the same time as Gil. Her rounded tummy bounced off Gil. He grabbed her so she wouldn't fall and then gave her a tender kiss.

WHEN Charlie called, the Chief was halfway out the door to go to the site of the plantation.

"Would it be okay if I brought the teens to Claudine's Quarters and gave them a tour?"

"Not a problem. I'm on my way there now. I have several grant proposals to get in the mail. I need to raise money for this place somehow."

"We won't bother you, I promise. Will you still be there after lunch?"

"I'll wait around for you. Charlie, I meant to ask you about the casing to your locket watch. Did Jake retrieve it when Roland Coombs was arrested?"

"He did, but it is evidence. I'll get it back sooner or later."

"Will that stop you and your family from looking for the so-called treasure?"

"It shouldn't, but I don't know where else to look. The fireplace in the cookhouse was shaped differently than the fireplace etched on the casing."

"In what way?"

"The casing showed that the fireplace was tall and arched. The fireplace in the cookhouse was tall and rectangular."

"Charlie, did you realize many plantations had fireplaces built into the windmills as well as the cookhouses?"

"Are you about to tell me something important?"

"There is very little left of the windmill on Claudine's Quarters. It does have a fireplace and it is arched."

"Ohmagosh! Victor, we'll be there as soon as we can get there."

CHARLIE dashed into the girls' bedroom. "Annie, Molly, get cleaned up. I know where the treasure is hidden!"

Jake heard his mother. "Where?"

"You'll know where when we get there. We're going on a treasure hunt."

"I haven't eaten yet."

"Tough munchies! Get that sling on properly to protect your arm."

Charlie sprinted for the phone and called Jeremy. "Join us at Claudine's Quarters. I know where the treasure is located."

"Where?"

"Are you going to meet me there or not?"

"Laurie is with me. We'll both be right there."

THE CHIEF called James to ask him what was happening with the Cort brothers.

"Murray convinced the district attorney to let Wizard go home with a bracelet on his ankle. With Roland Coombs and Zeke Cort handcuffed to their hospital beds, I have nothing on my mind for the moment except Elin, Greta Grace, diapers and formula."

"Did you know about the treasure hunt?"

"Chamaign mentioned something about the watch, but I wasn't sure what it was about."

The Chief laughed and explained. "Now Charlie thinks she knows where the treasure is located. The whole clan will be at Claudine's Quarters shortly. Wish to join us?"

The Chief overheard James tell Gil and Jeanette about the treasure. He heard Gil say, "Holy Moly! Let's go, Jeanette."

"Did you hear that, Chief?" James asked.

"Have them join the party. You, too."

"Chief, if you don't mind, I want to visit my wife and our new little treasure. Let me know how it goes."

ONCE in the car, Charlie looked around.

"Jake, where is the camcorder?"

"Mom, have you noticed my arm is in a splint?"

"Molly," Charlie said, "would you please go in the house and get the camcorder and a fresh memory card."

Molly scooted out of the car and into the house. One hundred and eighty seconds later, she returned with the requested items.

"My cell," Annie said. She hopped out of the car and into the house to return two hundred and twelve seconds later. "I'm sorry, Grandmom. It was in the hamper with my dirty clothes. It took me a while to find it."

Charlie put the car in drive and zipped down the driveway to the main road. She drove to Claudine's Quarters, and steamrolled her way up the narrow stone drive to the top of the hill. Victor was standing on the porch of the dormitory waiting for her. She had no sooner put on the parking break when Gil and Jeanette arrived. Seconds later, Jeremy screeched up the driveway spitting gravel. Once parked, he and Laurie popped out of Jeremy's truck.

Why do I feel something's about to happen, Missy?

Because it is. We're going to find the treasure.

But, there is something else, too.

Go find your Tarot cards and figure it out. I'm busy.

The Chief greeted everyone and said, "We are going to need to walk through some brush to get to the remains of the windmill."

Everyone trudged after Victor. Charlie had her camera stuffed in her Popsicle orange and lime green bathtub-size straw tote. Jeremy had the camcorder, the girls their cell phones, and Jake had his splint. Laurie and Gil helped Jeanette through the brush.

Within three minutes, the troupe was at the remains of the old windmill. Another minute later, Gil, Jeanette and Laurie caught up with them.

The only part left of the ancient windmill was its base. It was eight feet high in some places. The thickness of the rock wall was a good three feet. The thickness diminished as the mill got higher.

"Where is the fireplace?" Molly asked.

"It's in the rear," the Chief said as he led the way to the other side.

"I know this is all about love," Annie said as she followed.

When they saw the fireplace, everyone stood rooted to the ground like the indigenous hundred year-old walnut trees dotting the former sugar plantation.

Jake and Jeremy stepped forward to inspect the stones.

"I know this is about how much Christoffer and Claudine loved each other," Annie said with a sigh.

"I know it is about a gold treasure," Molly said with her voice filled with excitement and lips pursed into a grin.

"Jake, the *X* was in the upper left corner of the fireplace, wasn't it?" Jeremy asked.

"Around here someplace," Jake said as he felt the stones.

"The way you're touching the stones makes me think you've watched too many Nicholas Cage treasure hunt movies," Charlie said. "Somehow, I don't think there is a hidden button anywhere."

Annie's right. This is about love, Ms. Charlie.

Molly's right, too. This is about gold.

I'll take the love over the gold, Missy.

I'm greedy. I want both.

"Look at this mortar to the left of your hand," Jeremy said. "It's a little bit lighter than the surrounding mortar."

"Do you think it was patched here?" Jake asked.

"Yes, I do. What do you think, Chief?"

"I think these old eyes can't see a difference without a

magnifying glass."

"I have a tool box in my truck. Be right back, folks," Jeremy said as he dashed to the vehicle.

"I'm dying of curiosity," Molly said.

"My heart is pounding because this is so, so wonderfully and blissfully romantic," Annie said.

Jeremy returned with a small hammer and chisel. He glanced around at the group and said, "Shall I?"

"Hurry up, Jeremy. This is fun," Laurie said as she clicked on the camcorder.

Jeremy started to chisel the sand mortar away. It crumbled rapidly. When he was almost done, he handed the chisel to Jake. "Go ahead. You can finish with one hand."

Jake reached up and wiped the crumbled mortar away. He grabbed the stone with his working hand and wiggled it. The stone moved, but not much. After a minute, he said, "Finish up, brother, my hand is tired."

Jeremy wiggled the stone until it was loose. He pulled the stone out of the wall. Molly gasped for breath. Annie refused to breathe. "Mom, this is your treasure. Do you want to do the honors and check inside the hole?"

Charlie nodded.

"What if there is a snake in the hole?" Molly said.

"There are no snakes on the island. We have litters of mongooses instead," the Chief said. "The mongooses feast on snakes."

"What's a mongoose?" Molly asked her father.

"An animal, I suppose. We'll look it up later," he said.

Mongoose, Ms. Charlie? First it's an ostrich, then it's a bugaboo, and now it's a mongoose?

Welcome to the Zoo of Life.

Charlie reached in the hole and felt something. "There is something in here."

Everyone, even Victor, held their breath as she pulled out a small rough cotton bag closed with a drawstring. "Oh my, there really is a treasure."

Annie couldn't handle the excitement any longer. She almost

screamed at her grandmother, "Open it!"

Charlie sat on top of a large stone fallen to the ground from the wall of the windmill. She used a smaller stone as a little table. She opened the bag and let the contents fall into the palm of her left hand. No one could see what she had. "It's romantic, it's gold, and it's a treasure," she said.

Eight sets of eyes were glued on Charlie's hand as she placed two golden rings on top of the cotton pouch.

"They're wedding rings – I knew this was about romance!" Annie said.

"And they are gold," Molly said. "But, what makes them a treasure?"

Charlie picked up one ring and read the inscription, "To My Love 10 April 1844."

"What about the other ring?" Jake asked.

"To My Love 10 April 1844."

"Were Claudine and Christoffer married that day?" he asked.

"I never found information on their wedding date, but I bet so."

"Why are they in a stone wall, Grandmom?" Annie asked as she ran her finger around the edge of each ring.

Why, Ms. Charlie, why? I want to know, too.

I'm thinking, I'm thinking.

I feel strange things happening, Missy.

Stop with the theatrics, will you. Go swoon elsewhere.

"This is so awesome," Molly said. She picked up one ring and studied the inscription.

For the next few minutes, everyone took turns inspecting the rings.

"Jeremy," Laurie said, "we could use these weddings rings when we get married."

"They wouldn't match your engagement ring."

"That wouldn't matter. Imagine, these rings belonged to your ancestors. Obviously they were preserved in the stone wall for a reason."

Gil was the last person to hold the rings. He handed them back to Charlie. She carefully placed them on top of the pouch.

"But why are they here?' Annie asked.

"I might know the answer. Victor, you will have to help me with a history lesson. Wasn't it in the 1870s when the Labor Riots occurred on this island?"

"Yes, late 1878," he said.

"Christoffer Jakob Mikkelsen died in February 1879, so these rings were hidden before his death. However, between the riots and his death, he may not have had time to retrieve them because of illness."

"Mom, do you know if either of them was injured during the riots?" Jake asked.

"The archivist at the Landmarks Society showed me a document that named those residents who survived the fires. Christoffer was listed on it. I have letters written by Claudine in the late 1890's, so she survived, too."

"What fires?" Laurie asked.

"Charlie's ancestors lived in Frederiksted," the Chief said, "and at the time of the riots, half the town was set on fire."

"What the Chief just said is true," Gil said. "My dad was a young boy then. He and my grandmother went into hiding."

"My granny told me about the fires, too." Jeanette said. "I'm a bit ashamed to say it, but my grandmother actually set one of the fires."

Annie went pale. Her forehead crunched and her eyes squinted as she tried to understand. "Why did they set the fires?"

The Chief answered. "You see, Annie, slavery had been abolished a number of years before then, but there were many rules about how the freed slaves worked the land as employees. Many of these rules were unfair. In addition to that, there was an economic crisis around the world. There was very little work available for the former slaves. Just like today, men and women had to work in order to feed themselves. Many had no jobs. They rioted for five days out of frustration and anger."

Molly said, "So our ancestors buried their most valuable possessions behind the stones so they would be safe during the riots. Do you think that's the answer?"

"It's a possibility," the Chief said.

Annie continued Molly's logic. "And, if they were separated by the riots or one or both of them were killed, their rings would always hold them together. I knew this would be romantic."

"Gil, my love, the squabble over our wedding was so silly and selfish of me," Jeanette said. "I want the kind of love that Claudine and Christoffer had."

"Me, too. Want to elope?"

"Not without my wedding gown, bustle and train, we won't!"

Everyone oohed and aahed over Gil and Jeanette.

"Jeremy, I don't need a lace gown with train. We should elope instead," Laurie said.

He laughed, "We'll elope as soon as we get our bills paid."

The group laughed and then applauded.

"This is the most romantic story that will ever be told," Annie said. "And to think it is about my own great, great, great, great grandparents."

"You're right, Annie." Molly said. "This is far more about romance than about gold and treasure. I'm going to write a novel about this story and it will be a best seller."

Again, everyone oohed and aahed.

Jake asked, "Where did Mom go?"

Everyone looked around the site.

"Where is the Chief?" Jeremy asked.

Again, everyone looked around.

"Where are the rings?" Annie asked.